The door to his bedroom flew open

Both he and Barbara jerked back. She gasped.

In the archway stood Annabelle Crane—her tall, lithe body poised for action, her arms raised and her gun pointed at them.

It took Nathan a second to catch on. "Annabelle, I'm all right."

She surveyed the room—studied Barbara, glanced at the bed, the glasses, the dim lights. "I came home and Dan wasn't here. There was a strange car in the driveway. What the hell is going on, Nathan?"

He stepped in front of Barbara. "I asked Dan to leave Barbara and me alone. I need to talk to her about our situation."

"You're being stalked," she said tightly. "You could be killed. The alarm isn't even on ____ d you the windows could be ____

"Annabelle ____

"Oh, forget ____ going to work this wa____ f here."

Dear Reader,

Against the Odds, the story of Anabelle Crane and
Nathan Hyde, is the third book in my SERENITY HOUSE
series and wraps up the trilogy about girls who spent
some of their youth in a group home. If you've read the
other two, *Practice Makes Perfect* and *A Place to Belong*, you'll
remember Nathan, the charismatic congressman, and
Anabelle, the reserved undercover cop. And you'll
recognize other characters from the previous books.
But this novel stands alone, too. So if you're new to
Serenity House, welcome. I hope you enjoy your visit.

Anabelle and Nathan's story was an interesting one to
write. I enjoyed investigating Nathan's profession as a
member of the House of Representatives. The story line
also gave me a chance to include a suspense element in
my Superromance novel—something I haven't done since
my second book years ago; I'd forgotten how much fun it
is to write a multilayered villain. But mostly I enjoyed
creating the complicated relationship between the hero
and heroine and exploring issues such as: Should a parent
sacrifice his or her happiness for the sake of the child?
Can a woman ever truly forgive a man for hurting her and
changing her life irrevocably—even for a good reason?
Can people overcome their dysfunctional pasts? These
questions are explored in the book, though as with all
my work, there are no easy answers—just as in life. And in
the end, I hope you feel that this couple's future is bright,
despite the stumbling blocks ahead.

Please let me know what you thought of *Against the Odds*.
Drop me a note at kshay@rochester.rr.com, or at P.O. Box
24288, Rochester, NY 14624. Also, visit my Web site at
www.kathrynshay.com or the Superauthors Web site at
www.superauthors.com.

Kathryn Shay

Against the Odds

Kathryn Shay

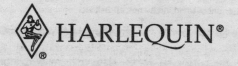

HARLEQUIN®

TORONTO • NEW YORK • LONDON
AMSTERDAM • PARIS • SYDNEY • HAMBURG
STOCKHOLM • ATHENS • TOKYO • MILAN • MADRID
PRAGUE • WARSAW • BUDAPEST • AUCKLAND

DEDICATION

To Candy Carlo, who's spent her career making the lives of troubled kids better, and much of that time being a colleague, partner-in-crime and unconditional friend to me. I hope this book always reminds you of Jamaica, Cand.

ISBN 0-373-71123-9

AGAINST THE ODDS

Copyright © 2003 by Kathryn Shay.

This edition published by arrangement with Harlequin Books S.A.

® and TM are trademarks of the publisher. Trademarks indicated with ® are registered in the United States Patent and Trademark Office, the Canadian Trade Marks Office and in other countries.

Visit us at www.eHarlequin.com

Printed in U.S.A.

CAST OF CHARACTERS

Serenity House: A group home for teenage girls in Hyde Point, New York

Jade Kendrick Anderson: Original resident of S.H.

Ariel Banks: New S.H. resident

Barbara Benton: Nathan's fiancée

R.J.: Barbara's ten-year-old son

Rick Benton: Barbara's ex-husband

Anabelle Crane: Police officer, one of the original residents of Serenity House

Zeke Campoli: FBI agent, Anabelle's friend

Porter Casewell: S.H. resident

Paige Kendrick Chandler: Original resident of S.H., pediatrician, Jade's sister, Ian's wife

Ian Chandler: Paige's husband, obstetrician

Charly Smith Donovan: Original resident of S.H., current operator of S.H.

Drew Hyde: Nathan's stepbrother and campaign manager

Kaeley Hyde: Daughter of Nathan

Nathan Hyde: Congressman, son of the town's founding father

Jonathan Jamison: Kaeley's boyfriend

Rob Kress: Anabelle's boyfriend

Trace McCall: Nathan's college friend, celebrity

Nick Morelli: Taylor's husband

Taylor Vaughn Morelli: Original S.H. resident, Nick's wife

Darcy O'Malley Sloan: Original resident of S.H., Hunter's wife

Hunter Sloan: Darcy's husband, bar owner

Dan Whitman: Police chief, Nora's husband

Nora Nolan Whitman: Dan's wife, founder of S.H.

Nathan's staff: Mark Macomber, scheduler; Karen Kramer, legislative assistant; Cameron Jones, press secretary; Hank Fallon, chief of staff.

PROLOGUE

February 1987

HER HEART THUMPING in her chest, Nora Nolan raced up the rickety steps of the Cranes' house with her friend, police officer Dan Whitman. She'd never seen him so upset. He practically ripped the screen off its hinges and began to pound on the front door.

"Anabelle, it's Sergeant Whitman," he yelled.

No response. He swore. The February wind whipped against Nora's face, chilling her.

"This is the *police*," he shouted. "Open the door."

Still no answer.

"That's it." He drew himself up. "Step back, Nora."

"Dan, I—"

Before she could finish, he slammed his body against the door, easily unhinging the dried-out, battered wood. It crashed backward like an old tree toppling in the wind.

Dan stepped inside. "Stay out here, Nora."

She didn't, instead she followed him into the house. The dim living room was cramped with a couch and a few scattered chairs that were worn and faded. The TV was on, but the screen was snowy and buzzing. The place smelled like burned bacon and mildew.

"*Anabelle?*" Dan yelled again. His voice vibrated with anger.

They heard a crash upstairs. Dan whirled around and catapulted up the steps, two at a time. Again, Nora followed. At the end of the long, dark hallway stood a big man, swaying drunkenly. He was slapping his hand on a closed door.

"Goddamn little shit…let me—"

He never got to finish.

Dan was on the guy in seconds, dragging him back, pushing him against the wall. "You son of a bitch."

"What the hell—"

"If you touched her, I'll kill you." For emphasis, Dan hoisted the guy up against the wall—none too gently—then let him go. He went down like a rag doll, the smell of stale booze emanating from him to where Nora stood.

Pivoting, Dan drew in a deep breath. He turned to the door. "Anabelle? Are you in there?"

No response.

"Anabelle, it's Dan Whitman. I got here as soon as I could. Nora Nolan's with me. Open the door."

Still, no answer. Dan shot a worried look at Nora. "Anabelle," he pleaded, gentling his tone. "You can open the door now. We're going to take you out of here for good. To Serenity House. Nora's got a nice room waiting for you."

After what seemed like an interminable amount of time, Nora heard a small voice ask, "Sergeant Whitman? A-are you sure? Is that you?"

"Yeah, honey, it's me. I promise, no one's going to hurt you again."

The lock clicked open. The door pulled back.

Nora gasped. Inside the tiny bathroom was Anabelle Crane. The sixteen-year-old's face was obscured by a fall of dark hair. There were hand-size welts on her arms. Her chin dipped to her chest, calling attention to a torn

T-shirt. It was ripped down the front as if someone had tried to yank it off her.

Someone had. One of her older brothers, Al Crane.

Dan stepped forward, as did Anabelle. He enveloped her in his arms and held her close. The girl's thin shoulders shook. "I—I was so scared."

"Shh, it's okay. We're here." He rested his chin on Anabelle's head as he gripped her in a solid embrace. "You're safe. You'll be safe from now on, Anabelle. I promise."

She nosed farther into Dan's shirt. "He tried to…" She couldn't finish. Dan looked helplessly at Nora. He'd brought her along just for this purpose.

Nora stepped forward and put her hand on Anabelle's shoulder. "Sweetie, do you need to go to the hospital? Did he assault you sexually?"

Gripping Dan's neck like a lifeline, Anabelle shook her head.

"Thank God." Dan's voice was gruff. "All right, I'm going to cuff him and call a black and white to come get him. Nora will take you outside to my car."

Still the girl held on. Dan let her. Nora waited, her eyes misting. Finally Anabelle let go. She stepped away and peered up at Dan, then over at Nora.

Nora bit back an outcry. The girl's cheek sported purplish bruises. One eye was swollen shut. Her lip was bleeding.

"We'll need the hospital after all," Nora said, taking Anabelle by the arm.

Dan's hands fisted and his eyes widened with rage.

Nora nodded to the crumpled heap on the floor. "Go make the call," she said with a calmness she didn't feel. "We'll meet you at the car."

Dan didn't move.

She touched his hand. "Dan, for Anabelle's sake, be calm when you arrest him."

Drawing in a deep breath, he turned to Al Crane. Nora slid her arm around Anabelle's shoulders and led her through the hallway, down the steps and out of her dingy surroundings.

Thank God for Serenity House, Nora thought. It was a place where she—and Dan—could keep Anabelle safe.

CHAPTER ONE

Fifteen years later

"HE'S THE MOST STUBBORN, hardheaded son of a bitch I've ever known." Dan Whitman's words drifted down the hallway to Anabelle. She halted when she heard his curse.

Nora's voice was low and soft. "And you love him as much as you loved his brother."

Anabelle tucked the lapels of her pink terry robe tighter around her chest and waited. They must be talking about Nathan Hyde. For weeks, they'd been worried about him, and therefore, Anabelle had worried about them.

"I'm pissed as hell at him now."

Silverware clinked, and as Anabelle got to the doorway, she saw that Nora was at the stove stirring hot chocolate. Its bittersweet smell filled the cozy kitchen. The clock overhead read 3:00 a.m. "You have every right, dear."

"Don't patronize me!"

Surprised, Anabelle stepped back into the shadows. Never once had she heard Dan speak harshly to Nora. He'd waited twenty-five years to marry Nora and most of the time they acted like Romeo and Juliet getting a second chance at happiness.

Nora turned from the stove. Her face was serene as she folded her arms over her chest, her satiny, blue robe and matching nightgown flattering her fair complexion. "I'm sorry, Dan. If you're upset enough to snap at me, Nathan's situation must be bad."

"No, love, *I'm* sorry. I didn't mean to yell at you." From the table where he sat, Dan ran a hand through his graying hair. His big, flannel-covered shoulders were stiff. Though he'd aged, Anabelle still saw him as the young sergeant who'd rescued her from hell. She owed him. She'd been thinking about that a lot since she'd found out about Nathan's problems. For once, Anabelle was in a position to help Dan.

"You're concerned about Nathan," Nora continued gently. "I understand."

Being privy to Congressman Nathan Hyde's life was one of the drawbacks of returning to Hyde Point, New York, after ten years away. That, and of course, seeing him in person. He and Anabelle had a painful history. Otherwise, Anabelle loved staying here with Nora and Dan. She had been a police officer in Seattle until last October, when she'd taken a bullet in the shoulder. Dan had insisted that she come back here to recuperate for a few months and she was only too happy to accept. She treasured her contact with the other original residents of Serenity House, too, and got great satisfaction from helping out Charly Donovan, who now ran the home for girls.

Nora crossed to the table and set two mugs on its sleek maple surface. Dan pulled her onto his lap. Anabelle turned and was about to leave them to their making up when Dan said, "Nora, I don't think it was an accident, what happened to Nathan tonight."

Anabelle stilled. Her police instincts went on red alert.

And in spite of the fact that Nathan Hyde was no longer a part of her life, a chill ran through her.

"What?"

"He said he was jogging by the river and had just come back up to the street when the car came out of nowhere. It sounded to me like somebody was waiting for him."

Anabelle gasped.

Both Nora and Dan looked to the hallway.

"Anabelle? Come in, sweetie," Nora called out.

She stepped fully into the kitchen. "Someone tried to *kill* Nathan tonight?"

Dan stared at her like a cop deciding how much to tell the family of a crime victim. "He doesn't seem to think so. I'm not sure."

"You just said this wasn't an accident."

When he didn't respond, she moved closer to him.

Nora slid off Dan's lap as he stood and took Anabelle's hand. "I didn't want you to know about tonight."

He was still protecting her. "Well, it's too late now. What's going on?"

Dan nodded to the table, so she dropped down in a chair. Nora got her a mug of hot chocolate and joined them. How many times had she sat at the scarred old kitchen table at Serenity House just like this with both of them…when they were trying to talk her into pressing charges against her brothers for attempted rape…when they found a job for her at the police station…when they recommended she go work as a nanny for the Hydes' daughter, Kaeley, after she graduated from high school.

And when she'd come to them, for the last time, broken and battered emotionally and told them she'd had an affair with Nathan Hyde, but he'd gone back to his wife, Olivia. She couldn't tell them the whole story, though, and because of that, Dan and Nathan had had some kind of showdown after she left town and things had been strained for a long time between them. They'd gotten through it, though, and regained much of their closeness.

"You know the basics from what Kaeley told you. Nathan got phone calls for a few months before the election, telling him not to run for re-election to his seat in the House of Representatives. Then, they stopped for almost a month after the election. On Christmas Day, he started to get e-mails."

She remembered Nathan's visit Christmas night. She thought he'd come to wish the Whitmans happy holidays. Since she'd returned to Hyde Point, Anabelle had avoided Nathan as much as possible when he visited Nora and Dan. That night, she'd been intent on steeling herself against watching him with Barbara Benton, his beautiful, sophisticated fiancée. After an acceptable period of time, Anabelle had retreated to the guest room. She'd been surprised when Kaeley came in and told her about the e-mails.

And asked for her help...

Annie, please, can't you do something? You're a cop. I know about those guys you protected, those women you saved in your undercover work.

How do you know about all that?

I heard Daddy and Dan talking. And I read the Seattle newspapers online. Don't worry, I think it's great. You're great. Couldn't you, like, protect Daddy until this is over? Since you're in Hyde Point and everything.

Gently but firmly she'd said no. First, Nathan hadn't asked for her help. Second, if Nathan needed a bodyguard, he could hire a professional.

But, truth be told, she *had* considered offering her assistance as a cop, since this kind of protection and undercover work was her specialty. And because Dan was worried. And also, for Kaeley's sake. But, in the end, she hadn't volunteered because of what had happened between her and Nathan years ago. Still, she'd wrestled with her reluctance, especially since Kaeley had begged her twice more for her help. Now it seemed as if the situation had escalated. How could she not help out Dan and Kaeley, the two people she loved most in the world?

And how could she let the man she'd once loved be endangered when it was well within her power to keep him safe?

Anabelle fell into cop mode. It suited her best. "What do the e-mails say now that he's been re-elected?" she asked. "Kaeley didn't know. Only that he got them and they were similar to the calls."

"That he shouldn't be in the House," Dan told her. "That he doesn't deserve to make laws for people. There were no direct threats."

Anabelle sipped the cocoa. It was warm and soothing on her throat, which had suddenly become raw. "Did he report this to his superiors in Washington?"

Dan looked frustrated. "Yes. But neither the calls nor the e-mails warrant Secret Service protection. They said this kind of crank thing is pretty common. They recommended that he hire a private bodyguard if he was really worried."

"He refused," Nora put in. "He said it would be too disruptive to his routine, and the caller would get tired of harassing him and would go away."

"Nathan always hated being backed in a corner," Anabelle said absently. "But he'll have to do something now, if he was run off the road."

"It could have been an accident. Maybe I'm overreacting." Dan squeezed Anabelle's hand. "In any case, this isn't your concern, honey. We'll deal with it. I know it's been hard for you to see him since you've been home.''

Anabelle shrugged off the comment. ''Actually, I've been concerned about all this mostly because of Kaeley.''

Leaving Nathan and Kaeley was the hardest thing Anabelle had ever done in her life. Though she'd had no choice regarding the man she loved, in the end she'd been unable to let the little girl go completely. With Nathan's approval, she'd maintained a correspondence and phone contact with the child. When Kaeley got old enough, they began sharing frequent e-mails. ''I still miss her.''

''We could tell. She spent a lot of time here with you before she went back to Syracuse.'' Kaeley was in her second year as a theater major at SU.

''She's worried about her father.'' Anabelle thought for a minute. ''After tonight, maybe he'll see he has to hire somebody.''

''Maybe.'' Dan didn't look convinced though. ''Preferably somebody who can pose as a member of his office staff or household. When he's been willing to discuss it at all, he's said he'd only consider the protection if it would be covert.''

''Why?'' Anabelle asked.

''For one thing, Nathan doesn't want the public to know he's been harassed.''

''That's ridiculous. It happens all the time to politicians.''

Again, Dan jammed a hand through his hair. ''There's another reason. From what was said, there's a possibility that the caller might know Nathan. He mentioned some things about Nathan's whereabouts, his movements, that lead us to believe the person knows him.''

"Could be," Anabelle said, "but politicians are often victims of one of the other types of stalkers."

"Types?" Nora asked.

"Yeah. I was on a case once where I helped catch a stalker. Usually they fall into three categories—intimate-partner stalkers, delusional stalkers and vengeful stalkers. Politicians tend to attract the last—somebody angry over a piece of legislation he helped pass, a criminal he was instrumental in putting away, things like that."

Dan frowned. "Well, this guy seemed to know a lot about him."

"It's a guy? You're sure?"

"He sounded like a guy."

Anabelle stood and crossed to the stove to get more hot chocolate. She knew so much about this kind of thing—had experience with tracing calls and e-mails, deciphering messages, ferreting out information. Maybe she could just give Dan some pointers.

They talked a while longer. It became clear to Anabelle that Nathan needed protection. At 4:00 a.m., she went to bed. Crawling under the covers, listening to the early-January wind howl outside, she thought about the only two men she'd ever loved in her life—Dan Whitman, as the father she'd never had, and Nathan Hyde, as the man she *couldn't* have. At 5:00 a.m., Anabelle began to think about Kaeley again. She'd always viewed the girl as a curious blend of daughter/sister. One thing was crystal clear—Kaeley loved her father. What would it do to her if something happened to Nathan? Anabelle knew only too well how close Nathan and Kaeley were. He'd practically raised her alone, except for the four years Anabelle was her nanny. At nineteen, just making her way in the world, losing Nathan was probably the one thing Kaeley Hyde couldn't handle now.

And at 6:00 a.m., sleep still eluded her. She thought of the last time she'd seen Nathan before she left Hyde Point ten years ago…

I love you, Annie, he'd said raggedly, holding the report in his hand. *But I have no choice.*

I know.

I'd do anything for you but this. Give up anything but this…

And I'd do anything for you, Nathan, give up anything for you… She'd walked out of his house then, and had not seen him again until she returned briefly to Hyde Point last June for Nora and Dan's wedding. But on this cold morning, sleep-deprived and emotionally ragged, Anabelle knew in her heart that she still meant what she'd said to Nathan. She'd do anything for him, even take the pain of being near him, if it meant she could keep him from harm.

Bleary-eyed and disheveled, she crawled out of bed at seven o'clock and made her way to the kitchen. Dan was there. He stood sipping coffee by the window. He was another man she'd do anything for.

"Dan?"

He pivoted, looking haggard and worried, as if he'd never made it to bed. "What are you doing up, honey?"

"I've got an idea."

"About what?"

She drew in a breath. "I want to be Nathan's bodyguard."

Looking horrified, he said, "You don't mean that, Anabelle."

"I do."

He shook his head. "No, absolutely not."

"Don't you trust me enough to do the job?"

"It has nothing to do with that. I'd never put you in a dangerous situation like this."

She chuckled and crossed over to the coffeepot. "Dan, I'm a cop. What exactly do you think I do every day?"

Staring at her shoulder, he focused on where she'd gotten shot. "I don't think about it."

"Do you believe I'm a good cop?"

"Of course I do. My cousin Herb says you're the best undercover operative he's ever worked with. But *this?* No way."

"Dan, Kaeley begged me to help out here. And I've got a lot of expertise in harassment, threats and protection. What's more, I could fit into Nathan's staff easily on the ruse that I worked for him before. It's perfect."

"Not for you."

"He's being stalked and you know it. He needs help."

Dan continued to list his objections until she stopped him with her ace in the hole. "You know, I'm going back to Seattle if you don't let me do this."

"Yes, of course I know."

"I might be working on a big case. Surveillance is being set up for Archie Glad."

"The Mafia guy?"

"Yes. He just got out of prison. He'll be back in Seattle by now."

"You're not…oh, God, I don't want to hear about it."

"They're going to plant some cops in his organization…female ones…"

Finally, Dan played his own ace. "Honey, it's not just the danger. I know what happened between you and Nathan. Are you sure you could handle being joined at the hip with him until the perp is found?"

"Of course I can. What happened between me and Nathan is nothing but a bad memory now." She grabbed

Dan's hand and squeezed it. "It was ten years ago, Dan. It took me a long time to recover, but I did. Besides," she said, winking. "I got me a boyfriend."

"The guy who calls here all the time?"

"Uh-huh." She smiled. "And Nathan's engaged. We can do this. We're adults." At his still-skeptical expression, she said, "Come on, Dan, you know it's the best thing for Nathan and Kaeley."

"It's not the best thing for you. That's what I'm concerned about."

"Don't worry about me. I'm a big girl now. I can take care of myself."

WHEN THE DOORBELL RANG, Nathan's Irish setter, Elly, barked loudly.

"Down, girl," he said irritably from the kitchen, where he was stacking dishes in the dishwasher. With no sleep and only coffee fueling his system, Nathan wasn't doing well since he'd been run him off the road at midnight.

He shouldn't have been out there at all, in the cold, so late. But he'd been trying to outrun the demons caused by Kaeley's little bomb before she left to go back to college yesterday.

Annie's got a boyfriend, Dad. I'm so glad. After she broke her engagement years ago, I was afraid she'd never find anybody. She misses the guy a lot. He's called her almost every day.

Banishing the thought of Anabelle's current love interest, Nathan left the kitchen and hurried through the living room to the foyer. He'd have to get the door himself. Mrs. Hanson, the kind old woman who'd been the Hyde estate housekeeper for years, was still visiting her daughter for the holidays.

His dog accompanied him to the foyer. Uneasy because of last night, Nathan checked the peephole. Damn, it was Dan. Were they going to go another round? The man almost had Nathan convinced he needed a bodyguard anyway. He should just give in graciously. But a stranger in his house? With him all day long? How could he live with that? And how would they explain this to the public? He sure as hell didn't want it to get out that some crazy person was after him.

He drew open the door and froze. Anabelle was standing to the right of Dan, where he hadn't been able to see her. She was dressed all in black, her hair pulled off her face. It had always been light brown but for her last undercover operation, she'd colored it blond. She was framed by the snow and the sun sparkling off it. He couldn't wrest his gaze from her.

"You look like shit," Dan said irritably.

That moved him, seeing calm, collected Dan—who faced down murderers and rapists with a cop's aplomb—so flustered. "Dan. Ann—Anabelle." The few times he'd slipped and called her Annie—Kaeley's old nickname for her—she'd gone stiff and cold on him.

Not that she didn't have the right.

"We need to talk to you." Dan stepped inside without being invited and brushed past him.

Nathan shot a questioning look to Anabelle. Her face was a blank canvas; it had been since she'd returned to Hyde Point two months ago. There was a time when he could read her every thought, when he spent hours just studying that face, which had only gotten more interesting with age.

"We want to talk to you is all." Her Demi Moore voice was still sexy as hell.

She paused momentarily before she stepped inside. When she did, he saw her straighten her shoulders and tilt her chin. It had always been her way of facing the unpleasant. Any good memories this house held for her were probably obscured by how things had ended between them.

Elly broke the tension by barking wildly and skittering around her, claws scraping loudly on the oak floor.

Anabelle's eyes widened. "You still have her? She was old back then."

"This is Elly, the third." He'd named her after Eleanor Roosevelt because he'd always admired the woman. "The grandpup of the dog I had when you lived here." He petted the animal's head. "She just had her own litter. We gave the last of them away a couple of weeks ago— to Serenity House."

"Oh." Anabelle started to drop to her knees. She'd loved Elly's grandmother. More than once he'd seen her burying her face in the dog's sleek red coat. At the end, Elly had been sleeping in her bed every night—and had moped around for months after she'd left.

So had Nathan.

Straightening, Anabelle looked at him blankly. "Kaeley didn't tell me about the dog."

No, you were too busy talking about your boyfriend.

Dan had gone into the parlor to the right and called out, "What's going on out there?"

Anabelle circled around Elly and crossed into the room. Her braid hung down her back onto her black leather jacket, swaying like a thick rope caught in the wind.

Nathan followed her inside, and after he hung up their coats, asked, "What's up?"

Dan and Anabelle exchanged looks.

"We have a proposition for you," Dan said. "It concerns last night's events."

"You told Anabelle about this?"

"She overheard Nora and I talking about it when I got home. And Kaeley had already told Anabelle what she knew about the situation."

"Damn it, Dan, Anabelle's the last person I wanted to know about all this."

Anabelle asked, "Why, because you're being so bull-headed about accepting help?" Though her tone was acerbic, there was a note of worry underneath. It was almost as if she was trying to disguise her concern for him.

Nathan faced Dan. Big and brawny, in a heavy sweater, jeans and boots, at fifty-five, Dan was still a force to be reckoned with. "Look, I agree we need to get an investigator on the case. I've called Washington and I'm going to meet with someone when I go down there this week."

"Well, that's good. But you need more than that now."

He probably did. In his sane moments, he knew he wasn't thinking clearly about this whole thing. "Maybe. But it's going to be hard getting somebody in here without alerting my whole district that I'm being harassed."

"We have a solution." Dan glared at Anabelle. "You tell him since it was your idea."

She grasped the long black scarf she wore around her neck and worried the cloth with her fingers. "I'm volunteering to be your bodyguard."

"*What?*"

"I'm a trained undercover cop. Several of my assignments have been in protection. I'm good at what I do."

"No way in hell."

"We could keep it quiet that way. Pretend I was joining your staff."

"No."

"That my shoulder hasn't healed right, so I might never be able to take up police work again. I might never *want* to after being seriously injured. I might want to settle in Hyde Point again. A staff position opened up, and since I worked for you in the past, I decided to take the job and figure out what to do with my life."

"Absolutely not." He faced Dan. "You planned this with her?"

"Hell no. But she's got a point."

"How can you even consider endangering her life like this?"

Dan's eyes widened. "Goddamn it, I don't want her in danger. But you're being stalked! Because you insist on keeping this situation quiet, because you're so stubborn about hiring a stranger, it feels like I'm being forced to make a choice between *your* safety and Anabelle's."

Anabelle gasped. Nathan swore.

"Oh, Dan," she said, crossing to him. "It's not that way at all. I won't be in any more danger here, protecting Nathan, than I would going back to Seattle and doing my job there."

"I know that in my head," Dan admitted.

Nathan didn't like the sound of that. "What the hell is she talking about?"

Dan got mad all over again. "Her next assignment in Seattle was to be bait for Archie Glad."

"What?"

Anabelle threw up her hands in disgust. "You know, you two are something. What do you think I've been doing all these years?"

"I try not to think about it." Nathan's voice was gruff. So was Dan's. "I already said the same thing."

She shook her head. "Listen, guys, I'm a highly respected police officer. I've participated in ten, no, eleven undercover operations. I've protected businessmen from the Mob, little boys from kidnappers and ferreted out criminals as a waitress, a high-school teacher *and* as a prostitute.''

"Oh, God," Dan said.

Nathan practically barked at her. "I don't want to hear this.''

"Well, you need to hear it because, believe me, watching over you will be a piece of cake compared to what I've done."

Both men quieted. Dan paced. Nathan went and stood by the window, peering out at the snow-covered lawns.

Finally, Dan said, "She *will* be safer here."

"Yeah, maybe," Nathan agreed.

"Damn it, you guys, I can not only take care of myself now, I've dedicated my life to keeping others safe."

Again, both men were silenced. Nathan glanced at Dan then faced her. He didn't want to broach this subject publicly, but hell, Dan knew some of the story anyway. He said gently, "What about everything else between us, Annie?"

Her lips quivered slightly before the cop mask fell back into place. "I asked you not to call me that." She looked at Dan. "Could you leave us alone a minute?"

He glanced at his watch. "Actually, I'm already late for an appointment. Can you get home all right?"

"I can *walk* home from here, Dan," she said, amused. "Hyde Point's still a small town."

"All right, I'll go." He crossed to Anabelle and slid his arm around her. She leaned into him, giving Nathan a flash of the girl she used to be. "I'm sorry, honey. I know you're all grown up now. I worry, though."

She kissed his cheek. "You're entitled. But be objective. Please."

Drawing away, he faced Nathan. "Listen to her, buddy," he said. "For me, and for Jack."

Nathan watched Dan go. "For Jack? That was hitting below the belt."

"He worries about you." Dan had taken Nathan's older brother's place after Jack was killed in a car accident when Nathan was young. According to Nora, since Nathan's father died, Dan had been even more vigilant. "You can't expect him to forget his big brother role now, just because you're some hotshot politician."

"Is that how you see me?"

She shook her head and stuck her hands in the pockets of her black wool slacks. With them she wore a black sweater and black boots. "I see you as a man who needs help, Nathan. Help that I can provide. I want to do it."

"Why?"

"For Kaeley."

"Kaeley?"

"At Christmas, she asked me to step in."

"I see."

"And I'm doing it for Dan. He and Nora would be devastated if something happened to you."

It shouldn't hurt. He knew that. But it did. "So this has nothing to do with me?"

The cop veneer cracked a bit. "Of course it does. I don't want anything to happen to you. If a few weeks of my time can prevent that, I'll do it." She raised her chin. "I do it for strangers all the time."

He studied her, wondering if she still felt anything for him. Her actions for the two months she'd been back in Hyde Point said no. But here she was...

"Don't mistake this, Nathan," she said quickly as if

she'd read this mind, "for anything other that what it is. I care about you, of course, like I'm sure you still care about me. But my feelings for you aren't what they were the last time I was in this house."

"So I've heard. You've got a steady guy."

"And you've got a fiancée."

They faced each other like adversaries. He remembered a time when she couldn't get close enough to him.

Anabelle cleared her throat. "I won't get involved, if you think otherwise."

"Otherwise?"

"That there's anything between us...that this could go anywhere. That we might pick up where we left off."

The moment was charged with electric emotion. "Of course I don't think that." He didn't, did he?

"Well, good then." She scanned the parlor.

"Let's sit," he said, indicating the couches. "And hammer things out."

After they took their seats, she asked, "Will there be problems with me moving in?"

"No. It will look respectable because Mrs. Hanson will be back after next week. Both she and Herman, my driver, still reside on the grounds. And my D.C. staff often stays over because the house is so big."

Anabelle nodded. "Is there anyone personally who might have a problem with this plan?"

He smiled fondly. "Drew. My stepbrother. He's my campaign manager. He's very circumspect about my actions these days."

"Why?"

"White House dreams, I guess. Sometimes I think he wants that more than I do."

"It's what *you* always wanted, Nathan."

"Is it?"

"I always thought so. In any case, you can't tell any-body the truth about my position, even Drew."

"Surely you don't suspect my stepbrother?"

"It's my job to suspect everybody."

He sighed deeply. "We have to tell some people."

"Who?"

"Kaeley has to know, since she begged you to help anyway."

"All right."

He hesitated a moment. "And I'll have to tell Barbara."

Anabelle's face was inscrutable.

"She'd wonder why you were here all the time, not just for work-related things. Social occasions and the like."

Not a flicker of emotion crossed her features. She must be great at staring down dangerous criminals without showing her inner feelings.

"Fine. But absolutely nobody else."

Nathan straightened on the sofa. "What about money?"

"Money?"

"Yes. I'd be paying a regular bodyguard."

"Okay. Give me what the government allows for an administrative assistant."

"No way. It's peanuts. And you're off disability now, aren't you?"

"Yes."

"How will you arrange the time away from your job?"

"Dan's cousin is my boss. He'll pull some strings."

"So you're not drawing a salary, right?"

She rolled her eyes. "I have money, Nathan."

"So do I. Private money. I'll be paying you a thousand dollars a day."

"That's absurd."

"Bodyguards make a fortune."

"I don't want to make money off the situation."

"Take it or the deal's off."

"Goddamn it, Nathan."

Arching an eyebrow, he folded his arms over his chest. "I've agreed to everything else. I'm insisting on this."

Her face lighted with challenge, like a kid who'd found a way to circumvent a teacher. "Fine, pay me the money. I'll donate it to Serenity House, or the new boys' home, Quiet Waters."

Nathan sputtered, but let it go.

"Then that's that," she said matter-of-factly. "Everything will work out fine."

But as he watched her beautiful eyes sparkle like amber jewels in the light that streamed in through the windows, he wasn't so sure he believed her. Could he really handle this proximity to her? Could he not let his old feelings surface?

After all, though he'd been married for several years to someone else, and was now engaged, Anabelle Crane was the only woman Nathan Hyde had ever truly loved.

ANABELLE HADN'T THOUGHT about the ramifications of being back in the house where she fell in love with Nathan. She hadn't thought about much except helping out Dan, Kaeley and, of course, Nathan himself. But when she told him that first on the agenda today was a tour of the house to check its security, starting with his offices, she knew she'd have to steel herself against the memories. The wing he'd appropriated for his offices and, when needed, for housing his staff, was the wing he, his wife, Olivia, and daughter had lived in when Anabelle worked as Kaeley's nanny and the elder Hydes were still in residence.

The former living area was now his office and conference room. "Well, this is different," she said when she entered the high-ceilinged, oak-paneled room. She crossed to the bank of windows facing the grounds.

As she sought out the locks, Nathan said, "Don't worry, they're all—"

A window slid up, silencing him. Glancing over her shoulder, she gave him an impatient look.

"Hell, I was sure they were locked."

"Most people are. A good number of break-ins are through unsecured windows." She methodically checked each window and then the door leading outside.

"Did you have any special training? In bodyguard work?"

"Some. Herb sent me for security training before I started undercover work." She focused on a loose lock. "This needs to be replaced. I could jimmy it with my eyes closed."

"When was that, Anabelle?"

She turned and found him sitting on the edge of his desk—a big, carved oak piece of furniture that shouted wealth and power like a neon sign. His grass-green eyes were fixed on her with a purposeful stare.

"When was what?"

"When did you get into undercover work? I know the basics of how you became a cop from Kaeley and the sketchy information Dan let slip. I always wondered how you got into covert police service."

Because after you left me I wanted to be someone else.

"About five years ago." She crossed to the door. "Good dead bolt. I'd like another one here, though, and on all the outside doors." She fished a notebook out of her jacket pocket and began to take notes. "First thing we'll need is a locksmith to do some work."

"You started out as a secretary for the Seattle police, didn't you?"

"Uh-huh. A lot like the reception job I had at Dan's office before I came to work for you."

"That's what got you interested in the police force?"

She studied the layout of the room, sketching it in her mind, ignoring his solicitousness. It was one thing she always loved about Nathan, his genuine interest in other people. "I liked the excitement. I asked Herb about the training academy. I went. End of story." She looked up at him. "I'm done in this room."

Sliding off the desk, Nathan nodded. He looked mildly annoyed, the way he used to when Olivia interrupted him at something he was doing. At the door he stood back.

She crossed to him. "I'll go first, Nathan, in and out of a room, for your safety. But don't mistake that for etiquette. Manners have no place in protective work."

"Yes, ma'am." His eyes flashed fire.

She ignored it. Partly because she hadn't meant the quip to come out so curtly. Partly because his face was etched with lines of exhaustion and she sensed, despite what he said, that he was worried about the stalking. This whole thing was not going to be easy on him.

Besides, Anabelle was very good at ignoring things and turning off unwanted feelings. The scowling man before her had been responsible for these acquired traits.

They toured an office, off of which there were guest sleeping quarters. "I'm going to need the names of your staff." She poised pen over paper.

"This is Hank Fallon's area. He's my chief of staff."

"Does he spend time here?"

"Yes. He's taking some certification tests in D.C. this

week. Things are slow over the holidays. Congress doesn't reconvene for a while, so this was a good opportunity for him to do that.''

"Who else stays here when you're in town?"

"My two aides when they accompany me back here. Drew, who as I said, is my campaign manager. Though he lives with his wife in town, he often stays with me at the height of things. And my administrative assistant used to stay here."

"Used to?"

"Yes. He finished his tenure with me before the last election then snagged a good job inside the White House. Hank and I have been discussing whether or not to replace him. We'd be able to cut some costs if we don't.''

She smiled. "Well, that solves one problem."

He nodded. "How you fit into my organization, right?"

His quick, incisive mind was another thing she'd admired about him. "Yep. You've decided you'll be needing an assistant."

He shrugged and she wondered what he was thinking.

They left the guest quarters and continued down a corridor. She smiled as she opened the next door. "I can't believe it."

She entered the twenty-by-twenty room and walked around, fingering the state-of-the-art workout machines, noting the beige walls that had once been decorated with Disney murals. "What does Kaeley think of this?"

"She uses it when she's home, a lot like she did when it was her playroom."

"Why did you put an exercise room in your office wing?"

"So all my staff could benefit from it when they're here."

Nathan had always been thoughtful of those in his employ.

Anabelle wandered around the room, picturing Kaeley at five. Poised at the top of a small slide, dressed in cape and suit like a superhero's, she'd whiz down the ramp. *Look, Annie, I can fly.* Either Anabelle or Nathan was always there to catch her.

"Anabelle?"

"Kaeley was an adorable kid, wasn't she?"

"Yeah. Remember the hours you spent in here with her?"

"Uh-huh." Shaking herself out of the memory and pulling into herself to stop further reminiscences, she went to the windows and checked them. And let anger replace the poignant emotion that surfaced. "Damn it, Nathan."

"Another's unlocked?"

"Yes."

He sighed heavily. "Somebody probably was working out and it got hot."

She pivoted. "Do you spend time in here?"

"Every day that I'm in Hyde Point."

She believed that. Her gaze dropped to his chest. He had a runner's body, tall and lean, but the tan cashmere sweater and brown jeans concealed, or used to conceal, a road map of muscles. "Then you should be more careful with the locks," she said with intentional coolness. "And clearly, use this room instead of running outside now."

"I'm sorry. I'm not used to being stalked!"

His tone spiked her temper. "You've been getting letters since the fall. Pretty careless to ignore all this."

"I—"

"Many stalkers know their victim."

"Annie, I—"

"But a significant percentage never know them." She slapped her hand on a machine, sending the bar crashing and clinking against another. "We don't know what you're dealing with, Congressman. You need to be more careful."

"Fine!" Turning abruptly, he strode to the door.

She followed. Saying little, they toured the rest of the wing: Kaeley's old bedroom, now a sitting area; a small kitchen; another bathroom. The last two rooms, at the end, had been Nathan and Olivia's bedroom and the nanny's quarters.

She tackled the former first, easing open the door. "This room hasn't changed much," she said, scanning the interior, ignoring the stab of pain that surprised her like a mugger hovering in the shadows.

"It's a guest suite now. There was no need to change the space."

For a minute, her gaze riveted on the bed. His and Olivia's.

Then, quickly, efficiently, Anabelle checked out the windows. Chiding herself for her discomfort—and vowing to get over it—she strode out of the former master suite.

The last was her old room. She eased open the door. She didn't know what she expected, but it wasn't a complete rearrangement of walls and spaces. The cozy window seat where she'd curled up to read was gone. The walk-in closet she'd played hide-and-seek in with Kaeley had been torn out and there was a desk and computer in the nook. Window treatments, everything, had been redone. "What happened here?" She tried to keep her voice neutral.

"Olivia had it remodeled."

Ripped apart, he meant. Olivia had erased all trace of her. Her eyes strayed to where the bed had been. There wasn't even a wall there now. Still, she remembered lying in that bed, dreaming of making a life with him.

Nathan came up behind her. "Annie?" He grasped her shoulders, and for a moment she was bombarded by the...familiarity of it all. He whispered. "Are you all right?"

"I..." She just stood there, her heart constricting in her chest.

"Annie?"

She wouldn't do this. She *wouldn't*. "Give me a minute."

He squeezed her shoulders and stepped back.

When she could breathe easier, she schooled her face to reveal little and turned to him. "Don't do that again."

His eyes narrowed. "Do what?"

"Touch me."

"You went white. I was concerned."

"Being back in this house, in this room, is hard for me. I need you to promise you'll keep your distance."

"Why? Are you remembering things?"

She sucked in a breath. "When I do, it's only the bad things I recall."

His look was skeptical.

She raised her chin. "I won't do this job unless you promise me you'll treat me as a bodyguard only. We've gone on with our lives and I want it to stay that way. Besides, I need my wits about me. If you can't control yourself—" *like you couldn't back then,* she wanted to say "—I won't be able to help you." Brushing past him, she headed for the door. There, she turned. "Think about it, Nathan. I'm not the girl who loved you anymore. I'll be your bodyguard and that's all. If you want something else, I'm out of here.''

He drew in a breath. ''Fine, I'll keep my distance.''

CHAPTER TWO

NORA WATCHED Anabelle come up the walk, all grace and style these days, but with a purposeful, determined stride. She remembered the girl as a teenager, with her coltish legs and slender awkwardness. A lot had changed in fifteen years.

Opening the door before Anabelle had a chance to ring the bell, she smiled fondly at her former charge. "Hi, sweetie. Got a minute before you go to Serenity House?"

Anabelle searched Nora's face knowingly. Of all the girls, this one read people like a trained interviewer. That's probably why she made such a good cop. "I always have time to talk to you," she said dryly. "Besides, it's probably best to let you have your say. Dan already lit into me about this whole thing."

Cut to the quick, that was her Anabelle. "Well, I'm not going to *light into you.*" She nodded to the kitchen. "We're just going to have a nice little chat." As she led Anabelle back to the kitchen, she said, "How are the classes going at Serenity House?"

"Great. I'm so glad Charly asked me to do some self-defense with the girls."

"We could have used that in your day."

"You can say that again." They sat at the table and Nora poured the tea without asking Anabelle if she wanted any. Sometimes you just had to steamroll the girl into letting you take care of her. "Do you think about it much, sweetie?"

"Serenity House?"

"No, why you needed to go there."

"Sometimes. When I see girls there who were abused, physically and emotionally, it reminds me of my situation."

Thoughtfully, Nora sipped her tea, not appreciating the honey-flavored brew. "Al and Aaron are still in town."

"Yes, but I haven't seen them these two months. And even if I do, I'm no longer the girl they knew." Though she hadn't prosecuted them—she'd been too ashamed and embarrassed—Dan had made sure her stepbrothers stayed away from her.

"You aren't that girl. In some ways that's good." Nora set down her cup. "You're different because of your experience with Nathan. So tell me why you volunteered to protect him."

Anabelle stiffened. "I'm doing it for Dan mostly. I'd give my life for him, Nora, and he'd be devastated if something happened to Nathan."

"I appreciate that. He'll rest more comfortably knowing Nathan has protection. He'll worry about you, of course, but I trust you can take care of yourself. Dan will see that, too, eventually." She'd learned long ago to let her girls realize their potential, and Anabelle's talent was in protecting others. Probably because she'd needed protection when she was young—and only got it from Dan.

"The fact that I'm guarding Nathan instead of going into a Mafia sting operation in Seattle didn't hurt."

Nora chuckled. "I'm sure Dan would rather have you here. We're lucky his cousin is your boss and can let you go for a while. But I'm more concerned about the emotional upheaval you're bound to experience, rather than the physical danger you might be in. Nathan almost destroyed you.''

For a long time Nora had found it inexcusable that Nathan Hyde had had an affair with Anabelle and then gone back to his wife. It had taken years for her to forgive the man.

Anabelle toyed with the spoon on the table. ''It's complicated, Nora.'' She raised her eyes to the ceiling. ''What a cliché I was. A Serenity House girl believing she had a future with the town's fair-haired boy.''

''I can't figure out what happened, Anabelle. He was miserable for years after you left. Dan was furious that Nathan had gotten involved with you, but at the same time he worried himself sick about Nathan's state of mind.''

''He seems happy now. He's engaged.''

Nora waited for a moment. ''Are you sure it's just for Dan that you're helping him out, sweetie?''

''And for Kaeley. I love her like a daughter. She'd fall apart if something happened to her father.''

''Then that's all of it?''

Sighing, Anabelle got up from the table and went to the window. ''All right, it's not. I'm no longer in love with Nathan, Nora, and I'd never start up with him again, but I cared deeply for him at one time. *I* don't want anything to happen to him. If a few weeks of my time, and some discomfort being around him, will prevent that, I'll do it.''

Where, given the hell she'd gone through, had this girl ever gotten that kind of heart? Nora must have spoken the words aloud, because Anabelle turned to her and smiled.

''I got that kind of heart from you and Dan. I was fourteen when he took me under his wing. Sixteen when

I met you. You taught me to give, Nora. Both of you. I'm giving back now. To Dan, and you indirectly.''

"Thank you for telling me that. But I'm still afraid this will hurt you too much.''

"No, I can handle it. I've learned to turn off my feelings pretty good in undercover work.''

She's gotten cold, Dan had said when Anabelle came to stay with them.

It's self-protection. She needs to do this for her work.
I think she does it in her personal life. Damn Nathan. It's partly his fault.

"Nora? What are you thinking?''

"That Nathan is partly responsible for your learning how to do that.''

"Turn off my feelings?''

"Yes.''

"Maybe. It would be ironic, wouldn't it? Because of him, I've learned to do something that could save his life.''

"I think Nathan's getting the better of the deal.''

"He did before, too. His lovely wife, his beautiful daughter and his career in politics. Though I always wondered why he waited so long to pursue that.''

"Dan said the same thing. He didn't know why, either. Nathan wouldn't talk about it.''

Anabelle wrapped her arms around her waist. "I'd prefer to end this discussion, Nora. It's very unpleasant for me.''

"All right. Just let me thank you for doing this for Dan and Nathan. I only hope you come out unscathed.''

She smiled. "I will. I can take care of myself.''

"Yes, sweetie, I know.'' In everything but matters of the heart, Nora suspected. But she'd gotten what she wanted—a glimpse into Anabelle's state of mind. Maybe she'd be okay. The girl was tough, and pretty sophisticated now. Maybe she could handle Nathan Hyde this time around.

ANABELLE STOOD before Serenity House and stared up at it. The moon shone down on the building and the outside lights had been turned on, creating a halo around the house. Appropriate, since it had saved her fifteen years ago—almost to the day. Grabbing her gym bag, she left Nora's Sunbird parked in the long driveway and headed up the concrete walkway.

She noticed everything. New roof. The porch had been refurbished. She stopped and stared at the swing, now iced over and still. The first time she'd seen Nathan Hyde she'd been sitting on that swing. He'd come striding up the steps with Dan Whitman, so suave, and handsome and masculine in an expensive suit, his dark-blond hair cut to perfection even then. She lost her heart to him on that very day.

And got it back only at great cost.

Remember that, she told herself. *Especially now.*

She knocked on the door a little more forcefully than she'd intended. Ariel Banks flung it open. "Anabelle!" the young girl said. "We thought you weren't coming!"

Though she tried to distance herself from most people, teenagers seemed to infiltrate their way into her heart. Like Kaeley.

"Would I miss a session with you guys?" Anabelle asked, ruffling the girl's spiked blond hair. Ariel had bleached it in imitation of Anabelle's streaks.

The girl pouted. "This is the last one, isn't it?"

"Maybe not, kid."

"What do you mean? You're leavin' this hick town next week, aren't you?"

"Change of plans. Let me inside, I'll tell you about it."

Anabelle appeased Ariel with a quick explanation that she might not be returning to police work for health reasons, then they made their way through the corridor leading to the kitchen. Immediately Anabelle was bombarded by a sense of well-being so strong, she smiled. The living room to the right had new furniture, the steps leading upstairs to the left were stained a darker oak, but Serenity House's homey warmth remained. When they reached the kitchen, Ariel trundled down the basement steps where they were all meeting, but Anabelle halted in the room where she'd found such solace. For a moment, she reveled in it.

Charly Donovan appeared in the doorway, took in Anabelle's expression, then crossed to her. She put her hand on Anabelle's shoulder. Both Anabelle and Charly had been rescued from abusive family situations and placed in Serenity House. It was the best thing that ever happened to them.

"I feel it, too," Charly said softly. Calm, light-gray eyes soothed Anabelle's troubled spirit. For a moment they just stood there. Then Charly glanced to the basement. "Ready for your farewell class?"

"Um, we need to talk about that," Anabelle told her quietly.

"Talk about what?" someone from behind said.

Anabelle turned and flashed another smile. Jade Kendrick Anderson, another original resident of Serenity House, had come up from downstairs, dressed in hot-pink everything—tights, leotard, shirt. Her blond hair was pulled up in a ponytail and fell in artful curls to her shoulder. Her green eyes shone with mischief.

Charly said, "Anabelle, aren't you leaving Hyde Point next week?"

This was going to be tricky. She hoped she didn't choke on the lie she had to tell to people she'd come to care about all over again since Dan's wedding. "No, I'm staying a while longer."

"Really?" Charly hugged her. "That's great."

"How come?" Jade asked.

Anabelle removed her coat and sat down to put on her sneakers. "I'm going to stay in Hyde Point until I decide what I want to do."

"Do? You're a cop, kid. And a good one." This from Jade, who bent over to stretch.

Anabelle rubbed her shoulder. "Yeah, since I got shot, though, I'm not sure it's the life for me."

Jade looked up from a deep waist bend. "Since when?"

Since I decided to help Nathan.

"Oh, I don't know. I've been thinking about it a while. I like being back in town."

Charly and Jade exchanged a look. Anabelle had made it clear when she came home for Dan's wedding that Hyde Point held bad memories for her. At Nora's shower—a girls-only weekend at the lake—Anabelle had told them it was because of Nathan, though only Nora knew the details—and not all of them. Now Anabelle needed to convince her friends that Nathan wasn't a threat to her.

"Ana—*belle*." Ariel's voice drifted up from the cellar. "We're waiting!"

"Put all this on hold, okay?" she said to Charly and Jade. "We'll talk after the class." Anabelle escaped downstairs with Jade and Charly close behind. In the re-finished basement, she found eight of the ten current residents of Serenity House in various workout outfits. "Hi, ladies." She smiled. "Mrs. Stanwyck."

Lila Stanwyck smiled back. "Hello, dear." A retired teacher—Anabelle had loved her—she currently rented half her house to Jade. When Charly told Jade that Anabelle was going to do some fitness/self-defense sessions at Serenity House, Jade had asked if she could attend. She'd brought Mrs. S. along with her.

Anabelle had just started to speak, when she felt something at her feet. She looked down to see a little auburn-coated puppy scurrying on the floor. "Oh," she said, leaned down and scooped up the dog. "Is this Elly's pup?"

Charly came forward. "Uh-huh. This is Franklin, aka Frankie. Our newest resident."

Nuzzling its warm puppy fur and receiving a couple of good licks, Anabelle reluctantly handed the dog to Charly and faced the girls. "Everybody ready for the quiz tonight?" she asked.

"Quiz?" One of the girls snapped her gum and scowled. "That's school stuff."

"Well," Anabelle said archly, "since I'm going to be staying in Hyde Point a while, I thought maybe we'd continue with these sessions. Get deeper into the self-defense now that you're in better shape." She winked at Charly. "But I gotta see how much you've learned." In the three sessions she'd been here, she'd devoted half of each class to physical fitness. Charly said many of the girls exercised together in between the classes.

The girls whooped at her disclosure. Then Ariel said, "I'm game."

The others agreed.

"All right, let's do some stretches and conditioning exercises first."

When they were done with the routines, they sat in a circle.

''Here's the quiz I brought. See if you can do it on your own and then we'll go over it. No grades, ladies. Just reinforcement of the ideas.''

As the girls worked, Anabelle tried to keep her mind on them and banish Nathan from her thoughts, but she couldn't. For one thing, Nathan's family charitable organization, the Hyde Foundation, had donated the funds for the renovation of the basement of Serenity House and installed this workout room last fall. He'd spent a lot of money on the home in other ways. Because of her? she sometimes wondered.

Then little Frankie crawled out of his box in the corner and onto Anabelle's lap. She stroked the puppy, thinking about its grandmother, and then inevitably about Nathan.

She wondered how he was doing tonight. Dan had agreed to go back to the house with him and Barbara after they had dinner at the country club. Anabelle was glad she didn't have to chaperon *that*. She wondered briefly how she was going to watch Nathan when he and Barbara were together. A sharp pain zinged through her. Damn it, she couldn't think about those things. She would concentrate on the girls.

They were so different from what she and the other original residents had been like when they lived here, yet so much the same. Cindy Le had been sexually abused by her stepfather like Charly had been; Porter Casewell, who wasn't here tonight, was a rich kid, like Darcy Shannon O'Malley, who couldn't get along with her parents. Sherah Wilson was pregnant, as Paige Kendrick had been when she'd lived at Serenity House. But there were no sisters, like Jade and Paige. And no one like Taylor Vaughn Morelli, who'd come to Serenity House with no memory of who she was. Ariel Banks reminded Anabelle of herself the most, though the girl was more outgoing and brash than Anabelle had been. A runaway, she'd come from a family of men who'd abused her physically and sexually, and they had that in common. It was one of the reasons Charly had asked Anabelle to do something with physical fitness and self-defense.

"Done," Ariel pronounced when she finished.

Anabelle smiled at her. Ariel smiled back.

When it appeared everybody had completed the task, Anabelle said, "All right. First question, Ariel. A twenty-one-year-old woman has what kind of odds experiencing a violent crime in her lifetime?"

"One in four." The girl was bright, and remembered things easily.

"Right on, kiddo. Next? True or false, staying at home most of the time virtually eliminates your chance of assault." Anabelle bit her tongue. Not at *her* home. She shuddered, remembering the night Dan rescued her and brought her here. She caught Charly's sympathetic gaze and returned it.

Sherah raised her hand. "No. A high percentage of rapes occur when a woman is in her own home."

"Exactly. Third, list the resistance techniques that we demonstrated on how to fight back if you're attacked."

The girls shouted out responses, getting into the gruesome images as only teenagers who reveled in movies like *Scream 3* could do. "Jab your fingertips into the base of his throat... Strike the base of your palm under the tip of his nose... Slam your hands onto both ears... Pinch and twist his upper lip... Squeeze his throat under the jawline... Grab his hair and pull his head over your shoulder and away from you... Strike him in the eyes."

Laughing at their gleeful violence, Anabelle held up

her hand. "Enough. I think *those* lessons were effective."
She looked back down at the paper. The last few questions were multiple choice. "Number one. If you're walking to your car in a deserted parking lot and you hear someone behind you who is quickly approaching, which of these do you do?" She read the alternatives.

Cindy raised her hand. "Put your hand on whatever defensive weapon you're carrying and turn around to look at the person." She glanced up. "I know that's the right answer, but why shouldn't you just run?"

"Because chances are," Anabelle said, "you won't get to your car before you're overtaken. You should walk faster, certainly, try to get away, but prepare yourself."

"And if you turn around," Jade added, "you'll be able to identify that person."

"Scenario two. You're coming out of a restaurant late at night. When you reach your vehicle, you encounter a man with a knife in his hand who orders you into his car. What would you do?"

"Who would pretend to faint?" Ariel asked disgustedly about one of the choices.

"Some people think going limp or fainting will make the person leave," Anabelle said. "It won't, of course. He'll get you in the car easier, is all."

"I think you should scream." This from Mrs. Stanwyck.

"Well, you should," Anabelle agreed. "But screaming alone won't do it. It's part of choice D, though." Choice D was refuse to go with the perp and resist in the strongest way possible. "If other people are around, scream. But that might make him use the knife, too. Of course, get away if you can, and always always run to other people if they're in the vicinity."

Emma Perry, a runaway who'd just been placed in Serenity House, and who'd been absent for the session where they discussed this, said, "I always thought you should cooperate and try to talk him out of it."

Please, Al, don't. It isn't right.

Anabelle shuddered. "No, cooperating is the worst thing you can do. And they don't listen to reason. Don't ever leave the area with him. Don't get into the car. Fight back. The place he's going to take you will definitely be harder to escape from than a parking lot."

She noticed the girls' confusion. "Okay, next week we're going to talk about carjacking and abduction. I have a whole bunch of stuff on that to clarify this point. Meanwhile, remember, resistance is the best course of action. We'll discuss next week, too, the different kinds of weapons you can legally carry."

Over snacks afterward, the girls chatted about what they'd like to learn from her in future sessions. Some of them hugged her before they left for their rooms.

As soon as they were gone, Jade donned her sweats and said, "Anybody want to go get a drink? Char, can you go out?"

Charly glanced at the clock. "Yep, it's my night off. Linda, the part-time counselor, should be in the office. Let me just tell her I'm leaving."

In fifteen minutes, after dropping Mrs. Stanwyck at home, Jade, Charly and Anabelle walked into Rascal's. The popular town bar in the Carlton Hotel was dim and quiet on a Monday night; isolated patrons were scattered throughout the place at the tables that ringed the perimeter around a big dance floor. From behind the long mahogany bar, a man looked up from washing glasses and flashed them a bad-boy smile. "Hello, ladies."

Jade grinned back at the dark-haired bartender. "Hi, Hunter. How you doing, buddy?"

"Super. Busman's holiday?" he asked. Jade worked at Rascal's, too, as well as at a diner in town.

"Yep." She grinned and reintroduced Charly and Anabelle to Hunter. "How's Darce?"

Hunter Sloan had eloped with Darcy O'Malley, another Serenity House original resident, right after Anabelle had come back to Hyde Point to recuperate from her gunshot wound. From what Dan had said, the two of them had a tough time getting together. Hunter had even left town for a while. But after coming to her senses, Darcy had flown down to Florida to find him and they'd come back married—and pregnant.

The man's smile was besotted. Sappy. Anabelle had never seen a guy more in love. "She's the light of my life," he said with mild chagrin.

"She feeling okay?"

"Great." He frowned. "But I gotta hog-tie her to get her to slow down." He glanced at his watch. "As a matter of fact, our kids will be here any minute. I arranged for their favorite baby-sitter to take them to an early movie tonight to give Darcy some time to herself. The sitter's dropping them here and I'm getting off early."

Jade squeezed his arm. "You're a sweetie, big guy."

He rolled his eyes. "Don't be so sure of that. What can I get y'all?"

They ordered beer.

"Go sit, I'll bring them over."

They took a table in the corner. Glancing at Hunter, Anabelle smiled. "Darcy's a lucky woman."

"He's a doll, isn't he?" Charly said.

Jade, however, got straight to the point. "All right, Detective Crane, what's this crap about not going back to Seattle?"

Anabelle knew that, of all the original residents of Serenity House, Jade was going to be the toughest to convince. Good thing Anabelle was so adept at dissembling. "My shoulder's healed, Jade, but my soul hasn't."

"What does that mean?"

"Undercover work can be bone-chilling. Often, you associate with the scum of the earth. Become one of them. I've only been doing it five years, but sometimes I wake up at night and don't really know who I am." That at least was true. "It was part of the reason my engagement failed."

Charly reached out and touched her hand. A Mother Teresa at heart, she'd been the peacemaker, and the most understanding of all of them. "It must be tough."

"It is. I've never been wounded this badly." Which was another lie. "It got me to thinking about my life. Then being with Dan and Nora—God, I missed them." Not usually demonstrative, she squeezed Charly's hand, then Jade's. "I miss all of you. And I love getting to know all your kids." Though only one original resident of Serenity House—Paige—had stayed in Hyde Point, Darcy and Jade had left and moved back, and Charly was working here now. Taylor lived only an hour away.

Charly looked totally convinced. "Well, I'm sorry you're doubting everything you've done, but it's great having you back."

Jade's green gaze was wary. "So what are you going to do, stay with Dan and Nora?"

"No, I'm taking a job on Nathan Hyde's congressional staff, as his administrative assistant."

Charly choked on her beer and Jade knocked her glass over. It ran in foamy rivulets across the table.

Anabelle jumped back and Jade reached for napkins. But Hunter was there in seconds with a bar cloth. "Got it, darlin'," he said easily.

Jade didn't smile. She just stared at Anabelle. After Hunter left—returning with a fresh drink—Charly said, "I don't believe it. When we were together for Nora's shower at the lake, you said you wished you'd never met Nathan Hyde."

"I know I did. But I had an epiphany when I got shot. I decided that wasn't as big a deal as I thought. And then being back here, and seeing him, I felt fine. Really." If that wasn't quite the truth, she'd just have to make it so.

"But why his administrative assistant?" Jade's tone was so skeptical it was almost mocking.

Anabelle rolled her eyes. "Actually, that was Dan's idea. You know how he watches out for us both. Since Nathan's re-election, he's needed more staff. And if I stay here, *I* need to support myself."

Charly's eyebrows formed a vee. "Honey, when we all went to the lake before Nora's wedding, you hinted that you were romantically involved with Nathan. Won't this hurt?"

She hadn't thought so until she'd spent the day with Nathan. Well, she'd just have to control herself more. "We were involved," she admitted. "But I was young, and he was unhappy. It's all in the past."

Still, Jade stared at her, stone-faced, so unlike the imp who meddled in everybody's business at Serenity House. From what she'd heard, Jade was still interfering—she'd dogged her sister Paige into letting Ian Chandler into her life, and needled Darcy about Hunter until Darcy acted on her feelings.

Anabelle was just about to ask Jade what she was thinking, when Charly's cell phone rang. "Hello?... Just a sec." She muted the phone. "It's Linda. I'll take this over there."

Charly left, and Anabelle squirmed in her seat under

Jade's knowing look. "Okay, Anderson, let me have it. What are you thinking?"

"That something's rotten in the state of Denmark."

"What does that mean?"

"It's a quote from *Hamlet*." Jade had excelled in only one subject in school—English. "Hamlet says it when he suspects his uncle might have killed his father. It means things aren't what they appear to be."

"Things are fine, Jade," Anabelle said. Then she added, "Even if you think they aren't, leave it, okay? Trust me."

Jade cocked her head. "All right. I don't believe your story for a minute, but I'll drop the subject if you tell me you know what you're doing."

"I do." God, she hoped she did.

Anabelle was glad for the reprieve when Hunter came back and asked if they wanted anything else before he left and his replacement took over. But her relief was to be short-lived. Jade nodded to his retreating back and said, "You know Hunter's working here and at Quiet Waters."

Nora had told them all about the new boys' home spearheaded by her and Dan. "Yeah. I know. I hear he's a talented craftsman."

"Yes." Jade hesitated. "He also did some work for Nathan. At the Winslow Place, honey."

The Winslow Place. The house that she had loved since she was a teenager. For a moment, thoughts of it stopped Anabelle's breath. No one, not even Dan and Nora, had broached this subject with her. She knew from Kaeley that Nathan had bought the house, but Anabelle never talked about it, and she'd ruthlessly repressed thoughts of it. "I don't want to talk about the Winslow Place."

"Maybe you should, given what you've just decided.

It's not coincidence that you loved that house so much and Nathan went ahead and bought it, is it?''

Cursing her inability to pretend that it didn't matter, she whispered achingly, "Please, Jade, don't go there.''

Jade clasped her hand. "All right. But only if you promise, if you ever need to talk, about anything, I'm here. I can keep a secret, and be pretty understanding when I want to be.''

Relieved, Anabelle managed a smile. "Thanks, Jade. You're a good friend. And a nice person.''

"Shh. Don't tell anybody.''

The poignant moment was broken when three whirl-winds flew into Rascal's and raced to their table to see Jade. There was a dog at their side. Hunter approached immediately. "Okay, guys, I'm ready to go.'' He glanced up at the teenager who'd brought them in. "Thanks, Por-ter, I'll take over from here.'' He faced Anabelle. "Have you met my kids?'' he asked.

She grinned. "No.''

"I'm Mellie,'' the youngest girl with hair like fire and a face dotted with freckles said. "This is my sister, Claire, and our brother, Braden.'' She hugged the dog. "And this is Tramp.'' The animal did indeed look like the mutt from *Lady and the Tramp*.

Claire, tall and ethereally pretty, with her mother's looks, moved in closer to Hunter. The dog moved with her. "Hi. You're Mom's friend, right?''

"Yes. How is your mom?''

"Tired,'' Claire said simply.

"And cranky sometimes,'' Mellie said.

"She's having a baby, dummy.'' This from the child Hunter had brought to the marriage.

"Hey, Brade, don't call your sister names.'' Hunter took his son's hand. "Let's go, before I have to referee you two again." He scratched the dog's head. "See you later, ladies."

Anabelle watched the entourage leave. It warmed her to see Darcy's family so...normal. She glanced at Jade, who stared wistfully after them, too. Anabelle had been comforted by her offer of confidence. Then Charly came back and hugged her again, and Anabelle thought just maybe with their support—and Nora's and Dan's—this whole thing wasn't going to be too bad, after all.

THIS *was not good.* Nathan rolled away from his fiancée in his big bed in the huge master suite of his house and sighed heavily. He couldn't get Anabelle out of his mind—and he was in bed with someone else.

"Nathan, what is it?" Barbara pulled the sheet closely around her and stared over at him. The light from the moon shone through his bedroom windows, accenting her feminine features. Petite and pretty in a classic way, she was a very attractive woman.

"I'm stressed. I'm sorry about this." Never before had he been unable to perform in bed, and he was faintly embarrassed.

Her dark eyes watched him. "That's all right, darling. Has something happened?"

"Yes." He climbed out of bed, found sweatpants in his drawer and pulled them on. "We need to talk."

He needed to make her understand. His life was with this woman. They were compatible in every way. Barbara was a top-notch lawyer with Hyde Point Electronics. She traveled extensively for the company, and since Nathan, too, spent much of his time away in D.C., things worked out fine for them. And Kaeley liked her. In turn, her ten-year-old son, R.J., who attended the same boarding school where Nathan had gone, adored him.

He grabbed his robe. "Here, put this on."

Sliding out of bed, Barbara donned the navy cashmere bathrobe. It was ridiculously big on her. She went to the sideboard and poured them each a glass of the Drambuie he kept there because she liked the liqueur. She handed him a snifter and took a seat in a leather wing chair in the sitting area. "Tell me what's upsetting you."

"Last night I was jogging and almost got hit by a car."

She gasped. "Oh, Nathan. You weren't hurt, were you?"

"No, it's just that I'm not sure it was an accident." He explained how the black sedan had come out of nowhere, and reexperienced the fleeting moment of terror.

"Oh my God. What did Dan say?"

"He's fit to be tied. He's been angry about my not taking action over the calls and e-mails."

"Smart man." Barbara had agreed Nathan should get some protection and had encouraged him to do so.

"I know. You were both right, I guess. I need some help."

She smiled. "It won't be so bad. I've worked with protective agencies in the past. The hulking bodyguard keeps his distance, stays in the shadows." She sipped her drink and her brown eyes sparkled. "And they're discreet about intimate encounters, if that's what's got you worried."

The thought of Anabelle sitting downstairs while he and Barbara...it made the alcohol pitch in his stomach.

What does that tell you, Hyde?

"I can get you names of some people I've worked with," Barbara offered.

"I've already hired someone."

"Really? Well, that's good. Where is he?"

"Barbara, I don't want it broadcast to the world that I

need a bodyguard. I've decided to keep it covert, hire somebody who pretends to be my administrative assistant so it will look like nothing's out of the ordinary.''

"Why? Politicians use protection all the time.''

"Not at my level.''

She smiled. "Not yet.''

He knew she had big plans for him. Hell, he had big plans for himself. "Dan suspects the stalker is somebody I know.''

Her lovely face paled a bit. "Why?''

"The guy has mentioned my whereabouts. Things in my past the public doesn't know. If that was him last night, he knew I was jogging.''

"I'm sorry, that must be difficult.''

"It is. In any case, somebody needs to fit into my routine and not alert the guy. We're not telling anybody about the bodyguard except you and Kaeley. Of course, Dan and Nora know.''

"All right.''

Nathan had to bite the bullet. "Dan recommended...and I agreed...to hire Anabelle Crane to do the job.''

The glass stopped halfway to her mouth. "Excuse me?''

"You remember Anabelle. She's—''

"Of course I remember her. The lovely young cop staying with the Whitmans.''

He nodded.

"The woman who got shot last fall and had you out of your mind with worry.''

Standing, he crossed to the decanter for a refill he didn't want. "Don't you think that's an exaggeration?''

"I rarely exaggerate, Nathan.''

"I was worried about her because she was Kaeley's nanny. Kaeley loves her to pieces. I told you all this."

"Yes, you did."

He leaned against the dresser and folded his arms over his chest.

Curling her legs under her, Barbara asked, "Is there something between you and this girl, Nathan?" She glanced at the bed. "Do you have feelings for her?"

"Of course I do. She meant a lot to my family years ago. I care about Annie. But not in the way you mean."

Barbara drew in a breath. Setting down the glass, she rose from the chair and came toward him. Slowly she slid her arms up his bare chest. "I mean to have you, Nathan Hyde. If I have competition, I want to know."

He smiled down at her. "No, Barbara, there's no competition." He lowered his head to kiss her.

And the door to his bedroom flew open. Both he and Barbara jerked back. She gasped.

In the archway stood Anabelle Crane, her tall, lithe body poised for action, her arms raised and her gun pointed at them.

It took Nathan a second to catch on. "Anabelle, I'm all right."

She surveyed the room—studied Barbara, glanced at the bed, the glasses, the dim lights. Her face was inscrutable. "I came home and Dan wasn't here. There was a strange car in the driveway. What the hell is going on, Nathan?"

For some reason he stepped in front of Barbara. "I asked Dan to leave Barbara and me alone. I needed to talk to her about our situation."

Her jaw was rigid. "We agreed Dan would stay with you tonight until I got back."

"Anabelle, I wanted some time to—"

"You're being *stalked*," she said tightly, as if she was trying to rein in her temper. "You could be killed. The alarm isn't even on, and I told you the windows could be jimmied."

"Anabelle, I—"

"Oh, forget it," she said heatedly. "I'm not going to work this way. If you won't cooperate, I'm out of here."

With that, she turned on her heel and strode down the hallway.

BY THE TIME Anabelle finished gathering what few belongings Dan had brought over for her and stored in her old room where there was a sofa bed to sleep on, she heard voices in the foyer, a car door slam and a vehicle drive away. She was just reaching for the doorknob when the door opened from in the hall.

Nathan stood there, big and intimidating. He was only a few inches taller than her five foot eight, but tonight he seemed larger than life...powerful. At his side was Elly, standing guard for her master. "I want to talk to you." Nathan's voice was deep and resonant with emotion.

"We have nothing to say to each other." She stepped forward, intending to brush past him, but he braced both arms on the jamb and filled the exit. "Yes, we do."

Anger rose up inside her, lodging in her throat. "I'm trained in self-defense, Nathan. I can take you down without getting winded."

"I'm sure you can. But I've got a few moves of my own and I'm not letting you out of here until we discuss what's happened."

Angry, Anabelle dropped her bag on the floor, not sure why she didn't follow through on her threat. Jamming her fists on her hips, she glared at him. He was still dressed in his sweats, though he'd thrown on a green-plaid flannel shirt. It was unbuttoned and she could see his chest, covered with curly dark-blond hair. She remembered memorizing every muscle and indentation there.

No. She wouldn't do this. "Fine. Here's the scoop, hotshot. We agreed you wouldn't be alone, without protection. Dan was here when I left. He was going to play watchdog for you and your date." She thought of the stark terror she felt when she saw the strange car, when she realized that Dan was nowhere in sight. Fueled by that fear, she added, "I come back, you're upstairs with your fiancée and no one's here to protect you." She went up on tiptoe. "Don't you have *any* self-control? Couldn't you forgo a little gratification for one night, if you were embarrassed by having Dan around?"

"It had nothing to do with that."

She gave him a disgusted snort. "I have eyes, Nathan."

"It wasn't—"

"She had your *bathrobe* on," Anabelle all but screeched. She sucked in her breath, appalled by her loss of temper. Horrified at letting Nathan's love life turn her into a raving maniac. And, somewhere in the inner recesses of her heart, hurt by their obvious intimacy. This would never do. "Get out of my way, I'm leaving."

He stepped forward and grabbed her arms. His grip was strong, unyielding. It shocked her—he'd never once touched her except with incredible tenderness. "You're not going, Anabelle. Until I make clear what happened."

She just stared at him.

"I wanted to tell Barbara about the circumstances in private."

"You could have done that with Dan here."

"No, I didn't feel I could. It was only one night, and I figured if we came back here, I'd be safe. After dinner with Dan and Nora, I asked him to leave us alone."

"I can't believe he agreed."

"He was almost as angry as you are."

She said nothing.

"I only wanted to make this easier on Barbara."

"At your expense."

"But I'm fine."

"Goddamn it, Nathan, somebody may very well want you dead. You can't take these chances every time you want to…" Her voice trailed off and she was embarrassed this time by the huskiness in it.

The dog growled at the palpable tension in the room.

Nathan's hands gentled and he rubbed them up and down her arms. She wore only a Seattle Police Department T-shirt, sweaty and stretched out, with ratty leggings. A picture of Barbara's Armani suits and heels flashed through her mind.

"Look, I didn't—I brought her here for privacy. To talk. I knew she wouldn't be pleased about the situation and I wanted to get it out in the open."

"What kind of woman is she if she doesn't want you to have protection?"

"She wants me to have protection. She'd suggested it a long time ago, just like with Dan."

"So what's the problem? Why did you have to soften her with sex?"

"The sex wasn't my—never mind. Damn it, *you're* the problem."

"Me?"

"I knew Barbara wouldn't be thrilled to have you as my bodyguard."

"Barbara barely knows I exist." Realizing he was still

touching her, soothing her, she stepped back and wrapped her arms around her waist. "What's going on, Nathan?"

He ran a shaky hand through his hair and looked away. "When you were shot, I...everybody was at the estate for a party. Dan got the call here. I...didn't handle it very well."

Despite her anger at him, his confession stopped her. "I'm sorry about that, Nathan," she said as coolly as she could. "I don't want anything to happen to you, either. That's why I'm here."

An arrogant eyebrow lifted. "I thought you were here for Kaeley. And Dan."

She silently cursed herself.

When she didn't respond, he finished. "In any case, Barbara had a lot of questions about you, my reaction to the shooting, my feelings for you, basically."

"Didn't you set her straight? Tell her your feelings for me—*those* feelings for me—are dead?"

He didn't answer.

"Nathan?"

"I explained what you meant to Kaeley."

"Oh, what does it matter, anyway? I won't do this job if you don't cooperate."

"I'll cooperate."

"You didn't tonight. And what's to stop you the next time, when you want to be alone with Barbara?"

Nathan hung his head, defeated. "I just wanted to break this to her gently."

Because they were covering the same ground, Anabelle turned her back and walked to the window. As if knowing she needed comfort, the dog followed her and rubbed up against her legs.

After a moment, Nathan came up behind her. "I'm sorry."

Absently, she scratched Elly's head. "At Serenity House, we used to say sorry isn't enough."

"What if I promise not to do anything like this again?" He was close. Too close. She felt his presence surround her; his scent—that very male, very unique scent that she still sometimes dreamed of—engulfed her.

Dear God, please let me handle this.

"I was wrong tonight. I'm sorry. I won't do it again. Stay—help me through this. I need you, Annie. Please stay."

Her throat clogged. She waited, praying harder for the strength to deny Nathan. Anabelle turned to face him, lifting her chin to look him in the eye. Even as she said, "All right, if you promise to do as I say," she knew she was making a very big mistake.

CHAPTER THREE

NATHAN LAY in his bed, hands linked behind his head, staring at the ceiling. The moonlight cast shadows around his room and he studied the vague outline of the ornate plaster and the crown molding above him. The soft light reminded him of something he tried not to think about these days—that this room wasn't him, this whole house wasn't what he wanted in a home. Was he even living his life as he wanted to? Sometimes he felt like an actor playing a role in the same movie, over and over again. It was one of the reasons he'd purchased the old Winslow Place, and had finally gotten around to renovating it. How had this happened to him?

He knew. When he'd lost Annie and discovered the lies his wife had told him, he'd been immobilized in many ways. He'd let his mother create his surroundings and Olivia orchestrate his personal life, what there was of it. He hadn't, however, let his father direct his career. He'd resisted running for the seat in the House of Representatives that Nathan Hyde the Second was to vacate. Instead, he'd taken the D.A. job when it opened. Ironically, when he finally pursued Congress five years ago, he'd discovered that being a legislator had given him more satisfaction than anything else he'd ever done. Professionally, he'd found his niche. Personally...

Who are you, Nathan Hyde? Annie had asked once.

I'm the man who loves you.

Maybe that was it. In his whole life, he'd only been his real self—not a son, husband, politician, or the town's fair-haired boy—when he'd been with her. What the hell were the odds that she'd end up back in his life, triggering this identity crisis?

"Arrgh," he groaned into the darkness. "You can't do this!"

But every time he closed his eyes, he saw her standing before him in that ragged T-shirt and those skintight leg things, her hair straggling out of its braid, her face flushed with glorious outrage. She had looked like a modern, vengeful goddess, smiting an underling.

She'd been mad as hell about his asking Dan to leave him and Barbara alone tonight. She said Nathan had been negligent with his safety. But there had been a vulnerability in her eyes, a catch in her voice, even as she railed at him.

Had she also been upset about his making love to Barbara?

Which, by the way, buddy, you couldn't do.

It had never happened to him before. Even right now, he felt the stirrings of arousal, hell, he got hard just thinking about…Anabelle.

Flinging off the covers, he climbed out of bed, grabbed the robe Barbara had worn and crossed to the sideboard. Still lit only by moonlight, he poured himself a healthy shot and sank into the gray leather chair. Propping his feet up on the matching ottoman, he closed his eyes and sipped the liquor that was the exact color of Anabelle's eyes. He'd seen those eyes wide and frightened when she met up with one of her brothers in town, laughing with delight at Kaeley's new antics, and glazed with passion from his touch.

She'd come to them at eighteen, after spending two

years in Serenity House. Quiet and unassuming, there had been a fragility about her that had endeared her to the entire staff. Mrs. Hanson was always feeding her; Herman, the chauffeur, didn't want her to walk anywhere; even the house cleaner, Mrs. Jones, tried to take care of Anabelle's quarters. Everybody had loved her but Olivia...

"She's a mouse, Nathan. I don't think she'll be a good influence on Kaeley."

"Then stay home once in a while and take care of your daughter."

Stunningly beautiful but a shallow woman—he hadn't found *that* out until after they were married—Olivia had laughed. That sultry, cultivated drawl was designed to reel men in quicker than the Sirens. "Sorry, darling, I'm off to my parents' house in Boston. I need the social life there."

"Take Kaeley. She needs you."

"Not this time..."

And so, for all intents and purposes, he'd been left to raise Kaeley alone, get his career as an assistant district attorney jump-started, and try to keep his sanity. Anabelle had been a lifesaver....

"What are you doing?" he'd asked when he'd come home late one night after a particularly grueling case that he'd lost. The aroma of spices had drawn him to the kitchen.

"Oh, I didn't think you'd be home." Self-consciously, she pulled at her ponytail and tugged at the towel she'd wrapped around her waist like an apron. "I hope you don't mind. I'm...cooking."

He settled his briefcase on the counter. "Mrs. Hanson cooks."

"She's got the night off." Her face had worn that uncertainty he hadn't seen in a long time, but had been etched there like grooves in marble when she first came here to live. "I won't do it if you don't want me to."

"No, it's all right." Loosening his tie and snagging a chair with his foot, he straddled it and smiled. "Do you *like* to cook?"

She'd given him that world-weary look that made him feel as if she was ages older than he was. In some ways, after what she'd endured, she was. "It's not a crime, Nathan."

In the dim light of the kitchen, he'd eaten her mine-strone soup and she'd talked about cooking—having the ingredients to cook, being allowed to cook without some-body yelling at her—and how it made the house smell, how it made the air feel warm and, above all, safe. Her husky voice and the homey things she was saying had soothed him like a balm. He'd ended up telling her about the case and his frustrations with the legal system.

He thought, whimsically, that's when he'd begun to fall in love with her. Thus began a routine. Late at night, when no one else was around, she'd fix him something to eat and they'd talk about his work. At first, he looked forward to those nights, then he'd begun to depend on them.

Angry at his ruminations, he tried to think of some-thing else…his job. A new session of Congress would start soon. It was an exciting time, a new beginning. He'd be the assistant chair of the Committee on Education and the Workforce this year and would continue on the Stan-dards of Official Conduct Committee. But when he thought of Washington, and the town house that he'd inherited from his father, he began to wonder if Anabelle would like it when they flew down tomorrow for a few days, after they went up to Syracuse and talked to Kaeley.

KATHRYN SHAY 67

Then he wondered how Kaeley would take all this—Kaeley who adored Anabelle. His mind drifted to what they'd been like together when Kaeley was little. Anabelle did everything with his daughter, but her favorite thing was drama. She used to take Kaeley to plays all the time, and act out the stories in the books they read together. He could still see them cuddled under the blankets of her bed, reading. Once, when Annie had been with them a year, Nathan knew he was in trouble when he wanted to just stand in the doorway and watch them...

"And then Zeus took his thunderbolt and flung it across the sky. 'I don't care what you say,' he shouted angrily at Poseidon.'' She cuddled Kaeley, who couldn't read yet, and whispered something in her ear, pointing to the words. "And Poseidon said...''

Kaeley took her turn. "I'm your brother. You can't do this.''

Wide-eyed, Kaeley had traced the words in the book with her chubby little finger. After she finished her line, she'd said wistfully, "Wish I had a brother.''

"Maybe you will, honey.'' Anabelle's voice had been tinged with sadness.

"Mommy says no.'' Five-year-old Kaeley's eyes had sparkled with love as she nosed into Anabelle's chest. "*You* could have my brother, Annie.''

Nathan's heart had started beating fast, like a drum gone wild. He must have made a sound, because Anabelle looked up. Her eyes rounded as big as Kaeley's—at the look in his?—and with a flash of insight, he knew she felt as he did....

Nathan got up from the chair and went over to the window. He'd managed to control himself, and his feelings for her, for another full year. He was in a position of trust, and Dan had given Anabelle over to him, not to seduce, but to care for. But things got worse with Olivia—she was never home, and when she was, she drank excessively. He stared out into the snow-covered darkness and traced the spiderwebs of ice that had formed on the outside of the glass. It was on a night like this that he'd succumbed.

Anabelle had gotten sick. Kaeley had caught a cold, and Anabelle had been tending to her twenty-four hours a day. Olivia was in the Bahamas with her parents, and Nathan had been involved in a big case. He hadn't been home much. One night he'd come in at midnight, feeling as if he could sleep for a week, and saw Kaeley's light on. He'd gone to the door and found Anabelle rocking his daughter.

The room had smelled like medicine, and a vaporizer emitted little puffs of moisture into the air. The hum of the motor was accompanied by the slight creak of the bentwood rocker. "What's going on?" he asked.

"She can't sleep lying down." Anabelle's voice was raw and her eyes were overly bright.

"Have you been holding her all night?"

"Pretty much." She smoothed his daughter's silky dark hair. "I sat in the bathroom for a while and ran the shower. It's an old remedy for croup." Anabelle coughed. "She's been out a while. I think she might go down now."

Nathan had walked toward them, leaning over to take his daughter. "Here, let me…" As he lifted Kaeley into his arms, he got a good look at Anabelle. "Anabelle, you're sweating." Usually he didn't touch her, didn't allow himself, but he'd felt her forehead. She was burning up. "Sweetheart, you're hotter than a furnace."

She shrugged. "I think I caught Kaeley's cold."

After he settled Kaeley in, he returned to the rocker.

Anabelle lay back against the headrest dozing. "Annie…"

She startled awake. "Oh, I'm sorry, I dozed off." She glanced at the bed. "Is Kaeley all right?"

"She's better than you are." He reached for her hand. "Come on, I'll help you to bed."

Standing, she said, "I don't need—oh!" She wavered.

Nathan grasped her arms to steady her. "Are you all right?"

"Hmm. Just a little dizzy. I haven't gotten much sleep lately."

"You're dead on your feet."

"Sorry." She took a step and swayed again.

Without thinking, Nathan scooped her up into his arms. "You're sick, Annie."

Her arms went around his neck. She closed her eyes and nuzzled into him. "Yeah, I guess." For a minute, he reveled in the feel and smell of her. She never used perfume, but there was a light wildflower scent that always surrounded her. When she moaned, the panic set in. He was afraid she was really sick.

She was. He'd taken her to his doctor the next day. She'd caught Kaeley's cold, which then turned into a nasty flu, with danger of progressing to pneumonia. She had taken two full weeks to recuperate. Mrs. Hanson and Mrs. Jones had cared for her, but Nathan had spent as much time with her as he could. He'd bathed her face and talked to her when she couldn't sleep at night….

Toward the end of her recovery, they were watching an old cop show on TV together in her bedroom. She'd gotten color back in her face and her light-brown hair was gleaming healthily again. Still, he made her stay in bed. "Nathan, really, you don't need to tend to me any longer. I'm better."

"I feel guilty I let you get run-down."

"You didn't let me. I was just doing my job. I'm Kaeley's nanny."

Maybe it was the scare of her being sick. Maybe it was the loneliness of being married to a woman he no longer could connect with. Or maybe it was simply that he was tired of locking up his feelings. But he'd taken her hand and brought it to his lips, kissed her knuckles and whispered, "You're more than Kaeley's nanny to me, Annie."

Wise beyond her years, she'd held his gaze. "Don't say it out loud, Nathan."

"I'm not sure I can deny it any longer."

"Please. Don't..."

He'd let it go then. It wasn't until three months later, after walking on eggshells around the house, avoiding contact and trying desperately to quell their ever-growing feelings for each other, that things had erupted between them.

Nathan's mother had surprised Kaeley and Olivia with a cruise. They'd given Anabelle two weeks off, and she'd decided to spend it at Dan's cottage.

"I don't want you to go up there alone," he'd said as she was packing in her room. He was sitting, sullen and frustrated, on the window seat. He remembered thinking that if she went away for good, he'd never survive his sterile existence again.

"I can't stay *here* with you alone."

"We're not alone. Mrs. Hanson's here. The whole house staff is."

"You know what I mean."

"It's cold. Why do you want to go to the lake in the middle of winter?"

She'd whirled around then, and what flared in her eyes

was honest anger. "How can you ask that? I need to get away from you. I—" She closed her eyes as if she was trying to stop what she was going to say. "I need to make some decisions, and I can't think clearly, with Kaeley tugging at my heart, and you..."

He'd crossed the room when she didn't finish and grasped her shoulders. "Anabelle."

"Please, Nathan, don't do this."

"What decisions do you need to make?"

"I—I'm not sure I can stay here at all any longer."

"Annie, I—"

Turning, she'd put her fingers to his lips and touched him intimately for the first time. "Shh, please, don't say it. It would be wrong. You're a married man. A father. A D.A. on his way to a political career. By all that's right, Nathan, don't say it."

He didn't, and she'd gone to the lake, taking Elly with her for company.

Nathan had managed four days before he went after her....

When he'd driven up, Anabelle was outside making angels in the snow, as she often did with Kaeley, so she didn't hear him. For a long time he watched her move her arms up and down, stop, stare at the sky. It was one of the things he liked best about her—how she took pleasure in simple things. Little things. Elly scampered around her in the snow, barking excitedly.

It was the dog who finally noticed him. She'd made a headlong dash for her master, calling Anabelle's attention to Nathan. Anabelle stood and turned toward the road. Her hair was full of snowy crystals from where it peeked out underneath the red cap Mrs. Hanson had knitted for her. Nathan had insisted she order the heavy red parka she wore from L.L. Bean and he'd paid for it.

With Elly at his side, he came toward her, his boots crunching on the snow. Breathing hard, her cheeks rosy, she stared at him. Emotions filtered across her face—fear, anger, a little bit of panic. Finally, resignation etched itself there, like someone who'd fought a valiant battle but didn't have the strength to go on. Silently, he stood before her, hands balled into fists at his sides, his own breath icy and visible before him. She just watched him.

Then, in a gesture he'd go to his grave remembering, she'd unzipped his jacket, stepped close and buried her face in the warmth of his sweater, her cheek resting as naturally as sunlight against his heart. He put his hand on her neck and held her close.

"I won't hurt you, I promise," he'd said.

"Yes, you will. But it doesn't matter anymore."

"It matters."

"Take me inside."

He did. He'd picked her up like a groom would his bride and carried her up the steps to the deck and through the sliding glass doors. In the big living room, there was a fire burning. He stripped her of her outdoor clothing, then removed his own. Pillows and blankets were mounded on the floor in front of the fireplace. An opened book lay on the coffee table. The air was redolent of smoky wood and hot chocolate.

After settling the dog in the bedroom, she sank onto the nest she'd made and drew him with her. "Make love to me, Nathan."

He did that, too.

Her skin was watered silk gliding against his palm. Her mouth was lush and yielding. Every inch of her had been soft and giving and...innocent. He was shocked, then humbled.

"Annie, no one's ever touched you?"

She'd shaken her head, smiling shyly.

"Oh, love." He'd kissed her deeply. "No one else ever will," he'd told her achingly. "I love you. I'll always love you...."

Little did he know then that other men would touch her...her fiancé of five years ago, the boyfriend she'd told Kaeley about, and who else? The thought drove him crazy.

Nathan heard his own moan in the darkness and it shocked him into consciousness. He glanced at the clock: 2:00 a.m. Had he drifted off to sleep? Or was he just remembering? In any case, the events had happened more than ten years ago; they had been real and remained branded in his memory.

He hadn't lied. Though no one could have predicted how badly things would go and the devastation that would befall their lives, he hadn't lied to her. He'd loved her deeply at that moment and had never, ever stopped. He'd just been so naive, so stupid, never even considering he couldn't have what he wanted.

Sadly, he got up and returned to the bed. Climbing under the covers, he closed his eyes and willed himself to sleep.

Instead, the feel and sounds and smells and utter satisfaction of making love to Anabelle wouldn't leave him, wouldn't let him find relief in oblivion. He lay awake with only the memory of her to comfort him.

ANABELLE GLANCED at the red numbers of the clock on the desk: 3:00 a.m. She drew in a deep breath, turned over and punched her pillows. "Go to *sleep*," she ordered herself. "*Now*. You've got a big day ahead of you."

But her body wouldn't obey her will. She never had

trouble sleeping at home. She'd mastered relaxation techniques and slow rhythmic breathing. Even when working on undercover missions, she could zonk out on cue. But being back in Hyde Point had destroyed her hard-won control. She felt like a newborn puppy, making its way in the world. And just as vulnerable.

Already.

What was continuous exposure to Nathan going to do to her? He'd always, always had power over her, from the very first time she'd seen him. She'd been eighteen and had experienced the darker side of men—a father who'd abandoned them after she was born, two brothers who treated her like a drudge and a punching bag until she was fourteen, and then had decided she could be their plaything. Except for Dan, she'd feared all men were scum.

Like a real father, Dan had protected her. He'd gotten her foster care for two years until the authorities had been assured her brothers were out of the house. She'd returned to her mother at sixteen. When Al and Aaron Crane moved back home, Dan had found a place for her at Serenity House. Then she'd met Nathan, and learned men could be good and kind and giving. Ironically, because of Nathan, she'd been able to have satisfying relationships with a few men she'd met. Though things hadn't worked out with her fiancé, Barry—they'd broken their engagement five years ago when she couldn't truly commit to him—her relationship with Rob Kress was going well. At least it had been until she'd come back here. Maybe she needed to see him. Maybe she'd call him to come and visit now that he was off his undercover case.

"That's it, think about seeing Rob."

But dark eyes and dark hair too soon gave way to sandy locks and eyes the color of wet grass. Nathan was still a beautiful man. His dark-blond hair was graying just slightly, and he had a few more character lines around his eyes. She remembered when he didn't have either of those signs of age. He'd been twenty-six when she'd gone to work for the Hydes. She'd been eighteen. An up-and-coming ADA from the best family in Hyde Point, he'd been everybody's darling son and done absolutely everything right—gone to prep school, on to Harvard and then Yale Law, married a debutante from Boston who'd attended Vassar, come back to take over the ADA's position, and went on to be district attorney. Then he'd entered Congress, which had always been his father's dream for him.

She hadn't been around for that.

He'd been a struggling ADA when she'd known him, though he'd loved the job with the zeal of Clarence Darrow. But his devotion to Kaeley had been what first drew her to him.

Slowly, she slid out of the sofa bed in her old room. By the light of the moon, she found her wallet on the dresser Dan and Nathan had brought in here. From its inner pocket, she pulled out the picture of Kaeley she always carried. It was folded in half—she only looked at one side of it—most of the time. But tonight, in the privacy of her old room, in Nathan's house once again, she smoothed out the whole photo. The pose was of Kaeley *and* Nathan lounging in a hammock. He was staring down at the latest Berenstain Bears book as Kaeley reclined into the pillows that filled the hammock, looking peaceful and content. Nathan wore jeans, a crew-neck sweater and thick socks. He also wore his glasses, and just after she'd snapped the picture, he'd looked up and smiled at her. Though they hadn't been lovers till that weekend at the lake, they'd known how they felt about each other for a long time.

In spite of her resolve not to, she remembered every detail of that idyllic time they'd been together. And when they returned, and were waiting for Kaeley and Olivia to get home from the cruise, he'd told her his plan…

They'd taken a walk in the snow-covered gardens. As they wended their way down the path, he'd reached for Anabelle's hand.

"You shouldn't, Nathan," she said, trying to free herself from his grasp. "Someone will see us."

He'd held on tight. "It doesn't matter anymore, Annie. When Olivia gets back tonight, I'm telling her I want a divorce."

She'd stopped dead in her tracks. "I didn't ask you to do that."

Gently, he'd run his fingers down her cheek, his touch always so butterfly soft it brought tears to her eyes. "I know, sweetheart. And I can't tell you how much I appreciate that sacrifice. But I love you and I can't keep up this charade. I *won't* keep concealing my feelings for you. And after this weekend…" He'd shaken his head. "I'm going to leave Olivia, no matter what the cost."

He'd been forthright about the ramifications of his decision. Olivia would balk, his parents would throw a fit. Maybe it would hurt his political career, but sometimes he wondered if those were *his* ambitions or other people's dream for him. Right then he only wanted two things in the world: her and Kaeley. Hell, he told her, he could be happy as a D.A. the rest of his life if he had both of them. And because he'd always gotten everything he wanted his whole life, he'd never questioned whether he could make it work for them. Knowing the other side of things hadn't kept Anabelle from believing him.

Anabelle sighed into the night, closing her eyes against the onslaught of ugly images that followed when Olivia returned...

Olivia had more than balked. No one else was at home, thank God, to witness her tirade. She'd come tearing into this very room—like the wronged wife she was. Nathan followed, trying to physically restrain her. "Olivia, don't."

But she barged in and strode directly to Anabelle. Nathan managed to step in between them, but Anabelle circled around and stood up next to him. She deserved this showdown for stealing Olivia's husband.

"You slut," Olivia screamed. "I knew the day you came here from that home you were bad news. Mousy little Anabelle Crane. The whole town knew those brothers of yours had *used* you. Everybody thought we were so generous to take you in. But your true colors came out, didn't they? You seduced my husband, let *him* use you. Well, no more. Get out of my house."

Nathan had grown furious. "She didn't seduce me. It was just the opposite."

That stopped Olivia. "Oh, hell, Nathan, couldn't you have picked somebody more suitable to slake your lust?"

"Olivia, I love Annie. I'm going to marry her."

Olivia laughed, long and loud. "Never in a million years."

Again, he stepped forward, faced her down. "I'm afraid it's not up to you. I know about your indiscretions. I'll use those if I have to. I want a divorce, and I want Kaeley."

His wife's eyes glowed with pure malice. "Kaeley? You want Kaeley? Not a chance."

"We'll see. I have a house full of staff who will testify

that since the day she was born you did nothing, *nothing* to take care of her.''

"That's what nannies are for, darling, not for screwing on the side. Really, Nathan, this is playing out like a Victorian novel. I won't have it. You can have your peccadilloes—like half of Capitol Hill—but not in my own home.''

She started to walk out.

Nathan grabbed her arm. "I'm getting a lawyer tomorrow.''

"No, you're not. Not if you want to see your precious *daughter* again.''

There had been something about the way she'd said the word, something secretive and vicious, that had set Anabelle's nerves on edge...

Trying to quell the images, Anabelle buried the picture in her wallet and left the room, intending to go to the kitchen. When she opened the door, she started. "Oh.'' It was Elly, waiting there. She squatted and buried her face in the dog's sleek coat, needing the comfort. "How are you, girl?''

Elly nuzzled her. Anabelle finally stood and headed down the corridor. But she found herself at the door to Kaeley's old playroom instead of the kitchen. Inside, she wandered around with the dog at her side. She and Nathan had been in here the day after their showdown with Olivia, helping Kaeley make a castle out of Play-Doh, when his father had strode in. Mrs. Hanson whisked Kaeley away and the elder Mr. Hyde asked to talk to Nathan alone.

Nathan sat on the toy chest that used to be against the wall and drew Anabelle down with him. "No, Dad, whatever you have to say you can say it in front of Anabelle.''

His father, who had seemed to like her, looked at Anabelle as if she'd just crawled out from under a rock. "Olivia came to see me this morning as soon as I returned."

"And tried to get you to change my mind."

"No, she blackmailed me."

"Blackmailed you? With what?"

Nathan's father held something in his hand. Anabelle remembered looking at the paper that, though she didn't know it at the time, had changed the course of her life. "This."

Snatching the form, Nathan had read it. And frozen on the spot. "This is nonsense," he finally said. "Something Olivia dreamed up to keep me in line."

Standing, Anabelle asked, "What is it, Nathan?"

He looked disgusted. "A fake birth certificate. It says somebody else is Kaeley's father."

"It's not fake. I had it verified."

"When?"

"Years ago, when Olivia first showed it to me."

"What?"

"She *presented* me with this one time when I chided her about her lack of maternal interest in Kaeley. When I called her out because of rumors I'd heard about her and other men. She said she'd use this to take your child away from you. That since Kaeley isn't yours, no court in the world would award you custody."

"That's ridiculous. Kaeley looks just like me. Besides, I'd know in my heart if she wasn't mine."

"I'm sorry, son."

They had tried to go on with their lives. Anabelle had moved out of the house, while Nathan had quietly started the process of DNA testing. Back then, it had taken weeks to get the results. Nathan and Anabelle had met surreptitiously during that time—optimistic, star-crossed lovers who foolishly made plans for a beautiful life together...

"We'll have more kids," he'd said one afternoon at the inn where they'd meet. He was dangling a long lock of her hair over her bare breasts. She shivered with the sensation. "How about a boy for you, and a girl for me?" He sang the line from the song "Tea for Two" from a play she and Kaeley had gone to see at the high school.

Anabelle had brushed the hair out of his eyes. He used to wear it longer then. "Two boys and two more girls."

"We're going to get her, Annie. Kaeley's mine, I know it."

He loved his daughter so much. Which was why the results of the tests had been lacerating. He'd sat in his office and cried wrenchingly when he read them. "I can't believe it. I can't believe it..."

Though her own heart was in shambles, Anabelle hadn't shed a tear; instead, she'd comforted the man she loved. "It doesn't matter, Nathan. She's more your daughter than Olivia's, despite this." She rapped the report with her fingers. "She has your sense of humor, your outlook on life, your decency. She's *yours,* no matter what a piece of paper says."

They both knew the damning document in his hands *did* matter. Olivia would use it to take Kaeley away from him. He'd never see his daughter again.

"I love you, Annie," he said raggedly. "But I have no choice. Not only couldn't I give Kaeley up, but I could never, ever leave her alone with Olivia."

Anabelle had been horrified. "I know you can't. I'd never want you to."

"I'd do anything for you but this. Give up anything but this..."

"And I'd give up anything for you, Nathan..."

As far as he knew, that was the end of it. That was the last time they'd seen each other. What he'd never found out was how Olivia had driven up just as Anabelle was leaving the house and caught her on the steps of the mansion. She'd stepped out of her Mercedes as if it was a gilded carriage and peered over at Anabelle like a queen facing a servant...

"Really, dear, did you honestly think you could fit in here?"

"I could be happy with Nathan anywhere."

"He'll be president someday. I can assure you, darling, *I'm* going to be the first lady, not some waitress's daughter who spent time in a home for wayward girls..."

Anabelle sighed and sat on the toy chest, the dog's head resting on her knees. Because of her insecurity, she'd nearly believed Olivia's words. A girl from the wrong side of the tracks. A Serenity House girl. Anabelle had left Hyde Point half convinced that Nathan didn't really love her.

She became fully convinced of that fact years later when Olivia had driven her car into the median on Route 15 and was killed instantly. The reports had been quelled, but Kaeley had told her they thought her mother was drunk.

That had been five years ago. Though Anabelle had been engaged to another man—a relationship that was good and healthy and a lot of fun—when Olivia died, she had secretly waited for Nathan to come and get her.

Like Dan had come for Nora after he was finally free.

But Nathan hadn't.

That was when she had really lost her innocence. That was when she went into undercover work. That was when she knew for sure that Olivia had been right. Nathan

Hyde didn't really love her. If he had, his feelings would have lasted through five years of separation.

Anabelle's feelings had lasted. She hadn't stopped loving him—until then. Until, when he was free to do so, he hadn't come for her.

CHAPTER FOUR

As HIS DRIVER maneuvered his way through the snow-covered streets, Nathan stared out at the sprawling landscape of Syracuse, New York. The university was located east of the city, on a hilltop. They climbed the incline and turned toward the campus, and Nathan was able to appreciate the setting—two hundred acres housing one hundred and seventy buildings of both old and new architecture to serve its fifteen thousand students.

"Have you ever been here, Anabelle?" Nathan asked of his grim and reticent companion. She sat stiffly in the back seat, hugging the opposite door. When she looked over, the smudges under her eyes indicated she hadn't slept much last night.

Neither had he. He wondered what she'd been thinking about, if ghosts had haunted her, too, because of their enforced proximity. Specters of their past had plagued *him* all night long. At least he and Barbara had parted on fairly good terms.

"No, I've never been here. I like the layout." All the classroom buildings were centered around a quadrangle.

"This is called the quad. The residence halls are easy walking distance from the classrooms."

"Kaeley loves this place." She glanced at him, her expression unreadable. "Why did you think I'd been here?"

"I thought maybe you visited her after she left Hyde Point."

"No. I didn't see Kaeley again until I came back for Nora and Dan's wedding."

Nathan knew Anabelle had stayed in phone and e-mail contact with his daughter. But she had used her undercover work, and the distance from New York to Seattle, as an excuse for not visiting Kaeley in Hyde Point. Even when Kaeley had graduated from high school, Anabelle hadn't come to the ceremony and Kaeley had been disappointed. However, he'd wondered if they'd seen each other since Kaeley went to college.

The car pulled up to Kaeley's dorm. "Here you go, Congressman."

Nathan smiled at the man who had been his driver since Kaeley was small. "Give us about an hour, Herman, then come back. Come on up, too, so you can see Kaeley."

"Yes, sir." Kaeley had had all the household staff eating out of her hand, and they still loved her.

They exited the car—Nathan first; he reached out his hand to help Anabelle.

"No, thanks. I can do it." She sidestepped him and climbed out by herself. For the drive here to see Kaeley, then their plane trip to D.C., she'd worn a tailored herringbone suit. Obviously of good quality, the slacks were tapered at the bottom, and emphasized the length and slimness of her legs. He deliberately suppressed the memory of what it felt like to have those legs wrapped around him. Underneath her wool overcoat, the jacket was long and formfitting; her curves had spiked his blood pressure—and other things—when he first saw her this morning. For a guy who couldn't get it up for his fiancée last night, he was randy as a stallion today.

Damn it.

Their boots crunched on the snow as they traversed the sidewalk. It was one of those rare and beautiful days in upstate New York, where the icy-cold weather coexisted with the January sun, which sparkled on patches of ice on the pavement. "Watch it, the sidewalk's—"

The words weren't even out of his mouth, when Anabelle slipped. Grabbing her before she went down, he clutched her arms. Still unbalanced, she held on to him and his hands slid to her waist. God, he loved the feel of her. "Steady."

For a minute, the vulnerability on her face poleaxed him. Then the mask dropped into place. "Sorry. I'm not accustomed to this snow."

"You used to love it."

"I did." Watching him meaningfully, she added, "I'm different now."

They crossed the sidewalk without further incident and pressed the bell for entrance to the dorm. Anabelle stayed at arm's length and waited for Kaeley to let them in.

The buzzer rang and they climbed the utilitarian staircase to the second floor. The sound of their boots clattering on the metal treads echoed through the halls, emphasizing the silence between them. Before they even reached her room, his daughter flung open the door.

"Hi, guys." She threw herself at Anabelle. "I'm so glad you're here. You've never seen one of my dorm rooms."

Nathan stood back and watched the two of them hug— the child he loved and the woman he gave up for her. His heart constricted painfully in his chest.

Pure joy lit Anabelle's face and she closed her eyes, as if she was savoring the physical contact with Kaeley. "Hey, kiddo."

Jamming his hands in his pockets, Nathan tried to ease the emotional turmoil inside him. "Well, I guess Dad doesn't rate any TLC."

With a big grin, Kaeley let go of Anabelle and launched herself at him. "Oh, Daddy." She hugged him tightly, too. She was tall and slender like her mother had been, with wheat-colored hair, artfully accented by blond highlights. She also had blue-green eyes. Ironically, Nathan's and Olivia's coloring were similar, so she resembled him, too. Even though...

Son of a bitch! He rarely thought about this, never let himself dwell on the fact that Kaeley wasn't the child of his flesh. With his father and Olivia dead, no one, other than Anabelle, knew the truth. Especially Kaeley.

As Kaeley dragged them both inside, her excitement at seeing them chased away some of the clouds that Nathan and Anabelle had brought with them. The suite she shared with three other girls consisted of four single rooms surrounding a kitchen/living area, offering the privacy kids needed yet the camaraderie of communal life. When Kaeley tugged Anabelle to her bedroom, Nathan waited on the couch because it hurt to see them together today.

"Want something?" his daughter asked as they came back out. "I could make coffee." She grinned at Anabelle. "Or hot chocolate." Something they'd always shared.

He glanced at his watch. "No, baby. We only have a small window of time before our plane takes off. Come sit here with me."

Crossing the room, Kaeley sank onto the cushions. "What's wrong? You look upset." She glanced at Anabelle. "You, too, Annie."

He noticed Anabelle didn't jump down Kaeley's throat

for using the nickname, the way she did when he used it. Nathan pasted on his politician's smile. "No, honey, not upset. We just need to talk to you."

As she always had when things were tense, Kaeley sidled in close to him. "Daddy?"

He took her hands in his. "You know I've been getting disturbing phone calls and e-mails."

"Yes." Her eyes widened and she glanced at Anabelle. "I'm worried."

"Well, you can rest easy, kiddo." Anabelle's voice sounded strained. He hoped Kaeley didn't notice. "I'm gonna do what you asked."

"Protect him?"

"Uh-huh."

"Oh, Annie." Kaeley stood, moved to the chair, and once again hugged Anabelle. "Thanks. I love you so much."

He saw Anabelle gulp back emotion. "I love you, too, honey."

Nathan glanced away briefly from the sight. It was too hard to look at. Against his will, his mind conjured other times Anabelle had said those words—to him—and they were equally difficult to think about…

I love you, Nathan. I've never said that to a man before… I'll always love you… And just before she left… I'll never love anybody like I love you…

She'd come back to Hyde Point a different person, though, with animosity replacing that love. Sometimes he wondered why. They'd parted like star-crossed lovers. He guessed that in the interim she'd suffered a lot. Maybe that was it.

He was distracted when Kaeley returned to the couch. "What made you change your mind about helping Daddy?"

Anabelle looked to Nathan.

He'd always tried to be as honest as he could with his daughter. "I was nearly hit by a car while jogging, and Dan Whitman's afraid it wasn't an accident."

Tears welled in those eyes now as he described the incident. "Oh, no, Daddy." She hugged him again.

He smoothed down her hair. "Anabelle's going to pose as my administrative assistant."

"I'll be with him all the time," Anabelle said. "I won't let anybody hurt him, Kaeley."

Nathan told her about the investigator they were meeting with in D.C. later today.

"Oh, good." Kaeley straightened her shoulders. "I won't worry so much now."

They gave her details about his safety and hers—to take care of herself a little more than usual, be circumspect, not to take chances. Used to being in the public eye, Kaeley accepted the advice stoically. They'd also make arrangements for campus security to watch her.

"Well, baby, I guess that's it."

"I—" There was a knock on the door. "I wonder who that is." Kaeley rose and crossed to the entry, which was just visible from the living room.

Nathan said, "Don't open—"

She flung the door back without checking the peephole.

From where he sat, Nathan saw a tall figure dressed in jeans and navy jacket. "Hey, babe. What's up? You missed my class so I came over to see if you were okay." The guy scooped Kaeley into his arms. He buried his face in her hair, nuzzled there intimately and whispered something only Kaeley could hear.

Nathan felt a jolt of parental chagrin go through him. When the guy's hands slipped to Kaeley's hips, the ra-

tional part of Nathan's mind warned him not to say anything, but a father's irrationality won out. He stood and
moved into lover boy's line of vision. "And you are?"

The guy stepped back from Kaeley but held on to her
arms. Dark eyes flickered with a bit of embarrassment
and a lot of amusement. Finally, he put Kaeley away
from him. "Congressman Hyde!" He held out his hand.
"I'm Jonathan Jamison. A friend of Kaeley's."

*Jon—this guy I know says… Just like Jon… Yeah,
Dad, I'm dating a neat guy now…*

"That's right, Kaeley mentioned you."

Glancing over at Kaeley, Jon put his hand on her neck.
"She better have." He focused on Nathan again. "I
wouldn't have interrupted if I'd known you were coming,
but it's nice to finally meet you."

"You, too." It wasn't, but hell…

Anabelle stepped forward and held out her hand.
"I'm—"

"Annie." The guy grinned. "Kaeley talks about you
all the time and she has your picture right next to her
bed…" He trailed off, his face reddening.

There was a meaningful silence.

"Come on in, Jon," Anabelle finally said. "You're
Kaeley's teacher, aren't you?"

"What?"

Nathan's gruff tone brought a scowl from Kaeley.

"Actually, I'm the grad assistant in her improvisation
class."

"How old are you?"

"Daddy!"

"I'm twenty-seven, Congressman Hyde. I'm finishing
up my Ph.D. in theater."

And sleeping with my daughter. They had that look
about them.

And he'd been in her bedroom.

Damn it. How was Nathan supposed to handle this?

Again, Anabelle intervened. "Well, it's nice to meet you." She took Jon's arm and guided him to the couch. "Sit with us. We only have a few minutes but I'd like to hear about your interest in drama. Kaeley says you're a regular Laurence Olivier on stage."

Nathan stood back. Kaeley dragged him aside. "Daddy, stop looking like you're going to pull out a shotgun," she said in a hush. "I'm almost twenty years old."

He stared down at her. His little girl had grown up. It made him sad and scared the life out of him.

AN HOUR LATER, at the Syracuse airport, Anabelle watched Nathan from where she sat in a stiff, vinyl chair across from him. He'd been silent on the drive from the SU campus. He'd snarled at the security guy who'd insisted on searching him when they went to the gate, and grunted responses when Anabelle had asked him questions about D.C. As they waited to board the plane, she hid a smile—the man who brashly resisted any protection, who argued eloquently on the floor of Congress and who handled reporters with the ease of a presidential press secretary was reduced to inarticulateness where his daughter was concerned.

"Did you know she was sleeping with him?" he asked without preamble.

Anabelle scowled. She didn't want to get into this with him for several reasons. "I don't think it's a good idea for you and me to talk about this, Nathan."

"She's my daughter. I want to know that she's all right emotionally with what's going on with that guy. That she's using birth control. That she knows what she's doing.''

Anabelle was intent on protecting Kaeley's confidentiality, but Nathan's distress tugged at her heart. ''She's sensible and levelheaded. She's mature, and so is he. They're careful, and responsible.''

''He's eight years older than she is.''

''She's in a good and loving relationship. He's crazy about her. She's head over heels for him. They're both deliriously happy. That should be obvious, even to her grouchy, retrograde father.''

''I have a right to worry. She's my little girl.''

''Maybe this is why she didn't tell you much about him.''

''Maybe.'' He frowned and messed up his exquisitely cut hair. ''I need to know if she has somebody to talk to about things. Somebody who can lead her through the murky waters of sexuality. As far as I know, she didn't have any sexual experience before this. Please, just tell me that.''

Anabelle swallowed hard. ''She's talked to me about everything she needs to, Nathan. I promise.''

His forehead creased. ''What is it? You sound sad.''

''No, it's nothing about Kaeley.''

''What then?''

Biting her lip, Anabelle looked away. ''She asked me how old I was when I first made love. She asked me if it was the right thing for me.''

His face went ashen. ''Oh my God. I didn't think... She's the same age you were when we—''

Unable to deal with the memory in the brittle light of day, Anabelle stood and crossed to the window.

After a moment, he followed her. Standing close behind her, he said, ''Annie...''

She shook her head.

"I didn't see the parallel. I'm sorry."

Sighing, she stared out at a 747 taxiing on the runway. "There isn't any parallel, really."

"He's the same age I was. She's as old as you were."

"Yes."

He was close. Too close. "And you were a virgin, too."

She had to harden her heart. "But he isn't married, Nathan. He's free to love her, court her openly, take this relationship to its natural conclusion, if that's what they both want."

"And I wasn't free to do all that."

"No, you weren't." She looked him in the eye. "You and I acted unethically. This relationship between Kaeley and Jon is wholesome and healthy in a way ours never could be."

Again his face paled.

"I'm sorry, I don't mean to hurt you. I just don't want to talk about our past."

"I'm sorry, too."

"Nathan, just be happy for Kaeley that she has something we couldn't have. You brought her up right. And it's time for her to have a serious relationship with a man. Things will be fine."

"They weren't fine for you."

"I survived." She angled her chin. "I've had successful relationships with other men, mostly because you showed me how to be intimate with a man. So you can rest easy."

Green eyes flaring, he stepped back. "Yeah. I can rest easy knowing you've slept with other guys."

He turned as he said it, his hands clenched. She could see his big shoulders, encased in navy wool, stiffen as he crossed to where they were seated and dropped down on a chair.

Damn it! She'd expected to feel anger at being thrown together with a man who was such a big part of her past. But she never expected to feel this depth of sadness.

They'd lost so much.

They landed in the early afternoon at Reagan Airport and, after thorough security checks, took a cab to Georgetown. Again, Anabelle was quiet on the trip, and Nathan had already said too much, so he stared out the window and watched Washington scroll by. Traffic was congested, as usual, and though it was milder here than in New York, the sky was gray and the atmosphere dismal.

A fitting backdrop to his mood. And the mood of the woman next to him. Shakespeare couldn't have written this dreary scene any better.

Nathan had tried to do some work on his laptop on the plane, tried to ignore the utter rightness of having Anabelle with him, but he couldn't concentrate. When she dozed off halfway to D.C., he was free to gaze upon her to his heart's content, shoulder in a bit closer and pretend things were different. He could smell the perfume she wore—something dark and a little dangerous. He remembered when she wore no scent, yet still smelled wonderful.

As they pulled up to his town house on Prospect Street and got out of the cab, she frowned. "This is pretty far away from Capitol Hill, isn't it?"

"No, only about ten minutes." He glanced at her. She shouldered her carry-on bag while pulling the big black canvas luggage on its wheels. He'd traveled lightly, as he kept clothes and personal belongings at two houses. "Here, let me help."

"Thanks, but I've got it." She stared up at the town house. "Did you buy this when you were elected?"

They covered the short walk from the curb to the front door. "No, it's another residence that's been in my family for years. My father lived here when he was in Congress." Nathan stood back, taking in the structure through her eyes. The exterior was all brick Colonial. Narrow like most Georgetown condos, it went up and back instead of sprawling to the sides. He unlocked the door, and once inside, he disarmed the security system while she stood in the foyer. "Want to look around before you go up?"

"Go up?"

He nodded to the stairs a few feet away. "You'll be staying up there, as if you're renting the rooms. It's a guest apartment really, with its own entrance off to the side." He shrugged. "It'll look better for both of us."

"I'll need access to you."

You can have all the access you want.

"Fine. We can open the security doors between the first and second floors, then."

After hanging up their coats and leaving her bags in the entry, they strode into the living room. "Lots of white," she said, nodding to the furniture.

He stared at the leather sofa and chairs a decorator had picked out. "I guess so."

"Maybe you should paint the walls, Congressman."

"It's supposed to be chic, Detective."

"It's boring." She nodded to the floor. "Nice rug though."

She indicated the geometric design of purples and mauves, which he'd picked out himself.

"Thanks."

Ever the cop, she began checking windows. She

crossed through a wide archway into the dining area, which was really part of an L. A huge oak table with thickly padded chairs—again white leather—took up most of the space. "You do everything in a big way, don't you?"

"Yeah, even get stalked."

She pivoted. "Are you all right?"

"Just peachy."

She waited a minute, then headed into the kitchen.

Here her eyes lit up. "Very nice." She nodded to the blond oak cabinetry, copper pots and sprays of green plants. "I like this room."

"Of course you do, it's a kitchen. Your favorite."

Someday, when we get our own house, I'm going to make love to you once a week in the kitchen.

Only once a week? she'd teased.

She checked out the windows and frowned at the lock on the back door.

Knowing the drill by now, he sighed. "I'll get a lock-smith out here."

She leaned against the countertop, the movement pulling the buttoned-down jacket of her suit taut against her breasts. "What's on the agenda today?"

"Get settled in. Stop over at my office to check on things." He glanced at the clock. "The investigator is due here at three."

"I'll go unpack, then." Her cell phone rang before she could start out. She flipped it open. "Crane." She smiled slowly. Sexily. "Well, hello." The smile broadened. "Yeah, I know. We keep playing phone tag."

Nathan crossed his arms over his chest and watched her. She finally caught his eye just as she said, "Um, me too."

Damn. Me too, what? Me too, I love you. Me too, I miss you? Me too, I'm dying to hit the sheets with you? Far as he knew, the boyfriend in Seattle hadn't visited her in the two months she'd been in Hyde Point.

Her face colored. "Wait a sec, Rob." She muted the phone. "This is personal."

"Yeah, I gathered."

"I'll take it upstairs."

"You do that."

She glanced around. "Don't go anywhere."

"Yes, ma'am."

Unreasonably angry, feeling like a teenage boy yearning for a girl who had left him in the dust, he strode to the front of the house as she went up to the apartment. Once inside his office, he booted up the computer and sat down, thinking about Anabelle with another man. Not really paying attention to what he was doing, he called up his e-mail and opened the first one.

And froze.

Oh, hell. Just what he needed. He stared at it a minute, then rose and went out to the bottom of the stairs. "Anabelle?" he called out. "Could you come here a minute?"

She trundled down the steps, still holding her cell phone.

"You need to see something." He glanced at the phone. "Sorry to interrupt your call." He knew he didn't sound sorry.

Quickly she said goodbye to Rob and looked up at him. "What's wrong?"

He ran a hand through his hair. "I got another e-mail."

Her eyes deepened to the color of honey. "I want to

see it." She preceded him into the den and, standing behind his chair, read the one-line missive.

Jogging can be hazardous to your health.

She swore under her breath, then said, "Save and copy it. We'll show it to the investigator." She turned to him. "You kept the others, right?"

"Most of them."

"Nathan..."

"Look, I thought it was crank stuff, so I trashed the first few e-mails. When they continued, I kept them."

"You wanted to think it was crank."

"Is that so bad?"

Her face softened. "No, of course not. I know this is hard."

He nodded to the computer. "It's not just the stalking."

"What else?"

"Don't you know?"

Her face reddened. "I don't want to discuss this."

"You shouldn't ask questions if you don't want to hear the answers, then."

"It just won't do any good to talk about the past." Her tone was exasperated.

"Isn't it hard for you at all, to be with me?"

"I'm trained for situations like this."

"Oh, and how many other men you've slept with have you guarded?"

She stared at him.

"Annie—"

The doorbell rang. Scowling, he glanced toward the foyer and took a step in that direction.

"Don't go. Don't answer your doors from now on. I will." She fingered her side. Where her gun was. Geez.

"It's the FBI guy," Nathan told her. "It's almost three."

"I'll still get it. Stay here." She strode out.

A pause. Then he heard the door open.

"Holy mother of God," a deep voice boomed. "I don't believe it. Ana-*bellissima!*"

"What the hell?" Nathan murmured and went to the doorway.

Just in time to see a tall, swarthy man scoop Anabelle up in his arms, kiss her hair and give her a hug that probably bruised her ribs.

And Anabelle hugged back just as hard.

When the guy finally set her down, he noticed Nathan. Looking a bit chagrined but still holding on to Annie, he said, "Sorry, Congressman, but this is the love of my life here."

Shit, not another one.

"Oh, really?"

Finally he let Anabelle go. "Sorry." He flipped out his badge. "Zeke Campoli. I'm your federal investigator."

"How do you know Anabelle?"

He chuckled and took hold of her again. This time he drew her to his side. Anabelle went with the ease of a longtime lover and stayed in his embrace. The guy's eyes danced with amusement. "At one time, I was her pimp."

NATHAN'S FACE was full of thunderclouds as Anabelle explained the undercover operation where she had worked with Zeke Campoli. The Seattle P.D. had been working on a case, and when it was discovered the criminals were involved in kidnapping, the FBI had been brought in. Zeke had been purposely inciting with his pimp comment—he was good at that—and Nathan had taken the bait. When it was obvious Nathan failed to see the humor in Zeke's joke, Anabelle turned to her friend. "Nathan's protective. I used to work for him when I was young and he's always felt this...need to watch over me."

Zeke's dark eyebrows formed a vee. Though he was boisterous and flamboyant, he was the consummate FBI agent when necessary. "Not a good attitude to have toward one's bodyguard."

Shrugging, Anabelle said, "He's managing." She smiled. "I had no idea you were on this case."

"Same goes." He reached out and tugged on a strand of hair that had escaped her braid. "You're lookin' good, babe. Love the blond streaks."

She smiled back and squeezed his arm. Affection was so easy with this man. She glanced at Nathan, who was staring at them. "Let's go in the office. Nathan can outline what's happened."

They followed the corridor to the den. Warm paneling and thick rugs filled the room. Huge rows of law books and other leather-bound tomes, as well as tons of paperbacks, graced the shelves. There was a stone fireplace in the corner. The Nathan she'd known years ago would have had an office like this.

Nathan sat at a small oval conference table and Anabelle took a chair across from him. She was trying to keep her distance after a morning fraught with emotional upheaval. Zeke dropped down beside her, close. She'd always appreciated his Italian warmth. It had gotten her through some harrowing hours of undercover work.

Drawing a notebook out of his jacket pocket, Zeke set it in front of him. "You're being stalked, Congressman."

"So they say."

"Tell me the progression of the incidents. Anabelle

and your cop friend must have reasons to want you to have protection.''

Nathan's green eyes darkened to jade. ''They do, apparently.'' He took in a deep breath, as if he were confessing to a crime. ''First there was a series of calls.''

''How many?''

''Maybe half a dozen.''

''What did they say?''

''No direct threats, which was why I wasn't sure what this was. The caller said I wasn't a good lawmaker. That I didn't deserve to lead the country.''

''I was told you thought the caller might be someone you know.''

''Yes.''

''What led you to believe that?''

''He seemed cognizant of my whereabouts.'' For some reason, Nathan glanced at Anabelle. ''Once, when I was doing some renovation on a house I bought in Hyde Point, I got a call there and the guy asked why I was slumming.''

Anabelle guessed he was referring to the Winslow Place. In spite of her staunch refusal to talk about it, a picture of the house invaded her consciousness…

I love that house, she'd said one morning as she and Nathan drove by it on the way back from taking Kaeley to preschool.

He'd pulled into the driveway. It was early, and no one was around. They got out and walked to the back of the grounds.

Oh, Nathan, look. A tower. I'd love to see the inside.

Everybody knew the house had been abandoned for years. Kids routinely broke in to explore the labyrinth of rooms or to party. Despite the fact that he was the town ADA, he'd jimmied the lock. He looked so young, so adventuresome and so sweet that she'd fallen in love with him all over again. They went inside. The turret was full of cobwebs and broken boards and peeling paint, but it had stolen her breath. *I'd feel like a princess if I lived here. No one could hurt me inside these walls...*

"Anabelle, baby, where'd you go?" Zeke's hand had slid to her neck again and rested there. "You okay?"

"Yes, my mind just drifted."

"That's unlike you."

Distractions could kill in undercover work. But this whole assignment was filled with distractions.

Yeah, I'll rest easier knowing you slept with other men.

After a searching stare, Zeke turned back to Nathan. "Tell me about the e-mails." Zeke listened as Nathan outlined their content.

"The last one is on the screen now."

Standing, Zeke said, "I'd like to take a look."

Nathan rose, too. She watched them cross to the computer. Nathan was fair-skinned, light-haired, lean and lanky, with muscles that were defined but not bulging. Zeke was a little taller, broader of shoulder, and his muscles always seemed to be pushing at the seams of his coat. Women fell all over him. Still, Anabelle's eyes kept straying to Nathan.

After Zeke read the e-mail, he said, "This is not good, Congressman Hyde."

"I know."

"Well, we've got our work cut out for us. Let's make a list of people who might want to scare you or hurt you."

"It could be a long list."

"Why?"

"I was a district attorney for a long time."

"Hmm."

Nathan glanced at his watch. "I have to check in at my office today. I'd like to get there before six."

"All right, let's start with categories. You can fill in the blanks with Anabelle and we'll meet again tomorrow to go over possible suspects."

Anabelle watched Nathan; she wondered what it was like to think about all the people who might hate you so much they'd threaten your life.

"What do you mean by *categories?*" he asked.

Zeke ticked off the information on his fingers. "Number one, anybody who stands out from your D.A. time. Criminals you helped put away. High-profile cases. We'll run them, see if the guys are still behind bars."

A muscle twitched in Nathan's neck.

"Number two, people in Congress you've pissed off."

"My colleagues?"

"Yep. Especially since the calls say you shouldn't be making laws. This could very well be professional jealousy."

"Damn it."

Zeke held up a third finger. "Next, discuss your staff."

"My *staff?*"

Carefully, Zeke eyed him. "Yeah. Any one of them could be angry at you for something. You fire anybody lately?"

"No, my administrative assistant quit."

"Why?"

"He got a better job."

"List that individual along with the others. I'll review their background checks."

"Fine," Nathan said tightly.

"Last is personal. You're engaged, right?"

"Yes."

"She got a jealous ex?"

"No, they get along fine. They have a son they're very protective of. They both dote on him, actually."

"She got any ex-boyfriends?"

"I don't know."

"Ask her."

Again he watched Nathan, as if choosing his words carefully. "This is the sticky part, Congressman, and it won't go any further than the three of us. But I need to know if there's a woman scorned in your past who might come after you."

Nathan reddened.

"You had any affairs with a married woman?"

He paused briefly. "No."

At Nathan's hesitancy, Zeke asked pointedly, "*Any* affairs?"

Nathan and Anabelle exchanged a meaningful look.

Good agent that he was, Zeke caught the exchange. "What?"

"Nothing." Nathan's voice was calm.

Damn. Anabelle knew she had to do this. But the necessity didn't make it easy. Drawing on her cop's reserve, she faced Zeke. "I know of one affair he had."

"Yeah?"

"With me."

Zeke's eyebrows rose. "Shit, Anabelle. What the hell are you doing on this case then?"

THE MAN STARED DOWN at the photograph of the congressman. Nathan Hyde had stolen from him. There were a lot of ways to steal…money, power, love, reputation. A sense of belonging. His heart jerked in his chest as he took in the cocky grin, the *I'm-what-you-want* glimmer in Nate's eyes. The man had it all. Sometimes, life just wasn't fair.

But he was going to even the odds.

A drink—a Manhattan—was steady in his hand. It was tart, potent. He felt sure of himself. Being sure made him calm. Calmness made him think clearer. As always, clear thinking should get him what he wanted.

It was time to go beyond the ordinary. Phone calls. E-mails. A quick and innocuous sideswipe of the car. He needed more. He needed to step this up.

Putting the picture down, he walked to the window and looked out at the Norman Rockwell setting—the white blanketed lawns suggesting a coldness that he himself felt in his bones. Often, the man in the picture had been responsible for that, too.

Think. What's next? Something bigger, something that would make the congressman even more vulnerable. Something that would make him suffer, as he himself had suffered so often in the past.

CHAPTER FIVE

THE LONGWORTH HOUSE Office Building had been constructed on a sloping site, thus it appeared to rise out of its granite base. Faced in white marble with Ionic columns, the structure sported five stories of office suites. Because of several security clearances and checks, routine now, due to the events of September eleventh and its aftermath, Nathan and Anabelle were detained. Anabelle's gun had to be cleared by security personnel, who had been briefed about the stalking. Finally, Nathan strode into the building with Anabelle at his side. They rode the elevator to the third floor and found his suite, off a long hallway.

They were immediately greeted by Nathan's chief of staff, Hank Fallon, who was housed up front in the first office. Hank ran the whole shebang—overseeing legislative obligations, contacting major campaign donors, setting up political strategies. Almost as tall as Nathan, but more slightly built, Hank stood when they entered and held out his hand. "Welcome back, Congressman."

"Thanks. Nice to see you, Hank." Though he'd talked to Hank daily, he hadn't seen him since the holiday recess.

My staff?

Yeah. Any one of them could be angry at you for something. You fire anybody lately?

Glancing past Nathan to Anabelle, Hank raised questioning gray eyebrows, which matched a full head of hair that had gone prematurely gray when he was in his thirties. Though he was affable and good with people, he could also be very intense.

"Hank, this is Anabelle Crane."

"Hello, Mr. Fallon." Like a dutiful assistant, Anabelle smiled demurely and shook hands with his chief of staff.

Straight ahead was another office housing Nathan's scheduler and press secretary; to the left was the legislative section, occupied by his legislative assistant and all the correspondents who answered mail. Nathan nodded to the closed doors. "Who's still here?"

"Everybody. They were waiting to see you."

"Sorry. I had an emergency."

"Everything okay, Nate?" Hank's dark eyes were curious, probably at the omission of an explanation of who Anabelle was.

"Yes." Nathan walked into his own office off to the right, along with Hank and Anabelle. Light filtered in through the group of windows behind his desk. Bookshelves and cherry-wood furniture filled the room. "Could you ask the rest of the staff to come in here? I want to talk to you all together."

"Sure."

When Hank left, Anabelle crossed to the windows, checked their locks and studied the room. She said nothing; he guessed Zeke Campoli's reaction to her confession was probably still preying on her mind. It was on his. What the hell *were* they doing, allowing themselves to be thrown together like this?

His staff entered, chatting with each other. He shook hands with each of them, and they all gathered on couches surrounding a coffee table, in a sitting area that was sectioned off from the office space. Anabelle stayed by the windows. "Can I get you something, Congressman?" Karen Kramer asked. "You look tired."

"No, thanks. I trust everybody had a good break?"

Assents all around. Some chitchat.

"How's Drew?" Mark Macomber wanted to know. "We miss having him around here."

The staff loved Nathan's stepbrother. Drew was friendly and got along with everybody. Nathan often wondered why they never got along as boys. "He's great. His wife is glad to have him home more. He sends his regards." Nathan smiled at them. "I've brought someone else along with me. I'd like to introduce you to Anabelle Crane."

Four pairs of eyes focused on Anabelle as she approached the group.

"She's going to be our administrative assistant."

Hank scowled and ran a jerky hand through his hair. Karen smiled. The other two aides just watched her.

"Anabelle, this is Karen Kramer, my legislative assistant." In charge of supervising all legislative activity he was involved in, Karen met with lobbyists, introduced bills and advised him on all matters. People often underestimated Karen's sharp mind because of her slightly plump appearance and pleasant demeanor.

"Mark Macomber, my scheduler." Mark's boyish good looks—curly hair, toothpaste smile—won him lots of friends. He worked closely with Hank to plan Nathan's day and keep track of when he needed to be in D.C. and when he should go back to the District.

"And this is Cameron Jones, my press secretary." A tall African-American, Cam was as sharp as they came, but friendly and kind, and extremely well respected on the Hill as he went about his public-relations activities.

Nathan had surrounded himself with competent people whom he also liked.

Which made considering them as suspects doubly abhorrent.

Calling forth his politician's grin, Nathan tried to put his staff at ease. "We've been talking about replacing Ron since he left and an opportunity came up that I couldn't resist. So I seized it." He ducked his head, knowing he looked faintly embarrassed. It wasn't an act.

"I realize I should have run this by you, but I've known Anabelle for fifteen years. She's in the midst of a career switch, and was temporarily out of work. When I found out she was available, I hired her before she could change her mind."

Dead silence.

"She's had experience," he continued. He told them the story they'd worked out; after doing a stint as a cop, she'd clerked for some local politicians in Seattle and had been an admin assistant to a top local official.

"Well, we're lucky to get her then, aren't we?" Karen's tone was genuine. "Welcome aboard, Anabelle."

"Thank you."

Nathan said, "I'll be in charge of her schedule, Hank, and take some of the onus off you."

"Of course, Congressman." Hank's tone was stiff, reminding Nathan of a wife whose husband hadn't consulted her in an important decision.

"So," he said easily, "if all that's clear, tell me what I need to know before next week." He smiled at Anabelle. "Take notes on this meeting, okay?"

"Yes, Congressman," she said.

An hour later, he and Anabelle were sitting at J Paul's. The Georgetown pub, located on M Street not far from

Nathan's town house, was famous for recapturing the aura of the legendary speakeasies of the past. Walking through the doors was like stepping back a hundred years in time. Among other old decor, the place sported a mahogany shotgun bar, antique brass elevator doors and cozy booths.

Nathan and Anabelle settled into one of those booths and ordered beverages. "Well, that went okay, don't you think?" she said after the waiter brought their drinks.

Nathan loosened his tie and pushed up the sleeves of his suit. "Hank's pissed."

"Yes, but you can smooth that over, can't you?"

"I'll try, tomorrow. Springing a new member of the team on them without discussion isn't my style."

Her eyes averted, she toyed with the lemon in her soda water. He sipped a scotch. She wouldn't drink on duty.

"They like you, Nathan. I can tell you're fair with them. Most times, years of trust building can supersede one autocratic decision like this."

"Sure." He knew that, but with his whole life in upheaval, everything was blown out of proportion, as if he was looking at it through a magnifying glass.

"We can tell them the truth after the stalking's over."

"I can't believe it could be one of them."

"That must be hard."

"It's excruciating. They've been with me since I came to Washington."

"I'm sorry."

"Forget it." He looked around the pub. He'd always enjoyed the atmosphere, which was filled with the aroma of seafood and hickory ribs. "Do you want to order first, or make the list?"

Pausing to think, she finally said, "Why don't you

relax a bit. Have your drink, we'll eat, then we'll get down to business.''

He sighed and stared out the windows, watching Washington unfold around him. "I'm sorry. I'm being ornery.''

"You're entitled." She picked up a menu. "Let's make the best of it.''

He watched her while she perused the menu. Her hair was still pulled back, but it was tidier now; the style accented her high cheekbones. He was getting used to the blond and the braid, though when they were together she'd worn her hair down around her shoulders, framing her face, the way he liked it best.

She smiled. "Hmm, look. They have sweet potato chips.''

"Do you still eat like you used to?" He shook his head. "I never understood how you could shovel in food like a lumberjack and stay so slender.''

"I'm not exactly thin, Nathan.''

His eyes scanned her. She'd filled out since she was twenty. He took a long slug of scotch. "You look great, Anabelle.''

Her only reaction was a nod, then the waiter came back. They ordered appetizers.

"Tell me about your life in Seattle," he said.

She frowned.

"We're relaxing. I've wondered about everything.''

"Didn't Kaeley tell you about me?''

"For my own mental health, I tried not to pump her. And Dan got annoyed every time I asked him." He remembered something. "I did ask a former friend of yours from Serenity House about you—Paige—after Dan's wedding.''

"Really? Did she tell you anything?''

"No, she was too preoccupied with Ian Chandler." Nathan smiled.

Anabelle smiled back. "I got to see the babies they adopted. God, they're adorable." She shook her head. "And that dog they have, Scalpel? He's almost human."

"Yeah, Ian says he watches over the twins like he's *their* bodyguard."

"Is Ian nice?" Anabelle asked. "I know Paige is crazy about him."

"He's a great guy. And the feeling's mutual. He'd walk on hot coals for her. They consulted me about finding her child."

Paige had decided to search for the baby she gave up for adoption through Ian's Internet matching agency. "No luck with it so far, is there?"

"No. They registered on Ian's site, but no matches came through. They seem happy, though." Nathan remembered being as enthralled with a woman as Ian was with Paige. It was Anabelle, of course, but he tried not to let himself think about that too much. "Your life?"

"I have a small apartment on a quiet street in the city. I work out of a downtown office when I'm not on an assignment."

He leaned back in the seat. "Undercover work must be fascinating, even though it scares me to death thinking about what you do."

"There's usually backup."

"Like Campoli."

"Yeah." She chuckled. "Though I saved his life once, not the other way around."

"Really? No wonder he's so enamored of you."

She shrugged off the comment, but he noticed she didn't deny it.

"Tell me what happened."

Listening to her, he tried not to cringe at the details as she told him about the organized-crime kingpin who'd wanted the new pimp off the street. The Feds were brought in when it was discovered the ring had kidnapped several young girls to sell, so Zeke had posed as the pimp—and the bait—and Anabelle had been their connection. When the Mob guy went after Zeke, she had taken him out.

Nathan kept his mouth shut and ordered another scotch.

As they had dinner, she finished her police stories. Sharing bluepoint oysters, top-neck clams and spicy jumbo shrimp, they were like any ordinary couple out for a night. The normalcy of it brought on a surge of regret that washed through Nathan like a cold ocean wave.

So, when she finished her tales, he said, "You left out your private life."

She raised her chin. "Let's not get into personal stuff."

"I know you were engaged."

She frowned. "How?"

"Dan or Kaeley must have let it slip." He angled his head. "Didn't work out?"

"No."

"Why?"

"Long story."

"What about Rob?"

"It's working out."

"I see."

When the waiter cleared the meal, Anabelle took out her notebook. "All right, we need to make this list. Let's do it now and get it over with." She stared down at the pad. "It would be easiest to start with the district attorney stuff. First when you were an assistant."

"Jeez, my ADA days." He glanced out the window again, watching people hurry home after a long day's work. "I can hardly remember them."

Her face paled. It took him a minute to realize why. "Not you, Annie. I remember everything about you. And me, together."

"It's fine if you don't. Actually, it's best forgotten." She turned brusque. "Weren't there a few high-profile cases right at the beginning of your term? I remember you telling me about them."

"Yes, that scumbag Merko, who abducted the little girl in Elmwood."

She wrote it down but shook her head. "He can't be out of jail yet." She made more notations. "How about the fraud case for Hyde Point Electronics?"

"Right. That put away some top people. They'd be out by now, and since Hyde Point Electronics is local, they might be around town."

Carefully, she listed their names.

Nathan remembered other possibilities—a man who he'd help put behind bars but who had turned out to be innocent, a dirty cop who was probably free now, a bank robber.

"Well, they're certainly possibilities." She sighed. "Let's talk about your staff."

He stiffened.

Without thinking, he could tell, she reached over to squeeze his arm. But like a batter pulling a swing, she withdrew her hand before she touched him.

Over coffee, they discussed forty-year-old Hank Fallon, father, lawyer and Washington native who hoped to work in the White House someday. No, Nathan told Anabelle, he had no reason to think Hank wished him harm. The same was true for Karen Kramer, single mother, paralegal, popular with the House staff. Cameron Jones was easy to get along with, and was finishing law school. No family.

"How about cute little Mark Macomber?"

"You think he's cute?"

Anabelle smiled. "Boyish charm." She cocked her head. "A lot like you used to have."

"I was never that young," he said dryly.

"I know, me neither." She focused on her notes. "All right. Let's go personal for a minute. What about Barbara?"

Nathan practically sputtered his cappuccino all over the table. "You suspect *her?*"

"Not her directly, but you heard Zeke. Her circumstances are important."

"I still think that's ludicrous."

"Humor me. Tell me about her ex."

"Rick Benton is a nice guy. As a matter of fact, he and Barbara are traveling to Carter Prep together for parents' weekend."

"Sounds cozy to me."

He arched an eyebrow. "Are you trying to make a point?"

"No. I'm trying to make you aware of possibilities. Zeke will need to check Benton out."

They talked about other people. "You said Drew was your campaign manager."

"Damn it, Anabelle, he's my brother."

"Stepbrother. Who you never got along with when I knew you."

"Yeah, well, things change."

"How did they change?"

He looked away.

Waiting a moment, she finally said, "Nathan? What is it?"

"When you left, I...I was a wreck. I couldn't function. Dad was worried. He confided in Drew that I'd had an affair with you. Just that it didn't work out, though. Not why."

"And you got closer to Drew because of that?"

"I needed a friend. And Dan was livid. He wouldn't speak to me for weeks. Our relationship was more than strained for a long time after that."

"That was because you only told him half the story."

Nathan felt again the cold nausea that he'd experienced the day Olivia told him Kaeley wasn't his. "Just Dad and Olivia knew about Kaeley's parentage. And now that they're dead, you and I are the only ones with the truth."

Again, Anabelle reached over and this time she didn't pull back. She touched his hand. "I'll never tell anyone. Kaeley will never know, I promise."

He grasped her hand. "I trust you, Annie. It just...hurts still."

"I can imagine."

Sighing, he nodded to her notes. "Let's drop the subject and finish this up."

Anabelle pulled back her hand. "So, Drew knew about me. He could be pissed."

"Yes, but he'd never try to harm me."

"Nathan, somebody *is* after you. You can't dismiss everybody."

"You're right." They talked a while longer about the possibilities. Not wanting to bring it up, Nathan nonetheless had to make a point. "Annie, there's one thing we haven't considered. What about Aaron and Al?"

She dropped the spoon she'd picked up to stir her coffee. "My brothers?"

"Yeah, they hated me—especially after the show-downs we had, and how I served them with injunctions. Even though you never prosecuted, they were furious."

"But why, after all this time, would they..." She didn't finish. Placing her hand on her stomach, she whis-pered, "God, it makes me ill just to think about them."

"I'm sorry."

After a moment, she composed herself and scribbled their names down.

"Your experience with men hasn't been good, has it? First your father, then them. And me."

"I don't want to discuss us, Nathan."

"Letting you go was the hardest thing I've ever done in my life."

She just stared at him.

Something about the way she was looking at him...

"You still believe that, don't you?"

Setting down her pen, she tidied her napkin. "I said I don't want to talk about this."

"Just tell me that."

"I can't."

"Why?"

She faced him squarely. "Because I don't believe it was that hard for you, Nathan. Not really. And I didn't by the time I left Hyde Point, either."

As IF SHE WAS RUNNING for her life, she opened the door to the town house and strode in. Nathan stopped to punch in the code for the security system, then grabbed her by the arm before she could escape up the steps. "You can't just say something like that to me, and then not explain it." She'd refused to talk to him all the way home.

"Yes, I can." She yanked on her arm. "Let go."

"No." His voice dropped a notch. "Anabelle."

"I said *no*. We shouldn't have gotten into that, anyway. We shouldn't be sharing quiet dinners. I don't know what I was thinking."

Pulling away, she managed to get to the staircase. Once again, he stopped her. "I'm not giving up on this."

"Yes you are."

"No!" Dragging her around, he grasped her shoulders. "Do you have any idea how much I suffered when you left me?"

"I didn't *leave* you. Stop saying that. You made a choice."

"Between you and Kaeley. You said you understood." She didn't respond.

Green fire burned in his eyes. "What happened to make you change your mind?"

"Nothing."

"What?"

"Nothing."

"I'm not letting you go until you tell me."

Exasperated, overwhelmed by his nearness, by the conversation, by this whole bodyguard thing, she said, "All right, it was Olivia."

"Olivia? As far as I knew, you never saw her again after we said goodbye."

"I did see her." She swallowed hard. "When I left the estate house that day. Outside on the steps."

He swore. "What happened?"

Anabelle couldn't answer. Swallowing hard, she tried to look away.

Gently, he grasped her chin. Coaxed her to look at him. "Annie."

His touch on her face was so achingly familiar, she leaned into it for a minute. Then she admitted, "Olivia was her usual condescending self. She talked about my brothers...using me. About you, using me. She said I could never fit into your life. She was going to be first lady. What was I thinking that I could make you happy?''

He swallowed hard. ''You made me happier than I'd ever been, before or since.''

''Don't say that,'' she whispered.

''Why would you believe Olivia, after what you and I shared?''

''Because she was *right!*''

''No, she was horribly wrong. I loved you more than I ever loved anyone in the world but Kaeley. I would have given up everything but her for you.''

''Those are the operative words, Nathan. What you would have had to *give up* for me. All your plans and dreams...I had no place in them.''

''Don't say it like that.''

''It's true. I was a waitress's daughter.''

''Stop it.''

''From Serenity House.''

''No, no, stop it!''

''I had a hor—''

He yanked her to him. *''Stop it.''*

The minute he drew her close, Anabelle's head began to swim. So many sensations—the feel of his strong fingers gripping her shoulders, his heart thunderclapping in his chest, his legs and hips aligned with hers, as if the two of them had been fashioned out of the same block of clay. But it was his smell that robbed her of thought...and willpower. It was so male, a little woodsy. At twenty, she remembered nestling in the crook of his shoulder and neck and just breathing him in. The sense of security it gave her returned...and her thirty-one-year-old body responded similarly. He held her, his hand smoothing down her hair, murmuring to her. "Don't ever think I didn't love you, please, Annie, don't."

She wanted to pull away, to sever herself from him. But it had been so long since he'd touched her, since she'd felt this way in a man's arms.

Burrowing into his chest, she nonetheless said, "Please, Nathan, let me go."

"Not until you tell me you were wrong to believe Olivia. She was manipulating you. She was afraid of our relationship, it was so strong. Don't you see, love, the fact that she told you all this proves how much I loved you. She needed to be sure you'd leave. She shook your confidence in me because she *knew.*"

It made some kind of convoluted sense.

"Annie...please."

There was more. Should she tell him about how she felt when he didn't seek her out after Olivia died? No, she wouldn't tell him. Because way down deep, she didn't really trust him. She didn't tell him because she was afraid he'd come up with a shoddy excuse and she'd believe him. She was afraid she'd ignore everything else, the way she did before, because she *wanted* to believe him.

Oh, God, why were they going through this? What did it matter, anyway? He was committed to someone else now—someone suitable—and if Anabelle allowed herself to think otherwise, it would be repeating the same mistake she'd made all those years ago.

When his actions had come close to destroying her.

Finally, he let her draw back but didn't release her.

His face was flushed, his eyes fierce with emotion. "Annie, God, you don't know..."

Glass shattered somewhere in the house.

Anabelle sprang away from him. "Go into the den.

Close and lock the doors.'' She drew her gun. ''I'm going to see what that is.'' He opened his mouth but she said, ''I mean it, Nathan. Do what I say.''

As he went in the other direction, Anabelle headed out of the foyer. The house was dark and she chided herself for not checking it earlier. The sound had come from the rear. Silently, gun poised, she crept through the living room…the dining room…to the back of the house. It was church-quiet, except for the whir of the furnace from down below. In the kitchen, with the moonlight filtering in, she saw that the window by the table had been broken. She crossed to it. On the floor by a chair lay a softball.

Damn.

Nothing was moving outside now.

She scanned the interior and crossed to the back door. It was locked. She checked all the other windows. Leaving the kitchen, she hurried back to the den and found Nathan pacing behind locked doors.

As soon as he let her in, she flipped open her cell phone. ''We have to call Campoli. A softball came through the window.'' She punched in a number.

''At ten o'clock at night?''

''Yeah, and it's cold outside. Still, it could be an accident. Are there any kids around here?''

''Uh-huh, and there's a park back there.''

''Shit. If this is the stalker, he's pretty clever.''

''Are you all right?''

''Yes.'' She studied him as she waited for a connection. ''Thanks for doing what you were told.''

''It wasn't easy.''

''I know, but I can't protect you if you try to protect me.''

''I realize that. I—''

From the phone, she heard a brisk, ''Campoli.''

She held up her hand to Nathan. "Zeke, it's Belle. Somebody shot a ball through the town house's window. Can you come over?"

"Be there in fifteen, babe."

When she hung up, Nathan said, "Belle?"

"It was my cover. With him, I forget sometimes."

Nathan approached her. "Annie, about earlier?"

Ignoring the stricken expression on his face, she drew back. "It was a mistake. We can't do that, Nathan. No walk down memory lane. No confessions. And no physical contact."

"But I need—"

"No!" she shouted. "I can't. I *won't.*" She stepped farther away when he reached out. "This is a deal breaker. No more slips like that or I'm out of here."

"You'd leave in the middle of a job?"

"Yes. If you can't keep this strictly business, you'll have to get someone else to protect you. Think about it. What kind of bodyguard am I, cozying up to you? I didn't even check the house when we got back because I was so upset. If someone had been trying to break in just now…"

"Is that the only reason you won't discuss us…reconsider—"

"No, it's not. Our relationship almost destroyed me once, Nathan. I won't risk it again."

Damn. Talk about déjà vu.

CHAPTER SIX

DAN AND NORA ENTERED the spacious ballroom of the Hyde Point Country Club, where the final fund-raising event for the opening of their boys' home, Quiet Waters, was to take place. The money raised—a thousand dollars per plate—would go toward furnishing the home. Since Dan and Nora had led the project, they were acting as hosts to this black-tie gala.

"What time did Anabelle say she and Nathan were going to get here, Nora?" Dan asked.

"She said they'd meet us in time for the greeting line."

Nathan was speaking tonight as district congressman, as well as one of the home's benefactors, and had arranged for several dignitaries and celebrities to be here. He was an important part of this function.

Dan scanned the spacious setting—black-and-white linens on the tables, a peppering of candles everywhere and a red carnation at each setting. "What time were they getting back from D.C.?"

Nora brushed some lint off his dark tux. He looked handsome as sin in it. *Almost as good as he looks out of it,* Nora thought girlishly. "Late this afternoon."

"Did the FBI find anything out about the ball and broken window?"

"No. They couldn't conclude foul play." She shook her head. "Anabelle knows the agent. A Zeke Campoli."

"Really? How?"

"She worked as a hooker with him in an undercover operation."

"Oh, hell." Dan drew in a breath and shifted restlessly. "I worry about her in that job. And now this thing with Nathan. Being together so much."

Nora could tell from the strain in Anabelle's voice that being with Nathan the last three days in Washington had worn on her. "I think it's hard. But she can handle it."

"Maybe. I hope I didn't make a mistake in encouraging Nathan to take her up on her offer."

Concerned, Nora touched his face. "Dan, it's not your place to make decisions for Anabelle."

He leaned against the wall and closed his eyes briefly. "I know. It's just...I always saw her as sort of, you know, my daughter."

"I know. But even parents have to let go sometime."

"Yeah. Well, I feel like I've thrown her to the wolves."

"Nathan might object to the comparison." She heard noise behind her and pivoted around. "Oh, here they are."

Dan turned just in time to see Nathan and Anabelle enter the foyer. Once inside, Nathan reached to help Anabelle with her coat, as naturally as a husband would his wife. After a pause, she allowed the gesture.

"Holy hell," Dan said. "Where'd she get a dress like that?"

"Now you do sound like a father." Nora studied Anabelle's copper-colored silk outfit as the couple came toward them. It was a lovely dress that accented every one of Anabelle's curves. She was slender, but the dress's cut, the scooped neck and tapered long sleeves, made her look voluptuous. "She's lovely." A perfect companion for Nathan in his raven-black tux and snowy-white shirt.

When the four of them met at the perimeter of the room, Dan reached out and hugged Anabelle. "Hi, honey."

"Hi." She held on tight for a minute, as if for grounding. Nora knew Dan meant a lot to Anabelle, but at times like this she witnessed just how much.

Anabelle hugged Nora, then Nathan kissed Nora's cheek and shook hands with Dan. In a totally natural move—one he didn't even seem to know he made—Nathan stood very close to Anabelle.

"Where's Barbara?" Dan asked, as if to remind Nathan he had a fiancée.

"She's meeting us here. She had some phone calls to make, so she'll be late."

Anabelle stepped away. "I need to check out a few things, Dan. Stay close to Nathan."

As she walked away, Nathan stared after her; his expression was...hungry. Nora had seen a similar look on Dan's face all those years when they couldn't be together because Dan was married to someone else.

Dan must have caught the look, too. "Nathan, jeez, you gotta—" Dan halted midsentence when someone called out from behind them.

"Hello, Nathan." It was one of his constituents, who had contributed heavily to his campaign.

"Hello, Mrs. Mackey," Nathan said with a smile. "You look wonderful tonight."

They chatted amiably; the woman snubbed Nora and Dan, and only had eyes for Nathan. Who cared, though, if she was giving money to Quiet Waters.

After a while, Nora said, "Oh, Dan, there's Jade."

Mrs. Mackey sniffed, but turned. And her mouth

dropped open. "Oh my God, what's that girl doing with Lewis Beckman?"

Nathan's voice turned cold. "I understand he's a friend of hers from New York."

"Jade Kendrick knows the producer of *OnLine?* That play got two Tonys. I had a perfectly horrid time getting tickets the last time I was in New York."

"Jade and Beck are friends." Nora sent the woman a withering look. "And I'll bet if you're really nice to her, she might even introduce you." Nora could do a little of her own snubbing. "Now, if you'll excuse me, I want to powder my nose."

Though she tried not to, Nora fumed all the way to the ladies' room. She hated when anyone looked down on her girls. Several people in town took potshots at women like Anabelle and Jade.

Well, Nora thought, pushing open the door to the ladies' room, she'd stack up her Serenity House graduates any day against the likes of Victoria Mackey. They were wonderful women, who despite their beginnings, had turned into terrific adults.

One of whom was sitting alone in the lounge of the rest room, looking very unhappy.

"WHAT'S WRONG, sweetie?"

Anabelle just looked at Nora when she came through the door and hesitated. She didn't want Dan to know how wearing this whole thing was for her. Finally, she said, "I want to talk to you, Nora, but you have to promise you won't discuss this with Dan."

"Dan knows this bodyguard thing is hard for you. But I promise I won't discuss our conversation with him."

Anabelle stood, the penny-colored dress molding to her as she paced. "I don't know what I was thinking. Being around him—'' she messed up her hair that had been prettily styled ''—has been more difficult than I imagined it would be. Especially in D.C. In about five minutes flat he had me talking about the past, the men in my life, how I fared after I left here.''

Not to mention that cozy little embrace.

Please, Nathan let me go.

Not until you tell me you were wrong to believe Olivia. She was manipulating you… Don't you see, love, the fact that she told you all this proves how much I loved you…she shook your confidence in me because she knew.

''That's not good, Anabelle.''

''And then the shopping trip.''

''The what?''

''I needed clothes, for political functions and to wear on Capitol Hill. He had to come with me, of course, because I didn't want to leave him unguarded, and Zeke was busy…''

I'd love to shop with you.

Don't mistake this for anything else. You can't be left alone. I need clothes.

''We went out of the city, to a small town in Maryland, where he wouldn't be known.''

They'd been shown into a private dressing room with a waiting area just outside the stalls.

Sir, you can sit here while your wife tries on clothes.

As if he didn't notice the error, Nathan had cheerfully thanked the clerk.

Anabelle had gone inside frustrated. When the woman suggested she come out and model the clothes, Nathan had wholeheartedly agreed.

''He whistled at some outfits, Nora, like a kid.''

Like a young suitor in love. He'd nixed some, praised others. His taste was impeccable. What's more, she'd had

fun. For a bit, she'd forgotten what their circumstances were.

"You know, sweetie, it's not too late to alter the plan.
Nathan can go public, get a visible bodyguard."

Let him, a self-protective instinct warned. *Get away
now.*

"No, I feel better watching over him during this."

"Anabelle, you don't have to be so strong."

"Of course I do, Nora, I've always had to be."

When Nora went back to the greeting line, Anabelle
stared at herself in the mirror. She liked how she looked;
this, too, was thanks to Nathan. He'd always loved the
color of her eyes, the upturn of her nose. He'd praised
the long lean lines of her body. She was happy with how
she'd matured. An extra ten pounds looked good on her.
Especially in this dress.

It's...it shows...

What, isn't it appropriate for black tie events? she'd
asked.

Of course it is, but it's so...sexy, Annie.

She'd grinned, and put the dress in the buy stack.

To her mirror image, she said, "All right, Annie baby,
you can handle this. His smoldering looks. His possessiveness. Ignore it and do your job."

As she approached the greeting line, she saw Nathan
standing with his stepbrother and his wife. Tall and lean,
Drew Hyde was chatting easily with his older brother
while Marian Hyde listened politely. Something about the
scene made her uncomfortable. Maybe because Nathan
had told Drew about their affair. But she didn't think that
was it. Nathan caught sight of Anabelle and motioned
her over.

"Drew, Marian, you remember Anabelle Crane."

His brother's smile seemed sincere. "Yes. Hello, Anabelle. Welcome to our team.'' Though he only worked on campaigns, Drew was a valued member of Nathan's staff.

Marian echoed the greeting.

Drew gave her an intense stare. "I must say I was surprised to hear you'd come aboard."

Again, Nathan sidled in close to Anabelle. "I told you she was in town. She was free. She's had experience. She's perfect for the...oh, the senator's here. Damn, look who he's with."

Drew, Marian and Anabelle tracked Nathan's gaze. Just inside the door was one of the New York State senators—from the other political party—Jacob Jenkins. With him was a big man. He reminded Anabelle of a tree—huge trunk, arms she wouldn't be able to get her hands around, legs like the base of a mature oak.

For some reason, Anabelle felt for the gun in her purse. The men approached.

"Nathan," Senator Jenkins said easily. "Nice to see you."

"You, too. Glad you could come." Nathan eyed the other man. "Surprised to see you here, Olsen."

Up close, the big man was very attractive. Dark-blue eyes. Chiseled nose and jaw. "Why is that, Nate?"

"The NRA doesn't usually support small-town fund-raisers for out-of-the-way boys' homes."

"We do a lot of good works," Olsen said, his eyes glittering like shards of glass. "Jacob told me about this function, and since I was in Albany, I flew up with him."

Dan intervened. "Well, we're glad to have your money."

Nathan gave Olsen a last doubting look then said, "Jacob, you remember Dan Whitman. He's the brains behind Quiet Waters...and Drew Hyde, my brother."

The senator's smile was polished. "Nice job with the campaign, Hyde."

"It takes a lot of people," Drew said modestly. "And we have a star here in Nate."

Olsen turned to Anabelle, who had stepped back to avoid attention. "And who's this beautiful lady?"

"My new assistant. Anabelle Crane, meet Hawk Olsen."

She held out her hand and smiled. He shook it, but didn't let go. "Nice—" his gaze dropped below her chin "—very nice to meet you."

"How do you know Nathan?" Anabelle asked sweetly.

"I'm his bitter enemy."

Damn it, one he hadn't told her about. "Oh, really?"

"Olsen here is a big shot for the National Rifle Association. He's a lobbyist in D.C. for their proposals."

"Which you always fight, Hyde." Olsen flicked him a glance. "When are you gonna give me a break?"

"When kids stop killing kids with guns. When homicide with guns stops plaguing our everyday life."

Big shoulders stiffened. The man towered over Nathan. "Always the bleeding heart."

"Let's mingle," the senator said.

"Let's." Olsen looked at her. "I hope I see you again, Miss Crane."

She nodded. Let her eyes bat a bit.

Drew swore under his breath when Olsen left.

Nathan fumed.

And Anabelle watched the newest suspect walk away.

"WE'VE GOT to get inside." Nathan and Anabelle were the last to leave the foyer.

"In a minute." She drew in a deep breath. "Why isn't your archenemy on the list?"

"He gives himself too much importance."

Yanking at his arm, she tugged him out of view of the ballroom, over by the phones and rest rooms. "I saw the way he looked at you. Goddamn it, Nathan…"

"I saw the way he looked at you, too."

"What's that supposed to mean?"

"He ate you up with his eyes."

"Don't exaggerate." She started to walk away. He grabbed her shoulder.

"No, let's finish this." He was sporting for a fight. He hated seeing her flirt with other guys, hated seeing other men come on to her. His hand tightened on her.

"Get your hands off me, it's inappro—"

"Nathan, what are you doing back here?"

They turned to find Barbara watching them. Nathan stepped back as if he'd been found in an illicit situation. "Barbara, I didn't know you'd arrived."

Barbara's smile was strained. She looked classy in a long red sheath that set off her dark hair. "You were occupied." Graciously, she turned to Anabelle and held out her hand, where diamonds glittered from her fingers and wrists. They matched those at her ears. "Hello Anabelle. We met at Christmas."

And they'd shared the scene in his bedroom that first night. When Barbara was wearing Nathan's bathrobe. *Oh, forget it,* Anabelle had said disgustedly. *I'm not going to work this way. If you won't cooperate, I'm out of here.*

Anabelle assumed her undercover demeanor and smiled warmly. "Nice to see you again."

Anabelle turned to Nathan. "We need to go in. You'll be seated at the head table, near Dan. I'll be off to the side."

Nathan nodded. "Fine. Let's walk back in like we're just friends."

Barbara's eyebrow arched. She twined her arm through his. "Let's."

Anabelle accompanied them but stayed a few feet away from Nathan. Once inside, she waited until he was on his way to the head table and Dan. Nathan saw her turn away and bump right into Drew, who seemed to come out of nowhere from the right side of the room. His seat was on the other side.

"Oh, excuse me," Anabelle said. "I wasn't looking where I was going."

Drew eyed her, then his gaze shifted and Nathan caught his disapproving look. "No, you were focused…elsewhere." Drew then headed off to the left and Nathan raised his eyebrows in a quizzical retort to Anabelle.

She watched Drew for a minute, then headed for the Serenity House girls, who were grouped at one table, as were Lewis Beckman and a couple of other people Nathan didn't immediately recognize. Before Nathan could sit, he heard a stir in the crowd. In a minute he saw why.

His college buddy, and the nation's current heartthrob, Trace McCall, had arrived. Abandoning his seat, Nathan went to greet his friend. They met up in the middle of the room and hugged warmly.

"McCall, you bastard, how are you?"

"Just fine, Congressman." He glanced around. "Fancy shindig you got here."

"People paid good money just to see you. Thanks for doing this."

"I wanna do this." Trace's blue eyes grew dark for a moment. "I got a past, remember?"

"Yeah, I do." Trace had had a tough upbringing, but

had fought his way through the poverty to get a scholarship to Yale's drama and theater program. After they graduated, he had found his niche in music first, then in movies.

"Come sit at the head table."

"I'd rather not." Though Trace was the darling of the media, he was in many ways a private person. "Is there a seat somewhere else?"

Nathan noticed one next to Beckman. He wondered if Anabelle would like to have a star at their table. "Sure. You know who Lewis Beckman is?"

"Hey, I may be born and bred in the hills of West Virginia, but I can read. He here?"

"Yeah, and there's a seat at his table."

"It'd be fun to meet the Broadway whiz."

Nathan brought Trace to Anabelle's table. When Nathan introduced him, everyone was polite.

Except for Jade. "An honest-to-goodness star." She fluttered her eyelashes. "Be still my heart."

Beck laughed, but it was strained; Nathan didn't know their connection, but he seemed possessive of Jade. Trace took a chair across from Charly Donovan.

Nathan turned and was just about to go back to the head table, when the lights went out.

A murmur filtered through the crowd and a chill hurtled through him with the coldness of a February wind. Somebody came up beside him. Instinctively, he braced himself, until he felt soft curves align with his body.

He'd know those curves anywhere.

"Move ahead, Nathan, go slow. There's a small alcove about ten feet to your right. Nothing in between."

She kept her body tight against his as they crossed to the alcove. When they reached it, she eased him inside; all the while she stayed in front of him and against him.

Not that he minded. Until he realized she had herself stationed between him and anyone who might come after him.

Once inside, she urged him up flat to the wall and turned around. Still, she was as close as a lover. Her hair teased his nostrils. It smelled wonderful, like flowers. Leaning forward, he breathed it in, and despite the danger of the situation, he let himself enjoy the sensation of her angled up against him intimately.

"What do you think's going on?" he asked, his breath feathering her ear.

"I..." She cleared her throat. "I hope it's just a blown fuse. We'll stay here until we know for sure. We're shielded from view, so when the lights come back on, we can get out inconspicuously."

They waited, heard Dan's shouts, people running around.

Nathan rested his hands on her shoulders and squeezed. She didn't react. They stayed that way for a while.

Finally, the lights came back on.

She said, "All right, let's go." Replacing her gun in her purse, she glanced over her shoulder at him. There was something in her eyes. He couldn't decipher it. Had his nearness affected her as much as him? He glanced down his body. Shit.

Slowly, she peeked around the wall. "It's settled down. You'd better get out there before anyone misses you."

It's anything but settled down, he thought as he took a few deep breaths.

"What's the matter?"

He shook his head. "Nothing. Give me a minute."

"Are you all right?"

"Yeah."

"Were you afraid?"

"It's not that."

"What is it? Why aren't you moving?"

"Annie, I—" he glanced down "—got *aroused* with you plastered up against me."

Her face blanked. Then she said, "Oh."

Yanking the coat of his tux together, he ran a shaky hand through his hair. Took two more deep breaths. "Sorry. I think I won't embarrass myself now." He gestured into the room, "After you."

"When you get back to the head table, stick close to Dan," Anabelle said as she stepped into the room.

"I will."

All the way back to the head table, he thought about getting turned on by just a slight contact with Anabelle—and not being able to make love to his fiancée last week. Tonight was the first time he'd seen Barbara since then, as he'd left for D.C. and she'd gone to Connecticut to see her son.

An untenable thought worked its way to his brain as he reached the table and Dan approached him. Barbara would want to make love tonight while Anabelle was in the house. How on earth was Nathan ever going to deal with that?

"Jeez, he's even sexier in person." Jade, dressed in green silk that made her eyes shimmer, practically cooed the remark about Trace McCall as he ended a set of songs. Her comment earned chuckles from all the Serenity House women at the table.

Charly Donovan sighed. Her black pants and short beaded jacket were perfect for the evening. "Did you see those eyes? They're like a lagoon."

''And those shoulders.'' Paige gave a girlish giggle, looking lovely in a long pink sheath. ''I read that he lived on a farm in West Virginia. Must be they grow 'em big and strong there.''

Taylor Morelli laid her head on her husband's shoulder. ''Don't worry, honey, I think you're a lot sexier.''

Nick reached over and adjusted the strap of Taylor's dark-red dress. ''Thanks for the thought, babe, but I know you're lying.''

''Well, just a little, maybe.''

Darcy Sloan patted her belly. ''I swear, even the little one's rolling at his music. Must be a girl.''

''Aw, come on, love, it's too early to feel her movin'.'' Hunter's scowl was sham. ''Besides, I thought pregnant women were immune to other men.''

She whispered something in Hunter's ear, making him blush.

Ian stood. ''I can't stand this. Anybody want to join me in the billiards room? I refuse to sit here and watch these chicks moon over some freaking rock star.''

''I can't help myself,'' Paige laughed.

Anabelle rolled her eyes as all the men left, even Beck. Trace had taken a break to sign some autographs, so they weren't being rude.

''What's going on with Beck, Jade?'' Anabelle waited until the men were gone. Lewis Beckman was a married man—and the father of Jade's daughter.

''When Nathan found out I knew him, he asked if Beck would attend the fund-raiser. The more celebs, the better the turnout. There are all kinds of rich and famous here.''

''Things between you two seem strained,'' Darcy remarked. ''You said you told him you just wanted to be friends when you went to see him over Thanksgiving.''

"We *are* just friends. Nothing more."

Paige snorted. "Yeah, he touches you every chance he gets, sis. It's not *friends* on his side."

Charly intervened, as always. "Come on, you two, why are you arguing when you can just drool over Trace McCall?" The star was graciously talking to several Hyde Point citizens who'd gathered around him. "He was so nice during dinner. Not at all self-absorbed." She patted her purse. "He signed an autograph for each of the girls and asked a lot of questions about Serenity House."

Anabelle's gaze strayed to Nathan, who was still seated at the head table. He wasn't as big or classically handsome as Trace, but he looked wonderful in his tux.

And felt wonderful in the alcove when the lights went out.

Which is what she should be thinking about, not how attractive he is. She'd checked with the club's maintenance people and nobody seemed to know what had thrown the breaker switch to plunge the room into darkness.

Still, she couldn't tear her gaze from Nathan. Next to him, Barbara leaned over and whispered something in his ear. It made him smile; the intimate little gesture caused Anabelle's stomach to lurch.

"What's got that sour look on a pretty lady's face?" Anabelle glanced up to see Hawk Olsen had approached their table. He loomed over her.

"Indigestion," she said neutrally and noticed the senator was with him. Anabelle watched as Jade took over to make the rest of the introductions.

When they got to Taylor Morelli, Anabelle heard Charly say, "Taylor, are you all right?"

Taylor had turned pale. Dazed, she was staring at the senator.

Charly shook her arm. "Sweetie, what is it?"

"What?" Taylor seemed to come to. "Oh, I'm fine."

The senator was staring at Taylor, too. "Do we know each other from somewhere?" he asked.

If possible, Taylor went even whiter. "I don't remember."

Charly stood. "Come on, let's get some fresh air." She smiled weakly, murmured, "Would you excuse us, please?" and escorted Taylor away.

The senator said to Anabelle, "What was that about?"

"Did you recognize her, Senator?" Paige asked.

"No, not exactly." He frowned. "She just looked familiar for a minute. Who is she?"

Taylor's amnesia was not a secret to anyone in Hyde Point, or Elmwood, where she lived, so Paige explained the circumstances. "If you remember anything about why she looked familiar, we'd appreciate your calling us." Paige gave him her card and the senator moved on.

Trace began to sing again, and he invited dancing. Couples eased onto the floor. One was Barbara and Nathan. Dan and Nora joined them.

"Would you like to dance, Miss Crane?" This from Hawk Olsen, who right now was living up to his name. He studied her like a bird about to pounce on its prey.

Anabelle was good at being prey.

"Sure, Mr. Olsen. I'd love to." She slid her purse over her shoulder. "We can share our views on gun control."

BARBARA STOOD by the window of the sitting room in Nathan's bedroom suite and stared out at the January night. She was contemplative, and Nathan didn't blame her. He slouched in a chair, feeling the way he had when he couldn't decide whether to run for the House seat or not.

That had been right after Olivia had died. And when he'd discovered Anabelle was engaged.

Think about your fiancée, and what you did to her tonight. Should he try to explain what had happened? What could he say? Just brushing up against Anabelle in the alcove put him in overdrive, whereas the preliminaries to making love with his fiancée left him cold. Silence seemed wiser than that truth, or worse, some lame excuse.

Finally, she turned toward him. "This is a repeat of the other night, Nathan. I guess I need to know why."

He jammed his hands into his tuxedo pants pockets. He was shirtless and barefoot. "Maybe it's the stalking."

"Did the lights going out precipitate this…reaction?"

So to speak. "It's the whole thing, Barb."

"Does it have anything to do with the way you looked at your young bodyguard tonight?"

"What do you mean?"

"She was particularly fetching in that dress. You seemed drawn to her."

He sighed and took the politically correct way out. "Truthfully, being up here, with you, while Anabelle's downstairs is disconcerting for me." In reality, it was repulsive. He couldn't stop wondering what she was thinking. Was she picturing him and Barbara together? How did that make her feel? He knew just seeing Olsen's hands on her while they danced spiked his own temper.

"Are you suggesting we wait until this stalking is over to make love again?"

There's an idea.

"I'm asking for some time to get acclimated to this situation."

She eyed him carefully. "You don't want me to stay overnight, either, do you?"

He remembered the look on Anabelle's face earlier when they'd arrived home. Barbara had gone ahead of him up the steps and he'd stayed down to talk to Anabelle...

"I'll be upstairs," he'd told her, almost choking on the words.

"I need to know if she's staying the night. What I should expect."

"I...don't know."

"Fine." Anabelle's words were clipped but her jaw was taut, her eyes tumultuous. He'd seen that expression so many times in the past. "I'll be in my room. Just let me know either way..."

Remembering the look on Annie's face propelled him to say to Barbara, "Your staying overnight would be awkward."

Amazing, all his explanations were true, but in the back of his mind, he knew everything about them was about as false as it could get.

Barbara buttoned her dress and straightened the rest of her clothes. She found her shoes and stepped into them. Then she crossed to him, sank gently into his lap and slid slender arms around his neck. "I don't know what this woman is to you, love, and I suspect I don't want to. But, as I said before, she can't have you." She kissed him on the mouth. "Remember that."

"Barbara, I—"

She placed her fingers on his lips. "Shh. No more tonight. It's all right. I wanted to talk to Rick, anyway." She glanced at her watch. "I'll still be able to call him from home."

"Why?"

"R.J. isn't feeling well. He's been unusually tired and developed swollen glands this weekend. When I left Connecticut today, Rick decided to stay on for a while to see how R.J. fared, and maybe get him to the doctor if necessary."

Nathan knew Barbara's young son meant more to her than anything in the world. He respected her immensely for it. Their feelings for their children was one of the many things they had in common. "I hope he's all right."

"Thanks." She rose. "Now show me out." She arched an eyebrow. "And don't forget what I said about the lovely Ms. Crane. She can't have you."

She doesn't want me.

Suddenly, Nathan wondered what he'd do if Anabelle did want to pick up where they'd left off, if she did want to pursue what, for him at least, had been feelings that had never died.

What did it matter? There wasn't a chance in hell of her rekindling a relationship with him. He'd hurt her too much. Oh, she cared for him; he was pretty sure of that, although her remarks about protecting him for Kaeley and Dan were true, she was protecting him mostly because she cared about *him*.

But he'd killed any chance of their getting back together when he let her go at twenty-two. She had a boyfriend again. And he was engaged. Talk about doomed.

Best to remember that. Because if it wasn't true, if he hadn't destroyed all her feelings for him, God knew what he'd do.

"COME 'ERE, ROSY. Come sit in Annie's lap." Seated on the floor of the laundry room, Anabelle reached over and took the ten-week-old puppy into her hands. He fit, cra-

dled in her palms. His fur was so soft it tickled her skin.
"You are so cute. How could anyone not want to keep
you?"

Both she and Nathan had been shocked, on their return
from D.C., to find one of the six puppies from Elly's
litter had been regretfully returned by the family Nathan
had given the dog to. It turned out the child was allergic
to dander and they couldn't keep the pup.

Roosevelt, aka Rosy, licked her face and then settled
down to nuzzle her neck. The gorgeous Irish setter's
movement dislodged two of the buttons on the navy ther-
mal top she wore. Rosy's mother watched Anabelle with
soulful brown eyes from her plush bed of blankets, but
finally laid her snout on Anabelle's knee. She could feel
the dog's warmth through her flannel pj bottoms.

Tonight she needed the closeness. It was stupid, but
she couldn't help it and she might as well admit to herself
that she was affected by Barbara being here. When she'd
tried to settle down for the night, she kept picturing what
was going on one story above her. It hurt, almost as much
as it used to hurt when Nathan would disappear into his
bedroom with Olivia ten years ago. When she and Nathan
had made love at the cottage that weekend, he'd told
Anabelle that he'd stopped having sex with his wife
months before, when he knew he was in love with *her*.
She'd believed him, though at the end, Olivia had gotten
in a shot saying they'd been making love all along. She'd
never really known what the truth was back then.

Now he and Barbara were upstairs having sex.

God, her insides were pummeled by the thought.

So, she'd crept out of her room, down here to the laundry room off the kitchen, as she often had years ago, and
found the dogs. Their contact soothed her, made her feel

less alone. She closed her eyes to savor the smell of them, to relish the sound of their breathing.

She didn't know how much later she heard, "There you are."

Her eyes snapped open. Nathan stood before her. He wore his tux pants, and his shirt was unbuttoned. His hair was disheveled and his eyes were after-sex smoky. She had to look away. "What are you doing here?" she finally asked.

"You said to let you know if Barbara was staying."

"Oh, yeah, I wanted to lock up."

"I already did."

Fine. Go back to her. But she couldn't get the words out. She just nodded, the lump in her throat stealing her capacity for speech.

Instead of leaving, he dropped onto the floor adjacent to her. She was leaning against a wall, and his back was flush with the washer. He stretched out his legs and reclined his head against the machine.

"What are you doing?" she asked.

"Do you mind if I sit here a while?"

Oh, God, what was he trying to do to her? "Barbara might mind."

"Barbara left, Annie."

"Why?"

"A thousand reasons."

"I don't understand."

"Now there's the truth."

She adjusted the puppy to cuddle against her chest. Nathan's gaze followed her movements. His eyes narrowed and she looked down to see the action had pulled her shirt apart and the upper swell of her breast was exposed. Before she could fix it, the puppy nosed inside and buried his face there.

"Hey, Rosy, where you going, boy?"

"Smart dog, I'd say."

She looked up, her face reddening. "Don't do that, please."

"What?"

"Flirt with me." When he said nothing, she said, "This is hard enough as it is."

He sighed. "Is it hard, Annie, for you?"

"Yes. It's unbelievable." Defenses down, she whispered, "Is it? For you?"

"Excruciating. I'm…having trouble being near you so much."

She bit her lip. "I could tell in the alcove."

"Sorry about that. Proximity."

"Sure, a warm female body."

"Not quite."

"What does that mean?"

"Nothing."

"Why did Barbara leave?"

He stared hard at her, as if trying to decide what to tell her.

"Nathan, what's wrong?"

"I hated seeing you dance with Olsen."

"Because of your history with him?"

"No, because watching another man's hands on you kills me."

"You shouldn't say that to me."

"I know. That doesn't make it any less true."

"I'm sure Barbara made you forget about that."

"Barbara couldn't make me forget anything."

"Nathan…"

"I didn't make love to her."

"Nathan…"

"I couldn't."

She tried not to ask. "You mean emotionally? Because I'm here?"

"No, I mean physically. Because you're here."

Her gaze dropped to his lap. "But you were...in the alcove..."

"I was aroused. By you. I haven't...oh, God, I haven't made love to Barbara since you took this job, Annie. I haven't had the least bit of desire to."

"I don't want to know that. To know any of those things." But she did, really.

"I'm sorry."

"This isn't good for us."

"I know." Still, he reached out his hand. Held it palm up. She stared down at it, remembering the familiar gesture. It made her ache. She glanced up and saw his eyes, full of conflicting emotions. She knew the expression there would match the look in hers.

And despite the past that they couldn't change, despite the present that seemed to be stacked against them, Anabelle reached out her hand and settled it in his.

In the dim light, on the floor of the laundry room, he simply laced their fingers as he had a thousand times before and held on.

CHAPTER SEVEN

"I REALLY APPRECIATE your interest in all this, McCall. Last night, and now wanting to see the actual place." Dan's smile was warm and grateful. "This boys' home means a lot to me."

Trace wandered around the kitchen of Quiet Waters, taking in its gleaming appliances and practical layout. "I can tell. I reckon it'll mean a lot to the boys who'll live here, too."

"Hunter did a great job." Nathan ran his hand across a wood cabinet. "Just like the kitchen at the Winslow Place. The guy's an artist."

"I wouldn't go that far." The men turned to find Hunter in the doorway. He held out his hand to Trace. "Hunter Sloan."

"Trace McCall." They shook hands.

"Yeah, I know. My wife was swoonin' over your singing with the rest of the girls last night."

McCall eyed Hunter. "The feisty little redhead, right?"

"That's right. She's all mine." Hunter smiled.

"How's she feeling?" Dan asked.

"Great."

McCall frowned. "Is she sick?"

"Pregnant. Almost three months." His grin spread ear to ear. "I can't wait."

Nathan watched McCall study Hunter. "You're a lucky guy." Trace glanced at the cabinets. "And a talented one. Beautiful work."

"Thanks." Hunter handed Dan the file he held. "Here are the placement requests. I starred the kids I think need us the most."

"You work here, too?" McCall asked.

"Yeah. As a part-time assistant."

"Must be rewarding."

Hunter shrugged. "For me it is. I don't know about my contribution, though. I just started some psych courses at the college and they're driving me nuts." He smiled at Dan. "But I'm loving it."

Nathan was envious of Hunter. Town bad boy. Never had anybody to support or encourage him. And he was happier than Nathan ever thought of being.

"I'm heading over to the Winslow Place when I'm done here to look at that staircase you want replaced," Hunter said.

"Oh, good." Nathan glanced at Dan. "I'd like to stop there, if it's okay."

Dan shook his head. "I have a meeting shortly with Drew about some legal stuff for Quiet Waters."

"I didn't know he was involved in this."

"Yep, it looks like he's taking an interest in all your pet projects."

"That's great."

"So…I can't go to the Winslow Place."

McCall cast them questioning looks. So did Hunter. The other two men didn't know Dan was filling in as his bodyguard and Nathan couldn't go anywhere without him.

"I can give Anabelle a call…" Dan's gaze darted between the two other men, obviously not wanting to say too much.

"No!" Nathan didn't want to foist the Winslow Place on her. Not after last night.

This hurts so much...being around you.

But Nathan didn't know how to get out of meeting Hunter there without appearing crazy.

Dan asked Trace if he'd like to finish the tour of the house, and when they left, Hunter stayed put.

Dark eyes focused intently on Nathan. "Something's goin' on with you. I can tell. Things haven't been right for a while."

Nathan sighed. "Too much is going on. I can't keep up with it all."

Hunter's gaze was shrewd. "How's Anabelle doing?"

"Why do you ask?"

"Darcy's worried about her."

"She's...do you know I have a history with her?"

Briefly, Hunter glanced away. "Darcy's not too happy about her working for you, so I figured there's a lot I don't know."

"It's like I keep covering the same ground all the time. It's frustrating."

"I know the feeling," Hunter said. He straightened. "If you ever need to talk to somebody, I'm willing. I appreciate your help in getting me my kid, Nathan." Nathan had helped Hunter file papers and had flown to Florida to testify when Hunter sued for custody of his son. "If there's anything I can do..."

Nathan clapped him on the back. "Thanks, but I'm not free to talk about it. Except to say I'd appreciate if we could postpone the Winslow thing."

"Sure. Call me when you can shoot over."

Just as Hunter headed back to the office, Trace and Dan returned. Dressed in jeans and cowboy boots, Trace looked like anything but a multimillionaire movie star. He leaned against the counter and folded his arms across his chest, his tawny good looks sparkling in the light coming in from the windows. "Takes a lot to open a place like this, doesn't it?"

"Yeah. But your attendance last night doubled our expected income for the fund-raiser."

Reaching into his shirt pocket, Trace withdrew a check and handed it to Dan. "Here. Add this to your take."

Dan shook his head. "You don't have to do that, McCall. You already gave up your time to come all the way to Hyde Point."

"I'm enjoying myself." He smiled. "I needed to get away, too. I like the Boxwood Inn. I'm thinking of staying on a bit."

"No kidding?" Nathan remembered his plans for tonight. "I wish I had known. I'm on my way to see Kaeley in a play. You could come with us…"

Trace held up his hand. "It's cool. I want some peace and quiet anyway. I'll just chill out by myself." Trace glanced out the window. "I'd build a stable up here. Have horses." He nodded to the check. "With that."

Dan looked at the amount and whistled. "Now, there's a thought. I'll bring it up to the board of directors." He glanced at his watch. "We need to get going. I'll just go tell Hunter we're leaving, then we can drop Trace off and head over to Serenity House."

Trace's blue eyes lit up. "That the girls' home the women were talkin' about last night? I signed some autographs for the brown-eyed beauty that runs it."

"Yeah." Dan smiled. "Charly Donovan. She took my wife's place there. She's an angel of mercy."

"Maybe I'll just tag along," Trace said. "I'd like to see the girls' place, too."

Dan left and Nathan chuckled. "Brown-eyed beauty?"

"And sweet." He looked past Nathan's shoulder, his gaze far away. "Nothin' like the women I know."

Nathan smiled. "You love the women you know."

"Nah, not lately." He eyed Nathan carefully. "Speaking of women, what's going on with this Anabelle chick? She sticks like glue to you, but you shoot sparks off each other all the time."

"Long story."

"Care to tell your old buddy?"

"As soon as I can. Maybe I'll fly out to California when this is all over and you can console me."

"It's that private?" A valid question since he and Trace used to bare their souls to each other in college. Nathan hadn't realized how much he missed normal things like simple male friendship. Maybe that's why he gravitated to Hunter.

"I'm afraid so," Nathan said.

"Then you better watch how you act around her, buddy. You got your heart on your sleeve."

"I got my heart in my mouth most of the time."

Dan returned then, and Nathan pondered Trace's words all the way to Serenity House where Anabelle was to meet them and pick up as bodyguard.

Some secrecy. Everybody was noticing the whacky vibes between him and Anabelle. He needed to be circumspect. Nonetheless, he couldn't wait to see her today. She'd been gone when he woke up this morning and Dan was at the house.

He wondered how she felt about their honest confessions last night.

ANABELLE KNOCKED on the door to the room she'd occupied when she was a resident at Serenity House. From inside, Ariel said, "Go away."

"Ariel? It's Anabelle Crane. I'd like to come in."

"No."

"Please." No answer. "Maybe I can help."

She heard a grunt, some rustling around and then the door creaked open. Ariel looked terrible—she hadn't washed her hair, her clothes were wrinkled and her face was taut. She didn't speak to Anabelle, but crossed back to the bed, lay down and turned her head to the wall.

Anabelle took a minute to scan the room. It had recently been painted and the furniture was new—a light maple desk, bed and chair. Instead of Van Halen posters on the wall, there was a big ad for Trace McCall's latest movie.

Anabelle took the chair. "Want to tell me what's wrong?"

"You already know. That's why you're here."

"This is about your grades in school."

"Uh-huh."

"Charly says you're failing four out of five subjects."

"Charly's pissed—and she never gets mad. She says I'm wasting my potential."

Anabelle heard a sniffle. Oh, dear. She got up and crossed to sit on the edge of the bed. Lightly, she put her hand on Ariel's shoulder. The girl stiffened at first, then relaxed. Abused kids froze up at contact sometimes. And Ariel hadn't been as lucky as Anabelle. Her stepfather had molested her for a year before the authorities got her out.

"What's going on, honey? Is the work too hard for you? If it is, maybe I can help."

Ariel snorted. "The work's a snap."

"Why don't you do it, then?"

After a moment, Ariel turned over. Her eyes were bright and her face blotchy. "Why should I? I got no chance of college, and I'm just gonna end up in the electronics plant or married to some jerk who drinks his paycheck away at a bar on Friday nights."

Anabelle had forgotten the all-consuming despair she'd once felt when she lived in Hyde Point. "It doesn't have to be that way. I'm sure Charly's discussed this with you."

"Yeah. No offense, I love Charly. But she's a Pollyanna. She believes everybody can be anything they want to be."

Anabelle, you can do anything you want, Nathan had told her when she first went to live with them.

Can I?

"You should go to college," she told Ariel.

"I can't afford it."

I can't afford to go to college, Mr. Hyde.

The Hyde Foundation offers scholarships. I could arrange something.

And so she'd taken courses at Elmwood College, and over four years she'd gotten an Associate's Degree. She would have continued except for...

"There are scholarships. As far as I know, the Hyde Foundation still gives several a year. It's how I went to college."

A glimmer of hope lit Ariel's eyes. "No shit?"

"I could help you apply for one. But you'll have to raise your grades this quarter if you want to get it."

Ariel stared at the ceiling. Anabelle glanced up. There were tiny little stars glued up there. "Maybe."

Remembering what it was like not to want to get your hopes up, Anabelle patted her arm. "Well, think about it." She stood. "Meanwhile, get your butt out of that bed and come with me. We're gonna learn how to protect ourselves from kidnappers and carjackers."

Ariel didn't budge, just studied her. "You were here, right? In Serenity House."

"Uh-huh. As a matter of fact, I lived in this very room." She raised her eyes. "I put those stars up there." She focused on Ariel. "I'm doing these sessions because I know what it's like to be at the mercy of others. Women need to be able to protect themselves as well as support themselves. And it's why, young lady, you need a college education."

Slowly, Ariel stood and found her sneakers. When she turned around, she asked bluntly, "Why'd they put you in here?"

Hating to talk about those times, Anabelle steeled herself against the emotional onslaught. "For as long as I can remember, my stepbrothers knocked me around. At one point they decided to…use me in other ways."

I knew the day you came here from that home you were bad news… The whole town knew those brothers of yours had used you.

Ariel looked away. "Did they?"

"No, Dan Whitman got me out of there just in the nick of time."

"My stepfather…he…did it to me."

Anabelle felt horror swell inside her. "I'm sorry, honey. It must have been awful."

"It was. I vowed nobody'd ever do something like that to me again."

"Then you need to depend on yourself to be safe. And to live a happy life."

"Are you happy?"

"Mostly."

"How come you're not married?"

Marry me. Let me take care of you.

In his hand Nathan had held a beautiful gold ring set with rubies. Her birthstone. She never let herself think of that ring and how she'd worn it on a chain, close to her heart, believing Nathan would one day put it on her finger.

"I haven't found the right guy yet."

"Ever been in love?"

I love you, Nathan. No matter whatever happens, I'll always love you.

"Yes. Once."

"What happened?"

"Didn't work out." She crossed to the door and opened it. "Now let's go learn what to do if you're being carjacked."

And stop this unnerving conversation. She didn't need any more reminders of her past, after last night, when she and Nathan had broken down yet another barrier and admitted how difficult it was to be together.

A tacit admission of what they both still felt for each other.

NATHAN AND TRACE CREPT quietly down the basement steps of Serenity House; a cacophony of hoots and hollers was coming from the group down there. Because of the noise, he and Trace couldn't be heard. Because the stairwell was behind the crowd and off to the side, they couldn't be seen. Nathan seized the opportunity to watch the goings-on by putting a finger to his mouth to signal Trace, who nodded his understanding.

Anabelle stood in front of five girls and three adults—Charly, Jade, and her older friend, Lila Stanwyck. Anabelle wore formfitting black leggings and a Seattle Police Department T-shirt the color of plums. Her hair was in a ponytail and swung vibrantly behind her as she demonstrated some techniques.

"All right. You're alone going to your car. I could tell you never to do that, but we all routinely take that risk. So what should you do if you're attacked?"

Everybody answered at once. "Run... Scream and yell... Make as much noise as possible."

"Okay. If he's too close to get away?"

Mrs. Stanwyck raised her hand just like a schoolteacher would. "I downloaded those articles off the Internet that you suggested, dear. It says to throw the keys as far away as possible so he can't take you in the car."

"Great point, Mrs. S." Anabelle smiled affectionately at the woman.

"How about weapons?" Jade asked.

"A weapon is only good if you use it." Anabelle put her hands on her hips. "So it's got to be available."

"You could carry pepper spray," a redheaded girl suggested.

"If it's legal. It's legal here in New York, but it's not in all states. So you've gotta check it out first if you move from here." She scanned the room. "What else?"

Demurely, Mrs. Stanwyck said, "One of the articles

said to carry a weapon on your key chain because it's always handy. When you're heading for the car, you'll have it out.''

"Exactly. As a matter of fact, I've brought some samples of what could function as your key chain, or things you could attach to it.'' From her bag Anabelle pulled out several keys chains. "Come on up and look at them.''

They all gathered around and picked up the implements.

"These look like brass knuckles,'' one girl said.

"It's a plastic scraper for a car with a hole for your finger.'' Anabelle demonstrated the gadget's use. "It *does* function as plastic knuckles.''

The other objects were sharp things like pens, combs or a small Swiss Army Knife that might function as a weapon on a key chain.

"So,'' Anabelle said after they were done perusing the items, "if the attacker comes near you, you've got some umph behind your blow.''

Everyone sat again as Anabelle dropped onto the floor. Her T-shirt pulled taut against her breasts and Nathan remembered what she felt like up against him last night. He shifted uncomfortably.

"Now, what if the guy gets to you, and none of these things work—'' she indicated the samples "—and none of the other physical things I taught you work. What should you do?''

"Do not go gentle into that good night,'' Jade said, quoting Dylan Thomas and making Mrs. Stanwyck smile.

"Right. Again, the place the guy will take you will be worse than where you are. And if he's taking you somewhere, he's going to hurt you bad or kill you.''

The room got very quiet.

"What if you're in the car and he gets inside?" a pretty, dark-haired girl asked. "Or if he has a gun and forces you inside?"

Anabelle lifted her chin. "Then if you're driving, cause an accident. Steer the car into something off the road. If you're not driving, reach for the wheel and plow into something."

Trace, who'd seemed mesmerized by the whole scene, blurted out, "No shit?"

His slip caused nine female heads to swivel around to where he and Nathan stood. The girls were agog. Anabelle looked surprised. Comments slipped out.

"Oh, my God, it's…"

"Holy hell…it's him…"

Nathan knew they weren't impressed by a congressman.

Trace's light complexion reddened. "Aw, geez, I'm sorry to interrupt. It just popped out. I was really into your talk, Anabelle."

"No harm done. As a matter of fact," Anabelle said, mischief lighting her face, "come on up here, Mr. McCall. You can be our perp while we practice our resistance techniques."

Trace smiled, not his movie-star smile, but a genuine one. "Why do I think this is *not* a coveted role?"

The girls giggled. Anabelle bit her lip. "Why, whatever do you mean?"

Nathan's heart twisted in his chest watching the teasing girl who emerged from the sober woman. He'd done this to her, made her lose that innocence. The thought practically broke his heart all over again.

"Who's gonna be the victim?" Trace wanted to know.

Everybody's hand shot up.

Jade called out, "How about Charly?"

The girls gave sham boos and groans of disappointment, but eventually cheered on a reluctant Charly.

Dressed in baggy sweats and a T-shirt, Charly strode up front next to Trace. He gave her a grin and said, "Ready for this, doll?"

She shook her head. "I doubt it."

Smiling, Anabelle said, "Okay, Charly, turn around. Trace, come up to her from behind. That's it... Now grab her in an armlock."

Trace obliged and encircled Charly in an embrace. He mumbled something in her ear. She giggled.

Anabelle said, "Now, break the hold, Char, like I showed you."

The imp seemed to surface in Charly, too. She shook her head. "Why on earth would I want to do that?"

Everybody laughed. Anabelle caught Nathan's gaze and gave him an intimate smile...the way she used to when Kaeley did something cute and they wordlessly shared the pleasure of his daughter.

It clipped him behind the knees when he realized—admitted—he wanted that kind of connection from her again...the trusting, wholesome, we're-in-this-together look that people in love got.

He was almost leveled by the strength of that yearning.

"YOU WERE PRETTY QUIET on the way down. Did something happen?" Anabelle asked Nathan when they were seated in Syracuse University's auditorium waiting for *Brigadoon* to begin.

"No, not like you mean." He searched for Kaeley's bio in the program.

Kaeley had the second female lead. They'd taken Nathan's chauffeured car because Herman, the driver, had wanted to see Kaeley perform. Nathan had gotten last-minute tickets for Drew, but his brother had canceled out. So Herman took his ticket, which was a few rows down. Barbara couldn't accompany him because she was out of town.

Nathan leaned back in his seat and closed his eyes briefly.

Anabelle hesitated, adjusting her scarf over a white cowl-neck angora sweater. She'd worn black slacks to be comfortable. "Want to talk about what's bothering you?"

"No." He nodded to the stage. "I asked Trace to come with us, you know. He's staying in town for a few days."

"He's staying? Why?"

"I think he needs a break from his life in the fish-bowl."

"He flirted like hell with Charly during the demonstration. It was cute."

"Well, at least he didn't flirt with you, like every other guy you meet."

"What are you talking about?"

"Zeke Campoli can't keep his hands off you. Hawk Olsen was looking at you like you were a steak dinner. Even Mark Macomber tripped over himself when you were around."

She tried to ignore the pleasure his words, his noticing, engendered. But since last night, it was hard to keep him at a distance emotionally. She felt like a piece of marble being chiseled away a little bit at a time. "I think that's an exaggeration."

"Yeah. Sure." He shrugged out of the sports coat he wore over a turtleneck. The deep green of the sweater darkened his eyes to the color of a forest. Without further comment, he studied the program.

So did she. It was fun seeing Kaeley's name there, her picture with the cast. Anabelle hadn't attended any of her plays, and it had broken her heart to hear about them but be excluded. She perused the program and found Kaeley's cast bio. Her credits were impressive. When she got to the part where the actor thanked people, Anabelle gasped. ''Oh...'' Moisture formed in her eyes.

''Anabelle, what is it?''

She stared down at the words.

Nathan moved close and looked at her program. Finally he said, ''She always does that.''

Anabelle glanced up. ''She does?''

''Uh-huh, ever since her first featured role in high school.''

''I never knew.''

''It was hard, every time I saw it.'' A muscle in his jaw tensed. ''You should have been here all those times, to see her perform.'' He smiled gratefully at her. ''You instilled this love of theater in her, just like she says in the program.''

''It was fun taking her to plays. Acting them out.''

''Wait till you see her perform.''

The lights dimmed. Anabelle waited, filled with contradictory emotions. In a minute, she felt Nathan's hand discreetly cover hers on the seat arm.

She needed the support when Kaeley came on stage as the flirtatious, funny Meg, and spoke with a beautiful Scottish accent. She battled back the tears when Kaeley's clear alto voice rang out ''My Mother's Wedding Day.'' And when Kaeley got a huge groundswell of applause at the curtain call, Anabelle leaned into Nathan's shoulder.

She was proud of Kaeley's talent and success. Yet she felt a sense of loss so deep...for all that she had missed in the last ten years.

PERHAPS IT WAS the emotion of the evening that had their guard down.

Perhaps it was the strain of being together, and admitting how hard it was, that undermined Anabelle's vigilance and Nathan's circumspection.

But it caught them unaware when, nestled in the back of the town car, in the dim light of the ramp as they got off Route 17 at the Hyde Point exit, the sedan pulled up beside them.

They didn't catch on right away until the car, veering to the left, sideswiped them.

Once. Grate...grate...

Twice. Scrape...scrape...

Three times...bump...bump...bump...

And then their car careened off the road and headed for a ditch.

But Anabelle did see the embankment looming in front of them and had just enough time to push Nathan down into the seat and throw herself on top of him before they crashed.

The sound of glass shattering and the thump of hard contact with the side door were the last things she heard before everything went dark and still.

DAN WHITMAN RACED into the emergency waiting area, his clothes disheveled, his expression taut. From where he sat by the coffee machine, Nathan stood and called out, "Dan, over here."

Purposefully, Dan strode to him. He clasped Nathan's shoulder. "Are you sure you're all right? That she is?"

"Yes. I don't have a scratch. She's going to be fine. I've been with her this whole time. They kicked me out to do one last exam before they released her."

"Should she be released this soon?"

"Hell, no. But she's putting up a fuss. Says she's had slight concussions before." He looked at Dan. "I hate this, Dan. What she does."

"Tell me the details of the accident—or whatever it was."

Nathan's heart pounded in his chest as he retold the story of the town car being run off the road.

"How's your driver?"

"A few cuts is all. He's going to be fine. His wife already came and got him."

Dan swore and began to pace the room. "Did you report this to that FBI guy?"

"No, not yet. The police came, of course. Tomorrow's enough time to call Campoli. Dan, I've been worried about Annie doing this bodyguard thing, anyway. Now this…"

In fatherly fashion, Dan slid his arm around Nathan's shoulders. "I know it's tough."

"Annie's insistent that you stay at the house the rest of the night. She says she's not well enough to—" Nathan broke off and swore. "Hell, Dan, she got hurt because she tried to protect me. She literally threw herself over me."

"That's what bodyguards do, buddy."

"It wasn't real before. I never pictured the scenario. We need to figure something else out as soon as she's well."

"All right."

"Nathan?"

They turned to see Paige Kendrick and Ian Chandler dressed in scrubs coming toward them.

Paige asked Nathan, "What are you doing here?"

"Um...a car accident."

She touched his arm. "Were you hurt?"

"No, but Anabelle was."

Ian placed his hand on his wife's shoulder. "How bad?"

"A slight concussion. She's going to be released soon."

"Anything we can do?"

Dan said, "Go see her, Paige. Make sure she's okay."

"We will," Ian told him. "Both of us."

Five minutes after the Chandlers left, a tired-looking doctor entered the waiting area. "Congressman Hyde, you can come in now. Ms. Crane's...anxious to get out of here." He shook his head.

"What is it?" Nathan asked.

"She's not a very cooperative patient."

Dan sighed heavily. "Are you sure she can go home?"

"Yes. Someone needs to watch her, though, tonight. And she should rest for a few days." Again he shook his head. "That'll be easier said than done, I'd guess."

Twenty minutes later, both Dan and Nathan were cursing Anabelle vehemently. Cranky and in pain, she snapped at them all the way home when they fussed over her. She'd gone straight to the bathroom, changed into cute, baby-blue pajamas and come out ready to do battle. Only Dan's concern had gotten her into bed. Amidst a mound of pillows she began giving orders. "Go to bed, both of you. Dan, make sure the house is locked up. Bunk somewhere close to Nathan.''

"The first guest room on the right would be good." Nathan nodded. "I'll show him." He reached over and squeezed her shoulder, just needing to touch her. "Please rest.''

Wearily Anabelle sank back into the pillows. Her eyes were becoming glazed. "All right.''

Nathan led Dan down the hall and showed him into what used to be his old room with Olivia.

"This is fine," Dan said. "Where do you sleep?"

"I'm going to sit by Anabelle's bed for a while.''

Dan didn't object. He studied Nathan. "Are you sure you're all right?''

"Hell, no. But let's not talk about anything tonight... Go to bed. I'll see you in the morning.''

When Nathan returned to Anabelle's room, she was slumped under the covers, her eyes closed. He crossed to her and gazed down at her sleeping form. She looked remarkably well for what had happened. She was so tough, so independent, so much the cop. The young woman he'd known years ago was, literally, gone.

His stomach still feeling as if it was on rinse cycle, he watched her breathing even out. Bending over, he kissed her forehead, turned off the light and dropped onto a stuffed chair he'd pulled up to the bed.

Then he picked up her hand.

And, in the dim light cast only from the moon, in the stillness of the night, he admitted some truths to himself.

He was in love with her. Still. He'd always been in love with her. The admission hit him with sledgehammer force. When he realized what was happening tonight, he'd understood once again the tenuousness of life, the preciousness of it. When she was knocked out cold, not only was he frightened for her, but he'd had a clear and powerful epiphany.

This time, he wasn't going to let her go. Stretching out his legs, he propped his feet on the end of the bed and cradled her hand in his. It was long and slender, and fit his perfectly. As she did. As no other woman had.

He drifted off to sleep thinking about that.

Sometime later he heard his name muttered. He awoke with a start. "Are you all right, sweetheart?"

"My head hurts." Her voice was thick with pain.

He glanced at the clock. Five o'clock. "You can have another pill."

"Makes me groggy."

"Good. You need sleep." He crossed into the bathroom and ran some water, brought the glass back to her and gave her the medicine. She moaned as she sat up and gulped the pill. Her eyes began to close as she lay down again.

He switched off the light. "Go back to sleep."

Nestled in the pillow, she whispered, "Remember when you took care of me that time I got Kaeley's cold?" Her words were slurred and there was a slight smile on her face.

He soothed back her damp hair. "Uh-huh."

"It felt so good having you there."

"It felt good to be there."

"I'd loved you for a long time by then."

Again, he picked up her hand. Kissed it. "I know, I'd loved you, too."

Gingerly, she turned on her right side. The white bandage on her left temple shone in the darkness. "Hold me, Nathan."

She didn't have to ask twice. He climbed onto the bed, gently drew her to him and settled her onto his chest.

"Don't leave."

Ah, he didn't intend to. He smoothed down her hair. "I won't."

"Promise?"

Knowing they were talking about two different things, he said softly, "I promise."

UNSTEADY HANDS reached for the liquor bottle. Just hours ago, they had steered a car right into Nathan's automobile. His plan hadn't worked out exactly as it should have. Anabelle, the young assistant—was Nate doing her, too?—and the driver were hurt. Charmed as he was, Nathan had escaped without injury. But that was all right. Actually, that was part of the plan.

The liquor soothed his raw nerves. He sipped it, thinking of the power and attention Nathan always garnered. He wanted to do something with that power, redirect that attention. It would go a long way to achieve his goal.

Finally, Nathan Hyde would be where he should be.

CHAPTER EIGHT

ANABELLE SAT in the visitors' gallery of the House Chamber and studied her surroundings. The building was steeped in tradition. Set up in amphitheater style, its rows of seats and benches formed a half circle around the rostrum—a type of judge's bench—where Dennis Hastert, the Speaker of the House, was making some remarks. Behind him proudly stood the U.S. flag and two bronze fasces, which resembled Roman pillars. Off to the side was a sliver orb engraved with a map of the world with a silver eagle on top, called the mace. Next to it was a silver inkstand. Over the gallery doors were twenty-three marble relief portraits of noted lawgivers. Anabelle liked the room, its tradition, its grandness.

Nathan had settled into his customary seat on the floor. He was too far away to protect if an attempt was made on him, but the observers' gallery was about as close as she could get without being obvious. She could keep a watchful eye on the crowd—very light today—and hope Nathan was safe amongst the other representatives who flanked him. Years ago, the representatives had abandoned assigned seating and now grouped themselves by party, with committee members of a bill being discussed sitting at a table up front.

In any case, security had been tight here—as it was all over Washington since September eleventh—and only Zeke's clout had gotten her inside with her gun in tow.

Zeke had been upset to hear about the car accident, but he remained confident that Anabelle should stay on as Nathan's bodyguard. She touched her temple. She didn't look *that* bad. But both Dan and Nathan had developed the protective instincts of cavemen over the events of two nights ago.

First Dan…

Anabelle had awakened slowly the day after they'd been run off the road. Her head had felt as if a hundred jackhammers were pounding inside it. She'd become aware of something hard against her cheek. Muscular. Very male. For a moment she couldn't remember where she was. Then it all came back to her. The town car…she'd been hurt…Nathan had sat beside her bed.

When had he gotten into it?

Why?

She'd watched as his chest rose and fell evenly, signaling that he was asleep. Knowing she should wake him, or at least get up herself, she'd nestled in close and for long luxurious minutes she let herself enjoy the sensations, steeped herself in his male presence the way she used to do. His smell was so familiar it made her heart ache as much as her head. And she still fit him perfectly.

Lying there had been a mistake. Dan had knocked softly on her door before Nathan had awakened.

When Anabelle got up and answered it, Dan had gotten a glimpse of Nathan in her bed. "Oh, this is just great."

There ensued a row worthy of street gangs, Dan yelling at Nathan for staying with her, for endangering her to begin with, Nathan yelling back that the bodyguard duty had had *Dan's* seal of approval. Finally, Anabelle had entered the fray, but when she'd wavered on her feet— in need of medicine and food—their mutual tirade had stopped.

But the conflict was far from over...

"We're done with this, Annie," Nathan had said implacably later that day. "I won't endanger you again."

"We're far from done. This incident just shows just how much you need protection. I'm in place, and I'm going to stay here. You two can duke out anything you want, but I'll have my way on this." She scanned both of them. "After all, you're safe. I did my job."

"That's the *problem*," he'd shouted, genuinely angry at her.

In the end, they'd only come to consensus because of Zeke. Anabelle and Nathan were still at a stalemate when they'd flown to Washington the next day.

"Son of a bitch," Zeke had said when he inspected her still-purplish bruise.

She'd snapped back at him not to start on her, too.

Zeke had merely arched an eyebrow, then told them he'd ferreted out some new information. The innocent man Nathan had prosecuted was living in a small suburb of D.C. Also, two of the people from the electronics plant that Nathan had helped convict of embezzling were back in Hyde Point. Both D.C. and his hometown currently had people in residence who might want to harm Nathan. When Nathan suggested another bodyguard, Zeke had balked. It also seemed there was a problem with one of the staff's background checks. Information on Hank Fallon had been lost. Zeke was looking into it now. A covert bodyguard already in place was the best idea, at least temporarily. Even Rob had agreed she should stay on when she'd called to tell him about the accident. Injuries in police work were routine.

So, she still had her job.

Now, scanning the crowd, she caught some movement

out of the corner of her eye. Someone had entered the visitor gallery.

Hank Fallon.

He didn't see Anabelle, so she took the opportunity to study him. His expression was intense as he sat three rows away from her, staring at the House floor. At Nathan? The set of Fallon's shoulders was stiff, his mouth a grim slash in his face.

Slowly, he reached down into his briefcase. Her cop's instincts kicked into gear and Anabelle tensed, sliding her hand inside her jacket to finger the gun.

With nerve-racking precision, Fallon withdrew something from the briefcase...a pad and paper.

Anabelle let out a breath. Still, she watched him. He took notes, looking up from them when Nathan spoke on the floor.

After about a half hour, he stood to leave. Only then did he notice Anabelle. His face colored, as if he'd been caught at something inappropriate. Hmm. He simply nodded to her and left.

The rest of the morning was uneventful as Nathan participated in floor activities.

At lunch, all of Nathan's staff walked down to C Street to a diner they frequented. Squeezing into a booth, with Anabelle sandwiched in between Nathan and Mark, she listened intently to their conversation. As was their custom at these noontime get-togethers, they reviewed Nathan's schedule.

Mark Macomber pulled out a Palm Pilot after they ordered. "You have a Standards of Official Conduct Committee meeting right after lunch, Nate." His curly hair falling into dark eyes, Mark smiled boyishly at her. "Are you familiar with that committee, Anabelle?"

"I know it's like an internal-affairs committee, and that the tenure on it is only a couple of years."

"Yes, this is Nathan's second year, so he'll be off at the end of this session."

"Do you like being on that committee, Nathan?" she asked, genuinely interested.

Looking tired but handsome in a navy pinstripe suit, light-blue shirt and paisley tie, he regarded her question thoughtfully.

Before he could answer, Hank spoke. The man's dour expression softened. "Got to be beyond reproach when you're serving on that committee. Our guy here's a good choice."

Nathan avoided her eyes. His ethics hadn't always been beyond reproach and they both knew it. "To answer your question, in some ways I do, in some ways not. I find digging into the personal lives of my colleagues distasteful, but the job has to be done, so I'll take my stint."

Anabelle didn't look him in the eye, either. The affair with her ten years ago suddenly took on a different slant. She wondered if anyone could use it against him now. He hadn't been a congressman then, but who knew what would pique the nation's interest.

Mark continued outlining Nathan's day. "At four, you have a meeting with the congressman from Delaware. He wants you on his side for his student assistance bill. It's right at Longworth, in the meeting room on our floor."

"Fine."

"And tonight we think you should attend the fundraiser for Senator Mathison's pet project on defense."

"Yum," Karen said. "They always have a great buffet."

Everyone chuckled.

At Anabelle's puzzled look, Nathan explained, "Staff

members across the board are aware of who has the best food at social events. Sometimes I think my group here picks where I'll go according to the menu.''

There was razzing all around, except from Hank, who studied his notes. After beverages arrived, they reviewed Nathan's schedule for the rest of the week.

"And don't forget, Thursday you need to fly up to Seneca Falls for the Women's Rights National Historical Park talk.''

"Really?'' Anabelle asked. "Is that in your district?''

"Just on the edge.''

Cam said, "Good PR there. They want you to cut the ribbon for a new exhibition in the visitors' center. Your speech is on the needs of underprivileged women, right?''

"Yes.'' It had been coordinated with the new exhibit.

"Good.'' Macomber checked his notes. "There's a luncheon afterward. You should be back in Hyde Point by nightfall—it's only a couple hours' drive, isn't it?''

"Closer to an hour.''

"Your fiancée will accompany you?'' Hank asked, darting a quick look at Anabelle.

"No, I'm afraid not. I meant to tell you, but with the accident and everything, I forgot. Barbara has to go out of town on business for Hyde Point Electronics.'' He shrugged. "She's also worried about her son. He hasn't been feeling well.''

Anabelle hadn't known that. "I hope it's nothing serious.''

"There's concern over some blood tests. It could be something as simple as mono, but Barbara's worried.''

"Then take Anabelle,'' Cameron said. "She'll fill in for Barbara.''

The sound of that made Anabelle uncomfortable and

she was glad when their food arrived and cut off the discussion. The rest of the talk circled around Washington topics and they returned to Longworth by two o'clock.

Nathan was holed up in his office on the phone, and Anabelle was sitting in the reception area right outside at a desk, when Hank came out of his office. "Have you seen Cam, Anabelle?"

"I think he had a meeting."

Hank watched her with dark eyes. "Can I ask you something?"

She pasted on her best, innocent smile. "Sure."

Casually, he edged a hip onto the desk. Today he wore a conservative gray suit that accented his hair. If he'd smile more, he'd be attractive. "Do you have some special relationship with Nathan?"

She stilled. "Why do you ask?"

Fallon shrugged. "He seems to know you well. Treats you familiarly."

"He told you I used to work for him."

"Yeah, that's what he said."

A telling response.

"I was practically a member of the family. I was his daughter's nanny for four years. That's probably what you're sensing."

"Maybe."

Cocking her head, she faced him fully. "Hank, are you upset Nathan hired me without asking you?"

He folded his arms over his chest. "Yes."

"I'm sorry. It was spur-of-the-moment."

"Yeah, so he said. I just don't understand why." He stood. "Well, he's entitled to hire who he wants. See you around."

Anabelle and Nathan came back to the suite after his

meeting with the Delaware congressman. It was nearly six. He said, "I'm going to meet with Cam and Karen now. Want to come?"

Wearily, she sank into a chair; her head was beginning to throb and she was having trouble concentrating. "Should I?"

"Nah, why don't you go in and lie down on my couch. You look a little peaked." He reached out as if to lift her chin, then caught himself. Still, he examined her face. "There's more to go tonight and you're tired."

She fingered her bruise. "I'm fine." She could see fatigue in his green eyes and strain around his mouth. "You work a lot of hours."

"Ten or twelve a day." He angled his head toward his office. "I wish you'd lie down in there. On the couch." His voice was coaxing, sexy. "I'll be right here in that office with two of my staff. I don't need watching. You'll be fresh to keep an eye on me tonight at the fund-raiser if you rest now."

"I'll wait out here. I'm fine."

But she wasn't. She made it through fifteen more minutes, then her headache worsened. Deciding some aspirin and a few minutes to close her eyes would be in everybody's best interest, Anabelle stood and went into Nathan's office. Switching on the desk lamp, she poured some water from a pitcher on his sideboard and downed three pills. Glancing around, she caught sight of a picture on the credenza, she picked it up.

And froze. It was the same one she carried in her wallet—of him and Kaeley on the hammock. She'd forgotten she'd had a copy blown up for him. Slowly, she traced his mouth, his hair, the curve of his shoulders. She'd loved him so much then.

With a sigh, she set the frame down and scanned the

rest of the desk. There was no picture of Barbara. "Not your business," she whispered and turned off the light. Leaving the outer door open, she walked into the sitting area of his office. She lay down and closed her eyes, sinking deep into the leather cushions.

Though she tried not to, she recalled vividly what it felt like to sleep in Nathan's arms, to nestle into his shoulder. In the past, they'd only had a few opportunities to sleep together—after he'd told Olivia about their affair and Anabelle had moved out of the Hyde estate. They'd spent a handful of glorious nights at the Boxwood Inn, and she loved waking up to the feel of him next to her.

Blowing out a frustrated breath, she was about to get up when she heard the door creak, then rustling in the office proper. No light was turned on. Instinct warned her to wait, to not let her presence be known. She heard drawers open and close.

Quickly she felt for her gun. Sliding off the couch, she crept up to the archway. Concealed by the partial darkness, she peered around the wall.

A man stood at Nathan's desk. Tall. Slim shoulders. Mark Macomber. He opened one drawer, then another. He lifted out some files. Did he put something in? She couldn't tell. Finally, he closed the drawers and quietly left the office.

After waiting to see if he'd returned, Anabelle crossed to the desk and flicked on the lamp. She reached down to the second drawer.

Opened it.

Files. She lifted them as Macomber had. Nothing was there. She switched on another light, fully illuminating the room. Then she shut the door and went back and searched the whole desk thoroughly.

Still she found nothing.

Hmm. What had Macomber been doing in here in the dark?

AT THE TIME, the shopping trip to Maryland had seemed like a good idea. Tonight, at the fund-raiser for Congressman Mathison, as Nathan watched Anabelle across the room, wearing one of the dressy suits he'd suggested she buy, he was having second thoughts. She looked good in sage-green silk. It accented her coloring and complemented the blond streaks in her hair.

Apparently, Hawk Olsen thought so, too. The man's gaze roamed hungrily over the one-button jacket that molded to her breasts and the skirt that hugged her hips and swirled around her legs. Nathan's staff had noticed her, too. Macomber had practically drooled when she strolled into the stylish Hotel George near Union Street tonight. Interestingly, Anabelle had been oblivious to how she looked. Her lack of vanity made her all the more appealing. Not that Nathan needed her to have any more allure. She was like a Siren to him. He was caught in her spell, was powerless to get out. And he didn't want to. Which was why he'd tried to talk to Barbara before he left for D.C.

But his fiancée had been distracted. He'd gone to her office to tell her about the accident and she'd been on the phone. Her eyes had been bright as she motioned him in, speaking into the mouthpiece. "I know, Rick. I know." She listened. Gave a weak smile. "Yes. Thank God you're there." Swiveling in the chair so Nathan was at her back, her voice had dropped, intimately. "All right. We will."

Nathan took a seat opposite her and waited. "Everything okay?" he asked when she turned back around and hung up.

She nodded. He cocked his head. She sighed. "No, I'm worried about R.J. He really doesn't feel well." She pulled up close to the desk. "Rick took him to the doctor and they want to do more blood tests. Rick says we should do them at Elmwood Medical Center, so he's bringing R.J. home."

"Barb, blood tests are pretty routine."

"I know. I'm overreacting, though Rick says what they want to do seems pretty unusual." She shrugged. "It...I don't know...I have a bad feeling about all this."

"I think you're entitled to be overprotective. This is your child. Tell me about the tests."

She'd explained procedures that could reveal simple anemia, maybe mono, or could show serious cause for his fatigue and flulike symptoms.

"I'm sorry."

She looked fragile in a pretty, red suit. Her vulnerability tugged at his heart. Not only wouldn't he tell her what he'd come to say—that they needed to talk, that things had changed for him—but he had to be supportive of her. "What can I do? Would you like me to come with you to Elmwood?"

She shook her head. "No, especially not with what you're going through with the stalking."

Briefly he told her about the accident so she wouldn't hear it from anybody else.

"Well, certainly not, then." She glanced at her calendar. "I'm going to have to beg off the Seneca Falls thing."

"Of course." He reached across the desk for her hand. Hers was small, slight and trembled in his. "I'll send good thoughts," he said.

Then her shoulders started to shake. Nathan stood, circled around her desk and pulled her up. He held her, his chin resting on her head. "It'll be all right, Barb."

She nodded, then pulled back. "I know. It's just that I'm so protective of him." Collecting herself, she peered up at Nathan. "We should have a child, Nathan. You and I together."

His response caught in his throat. He stared down at her. "You're not trying to tell me anything, are you?"

She chuckled. "No, darling, I'm not pregnant. And at the rate we're going…" She shook her head. "Never mind. Let's talk about all this when the stalking's over and R.J. is given a clean bill of health."

Nathan had been disconcerted when he left her. Barbara pregnant. Oh, God, that was all he would have needed. He knew then, with undiluted certainty, that things were over between them. He'd tell her as soon as possible.

"What's that scowl for, Congressman?" Karen had come up to him and handed him a tonic and lime.

He took the drink and sipped it; he tried not to consume alcohol at routine fund-raisers. "Just tired."

"Is your brother coming tonight?"

"Drew? No, he's in Hyde Point."

"Really? I thought Senator Mathison said he expected Drew to be here. That your brother was in town."

"Not that I know of."

"My mistake, then." She glanced across the room. "Anabelle seems to be on top of things. In spite of that nasty bruise. I'm sure it hurts."

"Those roads in New York can be treacherous." They'd simply told his staff his car had done a tailspin on the ice and Anabelle had bumped her head.

Karen smiled. "I like her."

"Yeah, so do I."

''So does Olsen.'' She nodded to the couple. ''Why's she cozying up to him, do you think?''

To find out if he wants to harm me.

Zeke Campoli approached them. ''Nathan, how are things?''

''Thing are fine. Zeke, do you know my legislative assistant, Karen Kramer?''

''No.'' The agent held out his hand. ''Zeke Campoli.''

''Nice to meet you.''

Karen waited for an explanation of who Zeke was.

''Zeke's with the FBI. He's working on a case where I knew the suspect in my ADA days.'' They'd decided that partial truths were the best cover.

''Oh my. Is the suspect here?''

We don't know.

''Nah. Zeke's a buddy of Senator Mathison's.''

After Karen left, Zeke nodded across the room. ''Olsen wants to take Anabelle for a drink after the fund-raiser.''

Nathan gripped his glass. ''Like hell.''

''It's a good idea. I don't like his turning up so much.''

''Jesus, Campoli. He's a vulture.''

''Anabelle has handled bigger, deadlier prey.''

Nathan turned to him. ''Don't you worry about her at all?''

''She's a skillful, well-trained undercover cop. I can't afford to worry about her.''

''Well, I do.''

''Yeah, I guess the fact that I'm not in love with her like you are makes a difference.''

Nathan stilled. He didn't meet Campoli's eyes.

''Hmmph. That's my answer. You two are really making a mess of things, you know that? Back off for a while, Congressman, and let her do her job.''

Nathan stuffed a fisted hand in his pocket and said nothing.

"And I'm coming home to baby-sit you while she's sweet-talkin' Olsen."

Nathan's expletive was succinct and potent.

Campoli shook his head. "You got it bad, Congressman. I just hope this thing between you two doesn't get anybody killed."

AN HOUR LATER, accompanied by Campoli, Nathan stormed into the town house, furious with himself and with the situation. Watching Anabelle play up to Olsen had been torture. Watching her leave with the guy, his hand resting familiarly at her back, killed him. He headed right for the den and some scotch to take the edge off. Campoli joined him after he checked the house.

Nathan held up the decanter. "Want some?"

"No, I don't drink. You go ahead though. Maybe it'll defuse some of that jealousy."

"I'm not jealous."

"Yeah, and I'm the queen of England." He sank down at Nathan's computer and booted it up.

"What are you doing?"

"Checking your e-mail."

Dropping into a chair, Nathan loosened his tie and shrugged out of his suit coat. He sipped his scotch as he thought about Anabelle. For the first time he wondered how far under agents went in their cover. Would she let Olsen kiss her? Touch her? Shit!

He was searching for a diplomatic way to get the information from Campoli when the agent himself let out a colorful expletive.

"Not another one," Nathan said.

"Yep. Come look."

Nathan stood and crossed to the computer. He saw, in all capital letters, HOW WAS THE PLAY, CONGRESSMAN?

''Damn it.'' He ran a hand through his hair. A frightening thought hit him. ''Zeke, how safe is Kaeley in all this?''

Campoli drew a breath. ''I thought she was okay up till now. But I'm going to call my contacts in the Syracuse/Rochester offices. I already followed up with campus security. SU is pretty good about all that. Maybe get one of our men in the upstate office to keep an eye on her. I don't like the sounds of this one.''

Nathan sighed. ''I think I'll call her.''

''She got a boyfriend?'' Zeke asked as Nathan punched out her number.

''Yeah.''

''Maybe he should stick close.''

Oh great. Nathan had *that* to worry about, too.

After phoning Kaeley and relaying his concerns, she gleefully informed him that she'd like nothing better than to stick close to Jon. The guy said something from the background, which meant he was in her room at midnight! Kaeley assured him she'd keep an eye out for the local FBI man, and promised to call Nathan every day.

Nathan and Zeke were watching the late news, like anxious parents waiting up for their daughter to come home from a date—he didn't particularly appreciate that analogy—when Anabelle came in. She stood in the doorway of the den; her shoulders sagged and her eyes were pinched, as if she had a headache. ''Hi.''

Nathan stood, crossed to his desk, got out some pills, poured some water and brought them to her. ''Here, take these.''

Gratefully she accepted the medicine. Without thinking, he put his hand on her neck, and for a minute she leaned close, as if she needed the contact.

Zeke stood. "You found something out, didn't you?"

She nodded.

"Come in and sit." Nathan urged her to the couch.

She sat, and Campoli dropped down next to her while Nathan leaned against his desk and took another sip of scotch. His body tensed, as if he was readying himself for a blow.

"Olsen said something." She looked at Nathan. "That you shouldn't be making laws."

Zeke swore. "That's exactly what one of the e-mails said."

"I know."

"Why would he tell you that?" Nathan asked.

"I'm not sure. He asked a lot of questions about why I was working for you. How did I feel about your views."

"Particularly gun control," Zeke guessed.

Her hand went to her side. "Yeah. I told him I didn't agree with Nathan's stance on that one."

"Good move, Belle."

She sought out Zeke's gaze. "I'm worried."

"There was another e-mail." Zeke relayed the content of the newest one.

Her first concern was Kaeley. They told her what they'd done.

"You gotta stick close to Nathan up there in Hyde Point and Seneca Falls," Zeke warned. "My gut tells me this is escalating faster than we thought it would."

She sighed heavily.

"Want me to stay the night, babe?" Zeke asked. "You could zonk out better."

"No. I'll lock up and set the alarm. We'll be all right."

Zeke had a few more questions, then left. Anabelle sank back into the cushions and closed her eyes.

For a moment, Nathan watched her. "Want to go to bed?" he asked.

Her eyes flew open.

He rolled his. "I didn't mean it that way."

She shook her head. "Things have gotten complicated, haven't they?"

"Yes." He crossed his arms over his chest. "I tried to talk to Barbara today, but—"

Anabelle held up her hand. "Not tonight, Nathan. Please. Too much is happening."

"All right. But you and I need to talk soon."

Her cell phone rang, precluding her response.

"Who the hell is calling this late?" he asked.

She checked the ID. Cleared her throat. "It's Rob."

Nathan's face flushed. Anabelle watched the jealousy etch itself out there in bold emotional strokes. She was too tired to deal with all this. She clicked on the phone. "Hello."

"Hey, baby, how are you?"

"Right now, I'm exhausted."

"Yeah? Case goin' bad?"

Her gaze locked with Nathan's. She could read his feelings in his eyes. "Let's just say things are not turning out as I'd expected."

"Want some good news?"

"I'd love some good news."

"I'm coming to Washington. I want to check up on you after that accident."

Again, her eyes closed. "When?"

"Next Monday. I can only stay a day, but I gotta see you, honey."

"Monday?"

Nathan's shoulders tensed.

"Tell me you'll be in town."

"Just a sec." She covered the mouthpiece. "Will we be back here Monday?"

"Why?"

"Rob's going to be in town."

Through clenched teeth, Nathan said, "I have an important meeting Monday. We have to be back."

She said into the phone, "Yeah, I'll be here. What time will you arrive?"

"Around noon. Can you get free?"

"I'll check with my backup."

"Aw, come on, you're killing me."

"I'll try, Rob."

After some incidental conversation, Anabelle clicked off.

"The boyfriend's coming to town?"

She nodded. She tried to summon anger at his jealous tone, but she couldn't. After their confessions in the laundry room, after his tender care when she got hurt and spent the night in his arms, she was so confused about her feelings she couldn't think clearly.

Nathan looked about ready to erupt. "So, what will you do with him?"

"Excuse me?"

"Will you sleep with him?"

"Nathan, please, this isn't helping."

"What about Olsen, did you let him touch you?"

That sparked her temper. "I won't listen to this."

"I want to know, Anabelle. How far do agents go to get their information?"

She stood. Threw her head back. "You have no right to talk to me that way."

"I have every right."

"Why, because I'm guarding you? That gives you—"

"No, damn it, because I love you. I've been in love with you since I was twenty-eight years old."

Her eyes widened. "No, no, don't tell me that."

"It's true." Something fierce burned in his green eyes as he moved close to her and grasped her shoulders. But his touch was gentle. "I loved you then, and I've loved you since. I never stopped loving you."

"You're engaged to someone else."

"I started to tell you tonight. I'm going to break it off with Barbara."

"No."

"And you have to break it off with Rob. You can do it Monday when he comes down."

Anabelle felt claustrophobic. Images smothered her. How he'd bulldozed right through her objections the last time when she was twenty. How he'd said that he'd simply tell his wife he wanted a divorce and he and Anabelle could get on with their lives. And he was doing it all over again. Ten years later, he was backing her into the same emotional corner.

Thoughts of Olivia sobered her.

"You haven't loved me since you were twenty-eight, Nathan. I know that for a fact."

"What are you talking about?" He looked genuinely confused.

She shook her head, tried to pull away.

"Annie, tell me, what are you talking about?"

It was all too much. The pain in her head. The hurt in her heart. The memory of that black, black time after Olivia died.

"I...I..."

He drew her even closer. "Sweetheart, tell me."

It was the endearment that cracked her veneer. She melted like a candle left out in the sun. "You didn't come after me."

"What?"

"When Olivia died. I thought, deep in my heart, you'd come after me."

He simply stared at her.

"Dan and Nora. They couldn't be together for fifteen years. But when *his* wife died, he married her."

"Oh, Annie. Is this why you've been resisting me?"

"No. It's just another piece."

"You should have told me."

"No, I shouldn't have. It doesn't really matter, given the years that have passed, and that you've gone on with your life."

"The hell it doesn't. It matters. A lot."

She closed her eyes, unable to bear looking at him. Fearing, somewhere inside herself, where that young, shy, eighteen-year-old girl who fell hard and fast for this man still lived, that he was going to make some shoddy excuse and she was going to believe it. Maybe that was why she'd never told him—she didn't want to take the chance that he could explain that away with some stupid reason that she'd want too badly to believe.

"Look at me, Annie."

She shook her head.

"Look at me."

Reluctantly, she opened her eyes.

His face was sad. He said simply, "I did come after you. When everything was over—the funeral, the aftermath, and Kaeley was taken care of—I came out to Seattle to find you."

IT WAS LIKE SINKING in quicksand. She couldn't get her footing, couldn't find purchase on solid ground. She'd never, ever expected *this*.

His fingers on her tightened. "Are you all right? You went white."

She shook her head.

"Come to the couch."

She let him lead her there.

"Your hands are trembling."

Finally she got out, "I never expected this." She raised her face. "I'm not sure I want to hear it."

Just like last time, he ignored her objections. "You've got to hear this. For both our sakes."

Lying back into the cushions, she turned her face away.

The words came out in a rush. "After a few weeks I came to Seattle. I waited till everything was settled. Till Kaeley was okay, then I flew out to find you."

Slowly she faced him. He was perched on the end of the couch, his face ravaged.

"I don't understand. I never saw you there."

"I came to your apartment in the city."

She tried to think—five years ago, where had she been living? Then it hit her. "Oh, God."

"I'd just gotten to your place, was sitting in my car gathering my courage, when you pulled up in an SUV. With some guy."

"Barry."

"Uh-huh." Nathan raked a hand through his hair. "You got out of the car...laughing. He swung you around. You kissed him." Nathan cleared his throat. "I remember it like it was yesterday. Then he scooped you up in a carry. You were all over him." As if he couldn't stand the image, he rose. Began to pace. "I thought I'd die."

Vaguely, she remembered that day.

"I didn't know what to do. You'd found somebody else. You'd made a new life."

"We'd gotten engaged a few months before Olivia died."

"I know that now, but I didn't then. Apparently you hadn't told Kaeley or Dan yet. So I didn't give up. After you went inside, I came to the door. That's when I saw your name, and his, on the mailbox."

"We'd moved in together."

"Yes. So I left Seattle."

He shouldn't have. He should have given her a chance to decide. It made her angry.

"I didn't give up, though. I came home and hired a P.I. to check you out. To check out the guy and the situation. He was your age. A cop. A nice guy. Everybody seemed to think you two were meant for each other."

"We were."

"What happened?"

"Finish the story first. Is that why you didn't pursue me?"

"Not solely." He shook his head. "I was still being selfish. Still thought I could get you back. It was Dan who inadvertently put the stops on me."

"Dan Whitman?"

"Yeah. You know he and I had a tough go of it after you left. He blamed me for seducing an innocent girl and ruining your life. Then not going through with my promise to marry you."

Anabelle sighed. This was old ground. "He didn't know about Kaeley, Nathan."

"I know. But I'd lost you. Then I'd lost Dan. I thought I was going to crack. It took us a long time to get back on equal footing with him."

"What happened after Olivia died?"

"Dan came to see me. He told me he'd reacted badly to what had happened between you and me. That I'd really shown honor sticking by Olivia when I was so obviously unhappy with her. That he didn't understand why I'd let you go, but something else had to have been working here. If it hadn't, I wouldn't have been so miserable for five whole years."

"Well, that's good that he forgave you. I still don't get why that kept you from coming back to Seattle."

"Dan said that I'd given you a gift in the long run. You'd met a great guy. You were genuinely happy and had gotten engaged. He thanked me for cutting you loose from a seedy situation and ultimately letting you find real happiness."

"Do you think he did it on purpose? That he thought you might come and find me?"

"Honestly, no. Dan's not devious. He would have confronted the situation head-on."

"So that sealed it."

"That and Kaeley. She went on and on about your engagement, how happy you were. Nora did, too. I felt trapped. It seemed you'd made a new life, and I had no right to upset it again. The final straw was Drew."

"What did he have to do with this?"

"I…oh, hell, he and I drank too much one night. I was a messy drunk. I slobbered all over him about you. He set me straight. Agreed with Dan. Everybody seemed so sure leaving you alone was the right thing, I just acquiesced, I guess."

"I see."

He swallowed hard. His eyes were bleak. "Did I do the right thing, Annie? I agonized over my decision, especially after you never married the guy."

"I kept postponing the wedding. Six months turned into a year. After a year and a half, Barry gave me an ultimatum, and I was forced to admit to myself I didn't love him like I did you. I broke it off."

"I didn't find out for a while. By then it had been two years, I'd gotten the seat in Congress..." He shrugged. "I'd met Barbara."

She just watched him.

"I need the truth. Did you really want me to come after you? Would you have left him for me?"

Lie. Don't muddy this any more than it is.

Staring up at him, she said simply, "Yes. I *thought* you'd come. I waited for you to come. I would have given up everything, once again, to be with you."

CHAPTER NINE

SNOW DRIFTED DOWN onto the rented car as Anabelle drove through the streets of Syracuse and headed up the entrance ramp to Interstate 90—the way to Seneca Falls, New York. She and Nathan needed to be at the Women's Rights National Historical Park by eleven. Anabelle thought about the site, which celebrated women's freedom from the bonds men had put on them. Glancing over at the man in the seat next to her, she feared she'd never be free from *him*. He'd thrown his black cashmere overcoat in the back seat. Dressed meticulously in a gray pinstripe suit, pure white shirt and striped tie, he looked more attractive than ever. She'd offered to drive so he could make some calls.

What a week!

Now he spoke on the phone. "I know, Hank. I'll be back in Washington tonight. I won't go to Hyde Point, as we'd planned." He waited. "This Seneca Falls thing had been set for too long and I couldn't cancel."

Anabelle tried to concentrate on her driving. As the falling snow thickened, she speeded up the windshield wipers. Their swish was loud but didn't drown out Nathan's voice, nor the concern lacing it.

Another crisis had occurred. After their personal disclosure Tuesday night, Anabelle had asked for some time to assimilate what he'd told her. Reluctantly, he'd agreed.

They didn't know the sky would fall on one of Nathan's committees the next morning.

A picture had appeared in the *Washington Post* of one of Nathan's very married colleagues—he'd been caught in a compromising position with a female intern who worked for him. The Standards of Official Conduct Committee had been convened by 8:00 a.m. Even though similar incidents had occurred in the past with other members of Congress, and of course, a former president, adultery with a staff member was still big news, and a breach of ethics that the Standards Committee had to deal with.

"Yes," Nathan said, impatiently shifting the phone from one ear to the other. "I know I could be smoothing ruffled feathers there. I chose not to. Giving this speech is important to me." He waited another minute. "Keep me posted, all right?"

He clicked off and laid his head back on the seat. She felt the deep and feminine urge to reach out and soothe him.

"Hank's upset that we're not there. We can't go to Hyde Point like we planned." He smiled sadly. "You'll miss your dinner party with the girls."

Taylor had planned a dinner get-together for Saturday night to celebrate the good news for the original residents of Serenity House—Paige had located her adopted daughter, Charly was thrilled Serenity House was expanding and Jade was going to college to become, of all things, an English teacher.

"That's okay. I don't mind."

"I wish we *could* go to Hyde Point. Hell, I feel torn in a thousand directions."

"I know you do."

Glancing across the seat at her, he smiled weakly. "We haven't had a minute to talk."

She studied the road, staring through a hazy film of snow. "That's all right, Nathan. We both need time to adjust to what we've just discovered."

He reached over and squeezed her knee. Dressed in a long black wool skirt, pink knit sweater and wine-colored boots, she could feel his hand through the heavy material. The touching had started again—a brief squeeze of her shoulder, a clasping of her hand when he'd had a break and they were alone, even a quick kiss on her hair when they'd finally gotten home after midnight both nights. She hadn't been able to stop his affections and didn't know if she wanted to. Her feelings were in an emotional tangle that she couldn't seem to unravel. When the scandal broke, she'd been honestly relieved to put them on hold.

"I wish I'd been able to talk to Barbara before this."

Anabelle knew he hadn't spoken to his fiancée all week. She'd been out of touch, dealing with her son, and life had been a political zoo in Washington.

"To break it off?"

"Yes, of course."

The phone rang again. Wearily, Nathan answered it. She heard him say, "Yeah, Campoli. What's going on?"

The Buick edged up behind a salt truck and she pressed her foot on the brake pedal, checking the mirror to see if she could pass. Visibility was not good. The closer they came to Seneca Lake, the worse the weather conditions. She glanced at the sky. It looked ominous.

"Holy hell. What next?"

She glanced over at Nathan.

He shook his head. "Yeah, I get it." He clicked off.

"What happened?"

"I got a letter at the office. Cam opened it, and Zeke happened to be around. Since he's FBI, Cam showed it to him. It was one of those cutout things, the kind you see in movies where a threat is spelled out in different letters snipped from magazines. Campoli says it's more intimidating than the e-mails."

"What did the letter say?"

"People in glass houses shouldn't throw stones."

"Oh, God. Do you think he knows about our past?"

"I don't know anything anymore, Annie." This time he reached for her hand.

The car skidded. Anabelle gripped the steering wheel, pumped the brakes and turned into the spin. In seconds, she had the car righted, but her heart was thumping wildly in her chest.

"Are you okay?" he asked.

She nodded. "It's getting slippery. I need to concentrate."

"Want me to drive the rest of the way? You aren't used to the storms up here."

"Maybe. In any case, we've got to table this discussion. It's upsetting us both and we've got a lot to get through today."

"All right. Pull off at the next exit and I'll drive."

Anabelle exited at Weedsport to switch seats, wishing she could switch off her mind as easily.

THEY MADE IT to the homey streets of Seneca Falls at eleven that morning. By then the snow was a heavy curtain around them. Nathan had finished the drive, and Anabelle had dozed.

He was worried about her. The accident. The emotional bombardment of being with him and finding out they both still felt the same. He could barely think about what she'd told him, about how he'd hurt her unknowingly five years ago, and of all the time they could have been together. Could he ever make up for the harm he'd done her?

Soon, he would deal with it.

Right now, he had a speech to give.

"It's beautiful, here, isn't it?" she asked as he gingerly drove down Route 20.

"Yeah, there's nothing like upstate New York in the winter."

"No, I mean the town. It's quaint. Oh, look, there's the wall."

The Women's Rights National Historical Park consisted of more than seven acres of houses and museums celebrating the first women's rights convention in 1848. They pulled up to the visitors' center and parked on the street in front of the Waterfall Wall where the Declaration of Sentiments—the women's version of the Bill of Rights—was engraved on long granite slabs which, Nathan thought, resembled the Vietnam Memorial. It stretched a good block down Route 20, then another block at a right angle, where the names of those who'd attended the controversial meeting were listed. In the summertime, water fell over the wall. Now, it was encrusted in ice, but was no less impressive.

Inside, they were greeted as if they were royalty. After Nathan introduced Anabelle, an older woman, who identified herself as the director, said, "Oh, Congressman, we thought for sure you wouldn't make it."

Nathan put on his legislative facade. "I'm an upstate native, ma'am. A little snow shower wouldn't keep me away."

The woman smiled. "We're assembled in the theater upstairs. Would you like a minute to catch your breath?"

"No, thanks." He shrugged out of his coat, and Anabelle did too, handing the director the long, black leather jacket she'd worn. He said, "I'm ready."

They passed by the magnificent bronze statues of some of the more famous original attendees of the 1848 convention—Susan B. Anthony, Elizabeth Cady Stanton, Fredrick Douglass—and followed a winding staircase up to the second floor. On either side were huge posters of women and their accomplishments.

"The main exhibits are up here," the woman said proudly.

"I know. I've been here many times." Nathan had taken Kaeley for a tour when she was old enough to understand the park's significance and explained all the exhibits to her.

"Have you, Ms. Crane?"

"No, I researched it on the Internet, but I hope I get to see the whole thing before we leave."

"Be sure to take in the Stanton House and Wesleyan Chapel where the original meeting took place. It's been reconstructed on the site."

When they reached the auditorium, Nathan handed Anabelle his briefcase and she settled into a seat up front. Grasping his speech, he took the stage. He was surprised to see about a hundred people gathered in the seats. Upstate New Yorkers were stalwart, all right.

After a long and flattering introduction, focused mostly on Nathan's efforts for women and children, he approached the podium. He smiled warmly at the crowd before him. Without preamble, he said, "We hold these truths to be self-evident—that all men *and* women are created equal."

The audience burst into applause at the famous line from the Declaration of Sentiments. Nathan gave input to all his speeches, and for this one, he'd really carried the ball. He knew how he wanted to come across.

Anabelle smiled from her seat. Her approval warmed him.

He gave his attention to the audience. "Those words are truer today than they were on July 19, 1848. Thank God." He smiled engagingly. "She's been busy in the last hundred and fifty years evening the playing field."

Chuckles all around at his use of the feminine pronoun.

"Yet, in many ways, the history of mankind *is still* a history of repeated injuries and usurpations on the part of men toward women." Another famous line. "True, women are empowered to vote, married women now have civil rights, and in the area of education and the workforce, there's been progress. But, inequity exists, and it comes from the simple fact of money. Underprivileged women all over the country suffer from lack of education and are forced to take menial jobs and live at the poverty level."

He thought of Ariel, Anabelle's new young friend, and of all the girls at Serenity House.

"Our nation needs to open its eyes to this predicament." He motioned toward the door, out to the exhibit area, which waited to be officially opened. "This site continues to promote awareness of the needs of women. Hopefully, your cataloging of the educational and employment discrimination of the female sex will awaken the nation, today, as the Declaration of Sentiments awakened it years ago."

He went on to talk about specifics; what the country could do to give women—poor women like Anabelle had been—the tools to reach their potential. He cited legislation he planned to introduce or had already sponsored to propel this progress forward.

And when he was done he received a standing ovation.
Feeling good about this, at least, he took questions.

All the while, Anabelle waited for him, her big eyes watching him intently. Like a good assistant.

Or a spouse.

God, he hoped they got to talk soon.

Maybe on the flight back to D.C.

BELHURST CASTLE was about forty minutes from Seneca Falls, just outside the small town of Geneva. The committee had chosen the place for Nathan's luncheon when the weather was better. It took longer to get there than planned, but when they arrived, it was worth it.

The century-old, stone castle perched on the edge of Seneca Lake. Out the bank of windows, Anabelle could see the frozen water sparkle with crystalline beauty. She was reminded of another Finger Lake, Keuka, where she and Nathan had first made love twelve years ago.

It had been snowy like this, though not quite as stormy.

Turning away from the view, and the past that seemed to be irrevocably colliding with the future, she looked around at the fireplace crackling in the foyer, the miles and miles of oak comprising the interior—doors, staircase, panels, archways. There were several rooms downstairs, both larger dining areas and intimate lounging areas, providing a warm and cozy respite from the weather outside.

From reality.

Nathan came up to her. "There's a problem."

Her shoulders sagged. "Why am I not surprised?"

"The Syracuse airport just closed."

She shook her head. "It's pretty bad out. We should have left earlier."

"It wouldn't have mattered. We would have just waited in the terminal."

"What will we do?"

"Have lunch. Hope the weather clears for the planes to take off. If not, maybe we can make it back to Hyde Point, which was our original plan before all hell broke loose on the Standards Committee."

"They aren't reconvening until Monday, anyway, are they?"

"No, the legal subcommittee is meeting tomorrow. The full show is scheduled for early Monday."

"So we'll be back Monday?"

"I hope so."

"Me, too."

He stiffened immediately. "Rob is coming to D.C." His voice was grave, his eyes searched hers. "We have to talk about that, Annie. About everything."

Wrapping her arms around her waist, she backed away from him, coming up against the windows. She could feel the cold seep through. "I know. Tonight, okay?"

His eyes glittered with promises. She'd seen those promises before, shimmering in the same green depths. The thought chilled her almost as much as the weather. Suddenly, she wanted to touch him so badly it hurt. She wanted him to take her in his arms, tell her things were going to be all right.

That dependency was dangerous, though. She didn't really believe she could ever trust Nathan wholeheartedly again. Given her background, along with the fact that she *had* trusted him once and gotten burned, she wasn't sure that now she could make the leap he wanted her to. So she was grateful when they were called into the luncheon.

Despite her fear of him, and what he could mean to her once more, Anabelle enjoyed watching him with a crowd. He was such a good politician, so at ease, so sincere. Inwardly she marveled at the man who was under incredible personal and professional stress. He seemed relaxed, focused, and as interested in the topics the women brought up as if nothing was awry—as if the January wind wasn't howling angrily outside, as if he wasn't being stalked, as if one of his committees in Washington wasn't in an uproar.

And as if an emotional volcano hadn't erupted on them two nights ago that they still hadn't had time to wade through. She'd never admired him more.

Several questions about Serenity House were addressed to him while they ate. She was particularly interested to hear his comments on the home, surprised to hear all he'd done for the place, or intended to do, along with Quiet Waters.

Again, she wondered how much of his interest in homes for troubled teens had to do with her. His life had been so separate from hers for the last ten years, yet in so many ways inextricably connected. It overwhelmed her.

Lunch ended about three. Nathan phoned the airport again while she waited in the lounge off to the right of the foyer, in front of another fireplace. Lulled by the crackle and pop of the wood, soothed by the flickering flames, she relaxed into a heavily upholstered chair.

"Anabelle?"

She looked up. "No luck?"

"Worse. Not only is the airport closed, but Interstate 90 is shut down. Everything's getting socked in." He shook his head. "Someone's checking with the state police to see if Route 14's open so we can get back to Hyde Point."

A man entered the room. "Congressman?"

"Yes?"

The owner of Belhurst Castle stood in the doorway. "I'm sorry. The roads are all closed now. We're not even sure if we can get our people out of here and back home."

"I see."

"I'm afraid you're going to have to stay the night."

The words hung heavily between them. For a minute the snap of the fireplace was the only sound. Nathan didn't look at her. She was glad.

"Well, this is a lovely place," he said finally. "I'm sure you can make us comfortable."

"We're glad to have you. With such a hectic schedule, maybe you can catch up on some rest. Relax a bit."

Anabelle almost choked. Nathan's back was ramrod straight.

Relax? The tension in the cozy little room at Belhurst Castle had just about gone off the Richter scale.

IT ALL TOOK ON a surreal quality. Stranded in a fairy-tale setting. Cocooned by the snow and ice. Brought together despite their best efforts to keep their distance. As fate would have it, they even had connecting rooms, on the second floor, where they were the only residents. The proprietor had shown them upstairs, provided necessities—they had no luggage—and Nathan had said they'd be working until dinner at eight.

They wouldn't be leaving the inn tonight. And he knew, God help him, that he wasn't going to be able to keep his hands off her. If she didn't want it, didn't want him, that would be a different story. But he knew her well, he recognized the aching desire in her eyes that mirrored his own. After all that had been confessed in D.C., it was only a matter of time anyway. The January

blizzard had simply accelerated the progress of their jour-
ney back to each other.

He'd taken a shower and donned one of the castle
robes, loosely belting it around his waist. The garment
was made of plush, white terry, and gently abraded his
already too-sensitive skin. He held a scotch in his hand—
there was a full bar provided in this room—and sipped
it as he listened. The shower next door shut off. He pictured Anabelle naked, wet, and God please, willing.
Looking down, he saw that his hands trembled, betraying
a fragile control just waiting to snap. There was a
hum...the hair dryer? Would she abandon the braid, and
free those long, luscious locks? The thought of her hair
spread across his belly had haunted him since she returned to Hyde Point. His stomach contracted at the image.

No noise now. Just the crackle of the fire across the
room. Would she come to him? If she didn't, would he
go to her? He tried to calm the crazy mixture of hope
and fear rioting through him.

The breath whooshed out of him when he heard a
knock at the slightly ajar connecting door. Facing away
from it, he closed his eyes and thanked God for letting
her make the first move.

"Nathan?" Her voice was soft, sexy, inviting.

He turned around, trying to keep his raw emotions in
check. She stood in the archway between their rooms; his
response to seeing her poised there was completely visceral: pink from her shower, wearing a robe which
matched his, her hair wispy all over the place, and her
eyes shining with...love? Surrender? God, he didn't
know, he couldn't think straight. A tight knot of longing
had taken over.

She just stood there. Watching him.

Searching for some kind of sanity, he took a gulp of scotch. Honor seemed to surface with the punch of the alcohol. He said, "Nothing's worked out, I know." His voice sounded like sandpaper across steel. "So if you don't—" he drew in a breath "—if you don't want this, say so. Go back into that room and lock your door. Because I want you, Annie, so much so I can't breathe for it. I can barely speak coherently enough to give you one more out."

For a long—too long—moment, she watched him.

It happened almost in slow motion—a blur of white slipping inside the room…the swish of the door closing… Then she crystallized. Slowly, very slowly, she lifted her hand, undid the knot of the terry robe, and let it slip off her shoulders.

SHE STARTED TO CRY when he entered her; small involuntary tremors shook her body. She couldn't help it. It had been so long, and she'd loved him, all that time, hopelessly.

They were lying on a bed of huge, green pillows that Nathan had taken from the stack by the fireplace and spread on the floor in front of the blazing fire. They lay half on their sides, with Nathan partly on his back, her partly on her front. One of his hands encircled her waist, anchoring her to him, the other clasped her neck. She was clutching his shoulders. It gave them maximum access to each other and had been a favorite position of theirs before. His face was buried in her breasts, and he lifted his head when he heard or maybe felt the tears. His movement inside her stilled. "Shh, love. I'm so, so sorry," he said with melting sweetness.

She shook her head. Kept her eyes closed. "No, don't talk."

"Look at me, sweetheart."

She wouldn't. Couldn't.

His mouth whispered across her ear. "Please."

Powerless in so many ways, she opened her eyes—and was shocked when she saw his face. His cheeks were wet, too.

He swallowed hard. "I...I know. I feel the same way. How did we ever lose this?"

"I love you so much," she said simply.

"And I love you. More. More. So much more." His words flowed over her like warm honey and he began to move again.

Sensations bathed her—his hands gentle, kneading everywhere, soothing away hurts; his mouth skimming her neck, closing over her breast, scraping, tracing with his tongue.

She loved him back, kissing his cheeks, his head, running her hands down his arms, feeling his muscles leap and pulse beneath her fingers.

His strokes inside her were long, slow; he'd stop, partly withdraw, poise just at the entrance to her, tantalizing her. Then he'd begin again. Slowly, irrevocably, she climbed to the top.

Tenderly, reverently, he toppled her over.

Once.

Twice.

The third time, she met his thrusts forcefully. The world dimmed as he began to vibrate in her arms.

His body sought hers as deeply as it could, melded with hers with a rhythm and meaning it innately remembered from before. With one long powerful surge, he came inside her, groaning, his release mixed with a chorus of "Annie...love...Annie..."

She climaxed on his words, with his touch, with the

final surrendering of his body to hers. Wave after wave of pleasure rippled through her, matched by his own tremors.

And once again, Anabelle felt a sense of completeness she'd experienced only with him.

NATHAN LAZED BACK in the roomy chair with the pillows they'd lain on earlier placed under his feet so he could bend his knees and elevate his legs. Tugging her down, he drew her legs apart and positioned her to straddle him. He already wore a condom. Then he lowered her into the triangle of his lap.

"Lean back, so you're resting against my thighs." His voice was a husky command, a hushed plea. He bent her knees, then lifted them over his shoulders.

Her eyes widened. "Nathan, what are you...oh!" He'd secured her hips and entered her fully.

"Brace your feet on the chair back, love."

She did.

"Now rock...ah, that's it." He tilted forward, took tiny love bites out of the delicate curve of her inner thigh. His hand stroked her tummy, went lower, tangled in wet dark curls. "You are so lovely."

"You are *so* naughty."

"I think this is going to be my favorite position. I can see you." He scanned her body, then his gaze, shining with the excitement of a man finally winning the right to claim his woman, returned to her eyes. "I can touch you." His clever fingers skimmed everywhere. "I can have you—" he thrust forward "—for a long long time."

He groaned when she shifted, arched and discovered she was in control of the angle and depth of penetration. Shamelessly, she took advantage of it and drove them both over a stunning peak while their hands linked in yet another intimate connection.

Lying back, he let his head sink into the cushions. She slid her legs off his shoulders, bent them at the knees, and started to move away. He kept her where she was. "No, don't go." He reached to the floor and picked up the robe he'd placed there. Like a courtly lover, he wrapped it around her, slid her arms in it and tucked it in place. "Let me stay inside you for this."

She was boneless against him. "For what?" she managed to utter.

"I want to talk."

"All right." She lay back onto his still-elevated knees. He smiled at the wanton picture she made.

Brushing her hair from her face, he cradled her cheeks in his hands. "I love you, Annie," he began hoarsely. "I've always loved you. Olivia was being manipulative. She wanted to plant those doubts in your mind about us when you left." He kissed her nose. "I understand why you might have believed her, given your background, but she was wrong in what she said."

Amber eyes watched him like a doe wary of man.

"Tell me now that you believe me."

She swallowed hard. "I believe you."

"And tell me you understand what happened when she died. That I came for you, but ultimately let you go because I thought it best for you."

This was harder. He could see the struggle on her face, in the way her teeth closed over her bottom lip. It took a long time, but she finally said, "All right, I'll believe that."

"Thank God." He took her mouth, carnally, sealing her vow. "What we'll do is go back to Hyde Point as soon as the snow clears. I'll talk to Barbara this weekend.

Break our engagement. Then, when the stalker thing is over, we'll be together openly.''

Her eyes flashed with pain.

''What is it, love?''

''Nathan, you sound just like you did last time. You were so sure Olivia would give you a divorce, we'd get Kaeley, and live happily ever after. But we have to leave this castle. And real life doesn't work that way.''

For the first time, he gripped her without gentleness. ''It *will* work out this time. I promise.''

''You can't promise that. You don't know.''

''Yes, I do. I'll make it happen this time. There's not Kaeley to consider anymore, and she was the obstacle last time.''

''What about your job? Something could leak about us—for God's sake, even being here now could ruin you. The Standards Committee is in an uproar. You'd be slandered by your relationship with me.''

He locked his hand at her neck, forcing her to look at him.

''That's ridiculous. I'm not married. No one would care about my breaking off an engagement.''

She said nothing.

''And even if they did, I'd give up the damn seat in Congress. Go back to law, or even being a D.A.''

''*What?*''

''Don't you understand? I only went into politics after I lost you. I found that I love it, and I'm good at it, but I'd give Congress up in a heartbeat rather than let it split us apart.''

''Nathan...''

''*Nothing,*'' he said vehemently, ''do you hear me, *nothing* is going to come between us this time.''

He could see she wanted to believe him. He drew her

even closer, held her against his wildly beating heart. Connected in the most intimate of ways, he begged, "Please, Annie, give me this chance."

"I'm afraid," she whispered against his chest, as if she wanted to sink into him. "If I believe it, and it doesn't work out, I won't survive this time, Nathan. I know I won't."

"It *will* work out."

She drew in a deep breath. And held on tight. "All right. I'll believe you."

"I promise, Annie. I *promise*. Nothing will come between us this time. It's just you and me and we're going to be together for the rest of our lives."

HE REITERATED THAT VOW several times during the magical night that followed...

They forced themselves to leave the sanctuary of their room to go down for dinner at eight, so as not to garner gossip from the staff. He told her over food, which he didn't remember tasting, how good things would be.

When they returned to the rooms, they used those clever pillows once again. He built a mountain of them, stripped her, bent her over them and entered her from behind with surprising passion, with none of the tenderness of before, and he used his body to cement his vow.

They slept together through the night, awakened together, and he promised one more time to make it work between them. This time she returned the pledge.

But when morning dawned bright and crystal clear, they headed out of their idyllic fairy-tale castle and back to the real world of Hyde Point, having absolutely no idea that a snake awaited them in the garden.

CHAPTER TEN

THAT MORNING, the snow continued to fall, and the airports were still closed. Even Washington's airports were temporarily shut down due to unusual ice conditions. However, the roads had been cleared enough for Nathan and Anabelle to travel back to Hyde Point.

Nathan drove, finessing his way down Route 14 behind salt trucks and huge plows. He looked so handsome, even in his wrinkled white shirt and suit pants that he'd worn to Seneca Falls. Her skirt and sweater outfit was equally disheveled.

He shot a quick glance over at her and smiled. "We'll live in the Winslow Place."

Anabelle gasped, then clapped a hand over her mouth. *"Nathan."*

Reaching out, he cradled her knee with his big strong fingers. "Oh, God, don't cry, sweetheart. I'd never seen you cry before last night. I can't take it again."

She leaned into him, felt the soft cotton of his shirt caress her cheek. "I love that place." She kissed his shoulder. "I love *you.*"

He gripped the wheel. "I'll *never* take hearing that for granted. *Never.*" Eyes on the road, he pulled her even closer than she'd been sitting on the hour-plus drive.

They were silent for a while. When they came to the sign that announced Hyde Point, Anabelle fought the uneasiness that welled inside her.

I promise, this time, nothing will come between us.

Though it was hard to believe, after all these years and against so many odds, that she and Nathan were finally going to be together, she searched inside herself for the strength to trust him. She covered his hand with hers and squeezed. "Tell me what you did to the Winslow Place."

"Well, Hunter made some terrific cabinets. And the floors—they're a work of art." He named several other things, then shrugged sheepishly.

"What?"

"I'm doing the turret room myself."

She drew in a breath. "Because of me."

Sliding his hand up her thigh, he said, "Of course, it's all because of you. I bought the place as soon as Olivia died."

Emotion rose in her throat as she thought about his coming after her, and the years she'd suffered because she thought he really didn't love her. "We lost so much time, didn't we?"

"Don't think about that. Think about what's to come. We're still young…we'll have babies…we'll teach them to love plays just like Kaeley." As if he remembered something, he grinned boyishly and said, "A boy for you, a girl for me, right?"

They kept up the singing, and maintained the lightness, until they reached town. More snow had accumulated here, and the Southern Tier looked like a white-blanketed picture postcard. "I wonder how shut down they were last night."

"We should turn the cell phones back on."

"All right." She reached in her purse for hers.

He stayed her hand. "Wait, before you do." Checking in the mirror, he pulled off the road to a small rest area, drawing the car up under the trees.

In the clear, uncomplicated light of day, he turned to her. She was mesmerized by the change in him. His face was animated and completely missing that restless look it so often had. His green eyes were like newly polished emeralds. There was no tension in those big, beloved shoulders. "It's going to crash in on us in a few minutes."

"I know."

"We're going to hurt some people."

She nodded. "Barbara. Rob."

"Others will be angry."

"Dan."

"It doesn't matter. We'll do this as gently as we can, take our time with it, but we'll do it." He brushed her cheek with his knuckles. "I'm never letting you go, Annie."

Smiling sadly, she caressed his cheek. "I'm never letting you go, either."

"Promise, no matter what?"

Again, a chill ran through her. She remembered the afternoon he said he was going to tell Olivia about their feelings for each other. Not used to trusting men, Anabelle had had the same feeling then as she experienced now, a primal fear washing over her that she couldn't stop. Well, she wasn't a kid anymore. She could deal with this. She said, "I promise."

After a searing kiss, he put the car in gear and pulled back onto the road. "We still have to discuss the bodyguard thing."

She sighed. Where would they go on that? Could she protect him, loving him as she did? Sleeping with him?

A phone rang. Hers. He had yet to switch his on.

"Back to reality," she said, flicking on the machine. "Crane."

"Oh, thank God we reached you."

"Dan? What is it?"

"I've been trying your cell—and Nathan's—since yesterday."

We turned them off so we could make love in peace.

Hedging, she said, "There was a problem with them."

"Both of them?"

"Why have you been trying to reach us, Dan? Is something wrong?"

"It's Barbara. She's been calling Nathan. When she couldn't get him, she phoned me."

"Is she all right?"

"What is it?" Nathan asked.

Anabelle covered the mouthpiece. "Barbara's been trying to reach you."

He sighed. Anabelle knew he didn't want to handle telling Barbara the truth about his feelings on the phone. He glanced at his watch. "I'll go to her office right now."

"Dan, Nathan's going to her office right now. Do you know—"

"She's not at her office."

"No?"

"She's at Elmwood Medical Center."

"Elmwood?"

Nathan scowled and took the phone from her. "Dan, what's wrong?"

Anabelle watched as the blood drained out of Nathan's face. He said, simply, "I'll head there now."

After he clicked off, Anabelle asked, "What's wrong?"

"It's R.J. Her son. He's at Elmwood." Swallowing hard, he reached over and squeezed Anabelle's arm. "There's bad news."

As the January wind whipped around them, Nathan rushed through the front doors of Elmwood Medical Center with Anabelle by his side. All he knew was that Barbara's son had been admitted to the hospital after he'd had blood tests and the doctors had found some abnormalities, none of which looked good. Dan told Nathan the word *cancer* had come up, though any specifics were vague. But clearly, Barbara had been frantic when she couldn't get a hold of Nathan yesterday.

When he'd turned off his cell phone because he'd been making love to Anabelle. While he was engaged to someone else who had needed him.

He cringed at the thought.

"Don't," Anabelle said as they made their way to the desk.

"Don't what?"

"Feel guilty. There's no room now for guilt or second-guessing. Barbara needs you, and until we find out why, think of her and not us. Not what we did."

He stopped midstride and brushed his knuckles down her cheeks. "*You* are something else."

"I love you."

She smiled, then they approached the desk. They obtained R.J.'s room number and headed for the elevators. Taking one to the pediatric ward, they didn't speak. Just Anabelle's presence was enough for Nathan now.

They found R.J.'s room and paused at the entry. Nathan shared a quick *This is going to be hard* look with Anabelle, took a deep breath and knocked on the slightly ajar door, pushing it open with the action.

Barbara sat in the corner of the large, airy room on a padded chair, looking pale and small. Dressed in simple tan slacks and a sweater, she was hunched over, her knees touching the knees of the man who sat across from her on the small bed. The man was Rick Benton, and he had his hand locked at Barb's neck. He was whispering something to her.

Small sobs shook her body, the sad sound reverberating in the room. Rick continued to speak in inaudible, soft words.

Nathan watched them.

Apparently they hadn't heard the knock. It was Anabelle who knocked again. Rick sat back but didn't release Barbara. He glanced over his shoulder, giving her a view of Nathan and Anabelle.

Barbara was momentarily startled—as if he'd caught her doing something she shouldn't—then she stood.

"Barb?" Nathan said quietly. "I came as soon as I heard."

Like an automaton, she circled around Rick, who finally gave her space, and crossed to Nathan. She fell into his arms; he just held her.

For a moment, she nestled there, then pulled back. "I…" Tears welled in her eyes, and he handed her his handkerchief. "I…t-tried to call you."

"I'm sorry. we got stranded in Geneva. I'll explain it all, but first, tell me what's happening with R.J."

Rick stood and faced them. "Hello, Nate." He was a big guy, dressed in jeans and sweater, which outlined every tense muscle in his body.

Still in Nathan's arms, Barbara looked sideways to her ex-husband.

Rick's fists were clenched and his face wore a ragged expression. "R.J.'s blood tests don't look good." He threw up his hands in a helpless gesture. "The worst-case scenario is leukemia."

"Oh, no." Nathan drew Barbara close to his chest. "But we shouldn't assume the worst case, should we?"

"No, but, they...suspect something's really wrong," Rick said. "They mentioned leukemia to Babs and me when we demanded a range of possibilities, so we'd be prepared. From what they said—and considering all his other symptoms—leukemia is a strong likelihood." The man was clearly overcome and sympathy coursed through Nathan. He knew the value he placed on his own child, and from all of Barbara's comments, Rick was a storybook father.

"I'm so sorry, Rick." Nathan turned back to Barbara. "What can I do?"

"Can you stay today?" She glanced at Anabelle. "When I talked to you Thursday morning, you said you had to fly right back to D.C., but...I need you here, Nathan. You've got to help me through all this."

Rick Benton turned his back on them. He walked to the window and stared out at the still-stormy day.

Nathan said, "Of course we can stay."

Barbara's whole body stiffened. "Does she...does Anabelle have to...?"

Anabelle and Nathan stilled. Secrecy was vital. Rick Benton's name had come up as the possible stalker. Nathan bent over and whispered, "I don't think we should discuss this now."

Rick said, "I know about the stalking."

Nathan's head snapped up and Anabelle stepped forward. "What are you talking about?" she asked.

Benton had pivoted around to face Anabelle. "Barbara told me about your being Nathan's bodyguard."

Anabelle drew in a breath. Nathan could see color rise in her cheeks. This was a direct breach of their agreement with Barbara, but Nathan hoped Anabelle didn't take Barbara to task on it, as she was clearly hanging by a thread. He didn't think Barbara could handle much more.

Quietly Anabelle said, "Then you can see why I have to stay." She faced Barbara. "I won't get in the way, Barbara, I promise."

Nathan had never loved Anabelle more. She was clearly distressed by Barb's revelation, but hid it from a mother who was out of her mind with worry.

As if Barbara caught the nuance, she said to Nathan, "I'm sorry. Rick and I were trying to reach you. He had questions about why Anabelle was with you..."

Barbara and Rick exchanged a meaningful look. Nathan suspected more had been said in that conversation. Was jealousy at work here, or something more sinister?

"It's okay, Barb." He squeezed her tight. "Let's just get through this today. Nothing else is as important right now."

The morning dragged on. After a series of tests, R.J. returned to his room about noon, and Nathan was stunned at the boy's appearance. R.J. had always had healthy, redheaded, freckle-faced Opie kind of looks. But today...there were bruises on his arms, more than most little boys would incur in normal activity, and he'd lost considerable weight since Nathan had last seen him.

Clearly, he was not a healthy ten-year-old.

Nathan greeted him warmly. "Hey, tiger, how are you?"

"Okay." He yawned. "I'm tired." He smiled at Nathan. "I like seeing you."

Sitting on the edge of R.J.'s bed, Nathan ruffled the boy's hair. "I like seeing you, too. Settle in and you can tell me about school." Nathan helped him adjust the covers and fluffed his pillow. "Last I heard, you were thinking of going out for lacrosse at Carter, like I did."

From the corner of his eye, Nathan saw Barbara turn her back. If R.J. had leukemia, he wouldn't be playing lacrosse this spring. Immediately Rick went to Barbara and took her by the arm. "Hey, buddy, I'm going to take Mom for some coffee so you can visit with Nathan."

"Sure, Dad."

Rick and Barbara left.

Nathan said, "Come over here, Anabelle."

Anabelle approached the bed.

"This is Anabelle Crane, one of my staff workers. Anabelle, this is R.J."

R.J. smiled. "Nice to meet you."

"R.J.'s a big fan of police shows," Nathan told Anabelle. "R.J., Anabelle used to be an undercover cop in Seattle."

The boy's blue eyes brightened. "Yeah? Can you tell me about some cases?"

Anabelle smiled warmly at R.J. "Oh, I think I can manage that."

And so the afternoon went, and the evening, until R.J. was out for the count, and Rick convinced Barbara to leave the hospital. She, Anabelle and Nathan headed out for the long night ahead.

"I SHOULD HAVE STAYED with R.J.," Barbara said brokenly.

From the back seat of their rented car, Anabelle saw Nathan reach out and touch Barbara's arm. "Rick's staying with him. Only one parent can sleep in the room. You stayed last night."

"I don't care."

"You need your rest."

"You'll stay with me, right?"

Hesitating only briefly, Nathan said, "Yes. Of course."

Anabelle glanced in the rearview mirror. She caught Nathan's gaze. It clearly said, *Please, understand.*

She did. On a conscious, adult level she understood that it was right for Nathan to be with Barbara in any way she needed now. It was on a more visceral, throwback-to-her-youth level that the notion of Nathan staying with Barbara cut deep. Still, she nodded to Nathan in the mirror, much as she had when Rick insisted Nathan take Barbara home.

Anabelle turned to stare out the window. The weather was still stormy; thick flakes tumbled to the ground and accumulated into what was now about six inches of snowfall. She was exhausted herself, and she was still reeling from the events of last night. Now, to see that little boy so ill…it was a lot to deal with.

They reached Barbara's patio home on Spencer Hill in about an hour and a half, slowed considerably by the icy conditions. Her place was near where Paige lived, in a subdivision geared for professional couples who wanted a nice area to live in, with smaller homes and grounds maintenance. Barbara's house was a compact, cedar ranch nestled on a small cul-de-sac.

As they parked in the driveway, Anabelle dreaded what was to come. Slowly, somberly, they made their way to the front door, the biting wind a fitting accompaniment for their mood. In the foyer, Anabelle watched Barbara lean into Nathan as he took her coat, then gathered her in his arms.

Anabelle stood back, feeling emotion clog her own throat. Nathan was visibly suffering, too. His eyes were bleak and his mouth a tight line in his face.

"Would you like me to fix you something to eat?" Anabelle asked. "Or make you some tea?"

Barbara shook her head.

"What *would* you like, Barb?" Nathan wanted to know.

"I want to go to bed."

"Fine. I'll take you."

"You said you'd stay with me." Her voice was panicky and she clutched the lapels of his coat.

"I will, I promise." Over Barb's head, he stared at Anabelle.

She'd done harder things in her life than to tell the man she loved to take another woman to bed. A woman he was engaged to. She said, "Go ahead, I'll just bunk on the couch."

Barbara drew back. "No, of course not. There are guest rooms. To the left." She tossed back her head and wrapped her arms around her waist. "Take either one. There's an adjoining bathroom with things you might need in there."

"All right. Get some rest."

Barbara gripped Nathan's hand and together they went down a hallway to the right. For a moment, Anabelle was rooted to the spot, just watching them.

I hated it when you went to your bedroom with Olivia. I loved you even though we hadn't said anything…

I hated it, too. We didn't make love after I admitted to myself how I felt about you.

Banishing the ghosts, Anabelle secured the front door, left the foyer, crossed through a dining room filled with cherry-wood furniture and walked down the left corridor. Along the way, she checked windows and outside doors. Off the hall, she found two bedrooms, both beautifully appointed. Barbara had class, and taste.

What were you thinking? Olivia had laughed, that day on the steps. *A waitress's daughter…from Serenity House?*

"Stop!" Anabelle spoke aloud as she chose the first room. "Don't do this. These people's lives have fallen apart. So what if you're unhappy with the situation?"

Rick Benton hadn't been happy either, Anabelle thought as she switched on a small lamp in the corner, shucked off her boots and dropped onto the bed, covered with a stylish, silk duvet. She stared up at the ceiling, thinking of Benton. When Barbara had asked Nathan to stay with her, the man's face had gone from ragged to ravaged. From the looks of things, he still had deep feelings for his ex-wife.

Deep enough to wish her fiancé harm?

Who knew?

And now that he was aware Anabelle was Nathan's bodyguard...would he go underground, and not be caught? Or would he just work around her? What if something happened to Nathan because Rick knew?

She thought of last night, when she and Nathan had made love. When he'd promised her he'd break it off with Barbara today so they could be together.

Just like the last time.

I'll tell Olivia tonight, I promise. We can be together openly.

She closed her eyes. Oh, God, she didn't want to draw these parallels. Willing herself to sleep, she drifted off.

She stirred when the door opened.

"Annie?"

"Nathan? Come on in. I must have dozed off."

"Sweetheart, you're fully dressed."

She glanced at the clock. They'd been here more than an hour. Completely awake, she sat up against the brass headboard. "How's Barbara?"

Wearily, he sank onto the edge of the bed. "She finally

fell asleep. I made her take a pill. This was the first I could get away.''

Anabelle nodded. The sleepy fog had begun to evaporate. She noticed he'd changed his clothes—in front of Barbara?—and wore a beautiful silk robe and matching bottoms. In his hands, he carried sweats. ''I brought these for you. They'll be a little big.''

''Whose are they?''

He cleared his throat. ''Mine. I keep some things here.''

She just stared at him.

''And there are toiletries in there.'' He nodded to the bathroom.

''Fine.'' She watched him. ''How are you doing?''

''I'm in shock. I love that little boy.'' His voice cracked. ''There's something really wrong with him, I know it.''

''He doesn't look good.'' At Nathan's dark expression, she asked, ''When do they expect a report on the tests?''

''Tomorrow morning.''

She reached out and touched his hand. ''I'm sorry. This must be so hard.''

''It is.'' He scanned the room, not really seeing it. ''When something like this happens, I always wonder where God is.''

She didn't respond.

''Do you believe in God, Annie?''

No, I stopped when I lost you.

''No, not anymore.''

''I can't rationalize this, you know?''

''I know.''

He reached out and his thumb made a quick swipe of her lips. ''You seem exhausted.''

''It's been an...unusual twenty-four hours.''

His knuckles skimmed her cheek. "Last night, at this time…"

She turned her face into his hand.

"I don't want to go back upstairs." His eyes were troubled, torn.

"You have to."

"I want to hold you. All night. Every night."

"Barbara needs you."

"Tell me you understand."

Tell me you understand. About how it really was between me and Olivia.

"Of course I do."

"When this is over, or as over as it can be for Barbara, then I'll talk to her."

"All right."

"I need to be there for her now."

"Of course you do," she repeated.

He leaned over and kissed Anabelle briefly, and stood. "Good night, Annie." Then he added, "I love you."

"I love you, too."

Nathan left and Anabelle sat on the bed. For a moment she was swamped by familiar, jagged feelings. They were petty feelings, and she didn't want to let them in. So she grabbed Nathan's sweats, took them to Barbara's bathroom, changed into Nathan's clothes—that he kept at Barbara's house—and valiantly fought the demons of doubt.

But her unconscious mind gave up the battle when she fell asleep; she dreamed about Nathan making passionate love to Barbara on a bed of green pillows, then in a chair, while Anabelle stood by wearing his sweats and watching.

In the dream, tears streamed down her cheeks as she

said, "You told me, you *promised* me you wouldn't do this again."

In the dream, he took a moment to glance over his shoulder and say, "I lied. Don't you know, Annie, that you can't trust me? I did it once before, and I'll do it again."

CHAPTER ELEVEN

THE NEXT MORNING, holding tight to Barbara's hand, Nathan sat in the office of pediatric oncologist Donald Miller. Rick Benton, who looked even more haggard today, sat on the other side of them. Anabelle was with R.J.

The fiftyish doctor removed his glasses and encompassed Barbara and Rick in a sympathetic glance. "I'm sorry, Mr. and Mrs. Benton, it's what we expected. The tests show R.J. has acute lymphoid leukemia."

There was a stunned silence. Then Barbara began to cry wrenchingly. Rick buried his face in his hands. Quiet sobs escaped him.

Nathan slid his arm around Barbara and held her close, feeling his own eyes sting. He struggled against the emotion, but it was like trying to hold back the waves in the ocean—this was a devastating confirmation.

When the weeping subsided, Barbara looked at her ex-husband and he at her. "I...can't believe it, Rick." Her voice was raspy and raw.

"Me neither." After a few moments, he straightened and faced the doctor. "Tell us about this."

Miller's information was encouraging; he said that the type of leukemia R.J. had was the most common among kids, that the cure rate for this kind of cancer for children under ten, with moderately intensive treatment, was eighty-five to ninety percent. And he said that R.J. had other favorable features at diagnosis, such as a low white count, good appearance of the leukemia cells under a microscope and the presence of certain antigens on the cells.

Miller looked up from the folder. "I know this is difficult for you," he ended with. "But try to hold on to the fact that about ninety-eight percent of children with *newly diagnosed* ALL, which is R.J.'s case, attain an initial complete remission in four to six weeks."

Barbara swallowed hard. "Really? That's…that's wonderful."

"Yes, Mrs. Benton, it is." The doctor gave her and Rick another sympathetic look. "I'd like to start the initial round of chemotherapy immediately."

Barbara drew in a tremulous breath.

Rick took hold of her other hand and gripped it. Nathan could see her clutch onto him.

"We'll begin Monday, and schedule the treatment for three times a week." He outlined the procedure—they would go through R.J.'s veins with a regular IV; if that didn't work, they'd have to put a in shunt. He also told them how chemotherapy killed the cancer cells.

Again, tears coursed down Barbara's cheeks. Nathan battled his own as he thought about what he'd be feeling if this was Kaeley they were talking about. Hell, he was emotional enough about R.J.

"Does he stay in the hospital all that time?" Barbara asked.

"No, he can come home after the first round, and we see how he reacts. The rest of the treatments will be as an outpatient."

"How he reacts?"

"Side effects, honey," Rick said gently.

"Yes, although they may not appear right away. But there *will* be hair loss and nausea."

Barbara clapped a hand over her mouth. "Oh, God, my baby."

Miller looked to Rick and then to Nathan. "I think that's enough today. We'll schedule the first treatment for early Monday. Your son should be able to go home Tuesday."

It was almost surreal, standing, leaving the room, and going out into the hall. Everything was the same, but everything was so different. They all knew their lives would never, ever be the same.

THAT AFTERNOON, Anabelle sat in the waiting area outside R.J.'s room while Nathan was inside with Barbara. Sighing, Anabelle chided herself for her self-absorption last night in the wake of what they'd just found out.

Barbara's son had cancer. Of course the woman needed Nathan now. That's all that mattered. Anabelle was leafing through a magazine, when the elevator dinged and Nathan's brother came off it; he spied her and strode toward her purposefully. A little taller than Nathan, Drew had always reminded her of Kevin Costner.

"Anabelle? I just heard."

She cocked her head.

"I had a meeting with Dan. Nathan called him about R.J." He ran a hand through his short brown hair. "I wish like hell Nathan had called me. I would have come down here with him."

"They just found out a few hours ago."

Drew zeroed in on her. "You knew. Enough to be here. I don't know how to prove—" He cut himself off and dropped into a chair. "Never mind. Tell me R.J.'s prognosis."

When she finished sketching out the details Nathan had

briefly given her before Barbara pulled him away, Drew shook his head. "Poor Barbara. I really like her. I'd hoped she and Nathan were in for some smooth sailing now."

Anabelle said nothing.

"They love each other deeply, but I don't know how you can get somebody through something like this."

Anabelle turned away. This was tough to hear.

"Why *are* you here, Anabelle?"

"I…um…Nathan and I were in Seneca Falls and the airports closed. We made it to Hyde Point when we couldn't get back to D.C. When we found out R.J. was in the hospital, we came directly here."

"That was yesterday?"

"Uh-huh?"

"So, why are you at the hospital with him today?"

"To see if I could help out in any way." Even to her own ears, her explanation sounded weak.

"Does Barbara want you here?"

Less and less. All morning, Barbara had been curt and almost hostile. "Why wouldn't she? I'm Nathan's assistant. A lot's going on in Washington. We've been working whenever she hasn't needed him."

Skepticism flickered across his face. "Anabelle, is there something going on I don't know about?"

"Like what?"

"I don't know. Truthfully, I find it odd Nathan hired you at all, after your past relationship. Then you seem to be his constant companion. It doesn't add up."

If you're using the right formula, it does.

Just then Nathan exited R.J.'s room and made his way to them.

Drew stood. "Nate, I'm so sorry." Then he gave Nathan a big bear hug that looked genuine. As a matter of fact, Drew seemed overwrought. About R.J., a boy he hardly knew?

Hmm.

THAT NIGHT, Barbara cried all the way home. Anabelle had seen this reaction before. Barbara had been strong in the hospital, especially after the good prognosis for R.J.'s recovery, but now, in the presence of the man she loved, she could let her feelings show. She'd been put through an emotional wringer.

Rick had convinced her that she needed rest more than he did, and that he should be the one to stay overnight with R.J. again. Barbara only agreed since Nathan had to go back to D.C. soon, and she wanted to spend this time with him. That bit of information had struck a nerve with Rick and he'd curtly turned away. Barbara wouldn't leave the hospital until ten, though, and now she was a wreck. Exhaustion, and the reality of the mind-numbing report they'd received, finally caught up with her.

This time, Anabelle drove the car while Nathan sat in the back seat, holding his weeping fiancée in his arms. Anabelle was drained, too. Regardless of the good prognosis, it had to be horrible finding out your child had cancer.

At the house, Nathan had to practically carry Barbara from the car to the door and into the foyer, where she collapsed against him. Coat and all, he scooped her up in his arms and headed to the right. Once more, Anabelle watched them leave her.

They love each other deeply...

Shaking loose of the doubts, Anabelle made her way to her room, got ready for bed—she had her own things now—and waited for Nathan to come talk to her after Barbara fell asleep. They hadn't had any time together alone today. Seeing him now would calm her fears. Make her feel better.

But he never came. Instead, she lay awake, as she had so many years ago, wondering what was really happening in the bedroom he shared with Olivia, then berating herself for doubting the man she loved.

She slept fitfully—then awoke with a start.

Someone was in the house.

Reaching into her nightstand, she grabbed her gun. Slowly she crept out to the kitchen. A light was on. She heard crying. Peering around the hall corner, she found Barbara standing in the center of the room, dressed in ice-blue satin, staring down at a brown puddle at her feet.

"Barbara?"

Anguished eyes looked up at her. "I…I dropped it."

"That's all right."

"I was trying to make hot chocolate. I couldn't sleep." She straightened. "I need to clean up the mess."

"I'll do it."

"No! You won't. You won't do anything."

Uh-oh. Anabelle stepped back. "All right."

She watched as Barbara got a roll of paper towels and started to chatter as if Anabelle wasn't even there. "I couldn't sleep." She bent down, soaking the hem of her pretty nightgown. "Nathan's out cold. He always is after…" She focused on the stain on her nightgown. "Oh, dear…" She looked up, seemed puzzled to see someone else in the room.

Anabelle hoped her face didn't betray her. *He always is after…*

Then Barbara burst into tears. Her knees dropped into the puddle of hot chocolate, splashing more onto her gown. She buried her face in her hands. "Oh, God."

Anabelle went to her. "Barbara, let me help."

"Nobody can help. Nothing will ever be the same. I'll never make hot chocolate for R.J. like I used to... I'll never sleep well... I'll never enjoy sex again... Nothing can ever possibly be right after today."

Again, Anabelle ignored the innuendo of her words and reached out to comfort Barbara.

This time Barbara screamed, "Get away from me!"

"What's going on?" Nathan stood in the doorway. When he took in the situation, he rushed to Barbara. "Here, let me help."

She fell into his arms, and once again he lifted her up, cradling her against his chest. "Barb, you're overwrought and forgetting the good news we got today. This disease is ninety-eight percent curable."

Still, she burrowed into him. Anabelle knew that at 3:00 a.m. people didn't look at things rationally.

"Come on, honey, let's go back to bed." He spared Anabelle a glance. It was full of feeling.

Nonetheless, she couldn't help the devastating chill that coursed through her as she watched him leave with Barbara.

Several things clicked into place... He always falls asleep after... I'll never enjoy sex again... Come on, *honey*.

And...it looked as if Nathan had nothing on underneath the robe.

Oh my God.

"I WISH YOU DIDN'T have to leave tomorrow morning." Barbara took Nathan's hand as they made their way to R.J.'s room, where they'd left Anabelle and Rick playing with the boy. Barbara looked fragile in jeans and a sweatshirt as she leaned heavily on him.

"Me, too." Feeling helpless, Nathan said little, just as

he had in the cafeteria over coffee and the bagel he'd forced her to eat.

She wouldn't take time for breakfast at home and had insisted on leaving as soon as they were showered and dressed. They arrived at the hospital by seven. Only after R.J. had fallen back asleep about ten had she agreed to leave his side.

"I wish you could stay in Hyde Point."

"I would, Barbara, but the Standards Committee thing…"

"I know." She straightened. "Anabelle will be with you." Her phrasing was odd.

"Yes, of course."

And he couldn't wait to talk to her. He'd been planning to go to her room last night, but had dozed off as he waited for Barbara's sleeping pill to take effect. Then the scene in the kitchen had happened. This morning, there wasn't an opportunity to speak to Anabelle alone.

All he knew was that she obviously hadn't slept well, and there was something in her eyes when she looked at him…a wariness that he couldn't explain.

When they got back to the room, they found Anabelle, Rick and R.J. watching TV and laughing. Nathan smiled at the picture Anabelle made. She was wonderful with R.J., just as she'd been with Kaeley. He glanced over at Barbara, who was staring at them with wide-eyed anger. Barb said, "We're back, Anabelle. I'd like to visit with my son, if you don't mind."

Both Rick and Anabelle looked puzzled. R.J. cocked his head.

"Of course." Anabelle stood.

"Could you go out in the hall, please?" Barbara's tone was cool and dismissive, much like Olivia's had always been.

"I'll go too," Nathan told them. "Give you three some time alone—"

"No!"

Everyone stilled.

"What's wrong, Mom?"

"Nothing, son." She addressed Nathan. "I want you here with me and R.J."

Rick glanced at the ceiling and he jammed his hands in his pockets. "We'll go get some coffee." He and Anabelle left the room together.

R.J. lay back on the pillows. After some small talk, his eyes drifted shut. Barbara spoke little until he was asleep. Then she stood and paced the room. "I don't like her being here."

"Anabelle? Why?"

"She's in love with you."

"Barbara, please, you're overwrought. Let's not get into this, now."

"Get another bodyguard."

"Barbara."

"Have Dan stay with you tonight. I don't want her around you."

Psychologically, Nathan understood what was happening. The emotional rug had been pulled out from under Barbara and she was grasping onto what was safe and secure. Right now it was him.

"All right. I'll call Dan. He can stay at the house with us."

She looked after where Anabelle had gone. "I don't want her around R.J."

"Fine. I'll talk to her."

Both of them settled into chairs and stared at the TV in an uncomfortable silence. When Rick came back in, he asked, "Everything okay?"

Barbara started to cry. "Okay?" She stood, her eyes wild. "Nothing is ever going to be okay again." With that, she threw herself into Rick's arms.

He held on tight. "Babs, you're not thinking clearly. The prognosis is *good*."

After a moment, Barbara pulled back. "You're right. Sometimes it's just too much to handle. I'm afraid."

Drawing her close, Rick said, "I know. It's okay. I am too."

Nathan was overcome by their fear. He turned away from them and faced the window and thought about Anabelle. Barbara needed him. He felt caught between her needs and Anabelle's. He knew Annie's feelings for him were fragile. And right now he felt as he had when he was forced to chose between her and Kaeley.

God, was Anabelle drawing that parallel, too?

IT WAS LATE AFTERNOON before Nathan came out of R.J.'s room. Lines of exhaustion bracketed his mouth and eyes. Dressed in jeans and a forest-green sweater that set off his coloring, he approached her. The torn expression on his face was familiar. She tried not to remember when she'd seen it before.

"Hi." His voice was a soft caress. "You okay?"

No, she wasn't okay. First the dreams the night before last. Then Barbara's hanging on Nathan constantly. Her possessiveness. And finally what she'd said last night. It was all vague and suggestive. It might mean nothing. And, especially given the circumstances, Anabelle struggled to see things clearly. "Yeah, sure, I'm fine."

"Let's walk to the cafeteria." They made their way down the hall. He stayed close to her but didn't touch her. After getting coffee, they sat at a table in the corner.

"They came in and gave us the details about the chemotherapy." He told her about it.

"Oh, God."

"I wish I could be here to help Barb through it, but I
have to go back to D.C. tomorrow morning—we'll take
the red-eye. The Standards Committee won't wait."

"I know." She swallowed hard.

"Barbara's on the edge."

"Yeah, I can tell."

"I'm sorry, some of her anger is directed at you."

With good reason. She smiled sadly. "I can handle it,
Nathan."

"Are you sure?"

Please God, let me be able to. "Yes, of course."

"I hope so, because she doesn't want you at the house
tonight."

The thought came out of nowhere. *Olivia wants you
out of the house by tonight.*

"I see."

"And she wants you to stay away from R.J."

And she doesn't want you to see Kaeley.

Nathan blew out an exasperated breath. "I...I can't do
anything about this, love. Barbara isn't thinking clearly.
If it wasn't for what we just found out about R.J...."

If it wasn't for what we just found out about Kaeley...

"I understand, Nathan."

I understand, Nathan. I'll move out right now.

"I'll call Dan," she told him. "Hopefully, he can meet
us at Barbara's and I'll go..." Where would she go?

I don't have anywhere to go, Nathan, she'd told him
when she was twenty-two. Anabelle remembered vowing
never, *never* to be in such a vulnerable position again.

Physically, or emotionally.

And ten years later, here she was again.

"Go to my house, sweetheart."

"Oh, all right."

"Annie, I'm sorry." He grasped her hand and brought it to his lips. "I'm so sorry. If there was another way…"

I'm so sorry, Annie. I'd do anything for you but this…

She pictured him in his bathrobe last night…heard Olivia's triumphant laugh: *We've been sleeping together all along, when he believed he loved you… I'll bet he didn't tell you that… Barbara doesn't want you at the house tonight…*

No, she wouldn't confuse this time with the last. She'd confront her doubts outright. "Nathan, I need to ask you something." She gripped his hand. "Last night, you didn't come to my room. And Barbara said some things that…"

He held on tight. "What is it, sweetheart?"

"Did you—"

Anabelle's hand was wrenched from Nathan's.

Barbara stood at their table. Her eyes were a road map of red, her face blotchy. And her whole stance was…aggressive. "Get away from him," she said wildly. "Get out of here. Who do you think you are…I should have known…"

The past merged with the present. Olivia's tirade melded with Barbara's…I should have known…you're a slut…you're just pretending to be his bodyguard…you can't have him…get out…

Anabelle couldn't breathe. Vaguely she realized people were looking at them. She heard Nathan say something to Olivia…no, to Barbara… Anabelle's head spun, and she felt the cold nausea rise in her throat.

She had to get out of there.

Blindly, she rose, circled around Olivia…and headed out of the estate house… She was in the hall before she realized she was at Elmwood Medical Center. Her knees buckled. She sagged against the wall and battled back the tears.

She didn't know how much longer it was when she heard, "Anabelle? Is that you?" Someone gripped her arm. "Oh, God, honey, what's wrong?"

Not recognizing the voice, she slowly turned her head to the side. Taylor Morelli stood there, dressed in a pink smock that had Volunteer written on the front pocket.

"Anabelle, are you all right?"

She shook her head.

Taylor grasped her arm. "Come on, honey, let me help."

Anabelle stared at her. "Taylor…please, call Dan. I…" She glanced at the cafeteria. "Get me out of here."

CHAPTER TWELVE

NORA STUDIED the occupants of Taylor's dining room, where she and the six original Serenity House residents had finished the Morellis' famous Italian spaghetti dinner and were enjoying wine and coffee now. The night had been planned for weeks, to celebrate all the good news the Serenity House girls had gotten lately. Anabelle, however, had not expected to be able to attend.

"I ruined your dinner party." Anabelle shook her head and took a sip of Chianti. "Everybody was so happy about what was going on with them and I cast a pall on it." She scowled. "You didn't even talk about your news when the men were here."

"Nonsense. We had a perfectly lovely dinner." Nora hedged a bit. It had been tense at first, but eventually they'd enjoyed the meal.

"I chased the guys away. And after Nick cooked the whole meal."

Darcy, curled up in a big captain's chair, chuckled. "Are you guys crazy? Hunter, Nick and Ian were only too happy to go into town and catch the Super Bowl playoffs at Nick's brother's bar—and avoid cleanup, I might add."

Anabelle sighed and Nora worried about the lines of stress on her face. The scene at the hospital had been horrendous. She and Dan had arrived to find Anabelle huddled with Taylor in the corner of the waiting room

outside R.J.'s room. Anabelle and Dan went off to talk
privately and when they'd come back, Dan was quietly
furious but announced he'd be staying at the hospital with
Nathan tonight. Anabelle and Nora were to go home
alone. It was Taylor who convinced them to come to the
dinner party.

Overwrought, Anabelle hadn't objected. She told Nora
all she wanted was to avoid Nathan. Being with her Serenity House friends might soothe her. Sharing their good
news surely would. Nora didn't know what had happened
between her and Nathan—and Anabelle didn't want to
discuss it yet—but something had exploded and the fall-
out had caught Anabelle behind the knees. Nora had seen
her so devastated only once before, when Nathan had
stayed with Olivia.

Nora studied her girls. Like Anabelle, so much had
happened in their lives. Sometimes she wondered how
they dealt with it. Right now, they were trying to keep
Anabelle entertained. None of them had asked why Anabelle was looking as if she'd lost her best friend. They'd
just surrounded her with support. It was a tactic they'd
learned while at Serenity House, where sometimes things
were too tough to share and all the girls needed was their
friends around them.

"Anabelle can use some cheering up. Let's talk about
Paige's daughter." This from Jade, who smiled at her
sister. "Tell it, sis. It'll make her feel better."

"I found my daughter on an Internet matching site—
not Ian's adoption Web site, by the way."

"How did it happen?" Taylor asked.

Darcy was excited. "Where is she?"

Paige's smile was electric. "She's living in Rochester.
She goes to a small Catholic girls' school there. Her parents are an older couple who couldn't have children of

their own.'' She swallowed hard. "Her name is Amara.
It means beloved. They call her Mara. When Mara did a
paper for her English class on open adoption, she asked
her parents if she could search for her birth mother.''

Darcy's hand went to her stomach where her own future bundle of joy rested. "Were they receptive?''

"Not exactly. At first they forbade her to try to find
me.'' Paige shrugged. "But apparently she persuaded
them to at least think about it. They all got counseling
and agreed to post Mara's statistics on an Internet matching site last week. If they found a match, which they did,
they'd decide then.''

"Have you had contact with her?'' Anabelle asked.

"No, the parents are still hesitant. They're scared. I
understand. They're good people. And she sounds like a
wonderful child. She's happy and well adjusted. I don't
blame them for being wary.''

"Oh, honey, it's wonderful that you found her, that
you might be able to see her.'' This from Taylor.

"Ian and I want to go up there for her winter break in
February when we could have some time together. Her
parents said they'd consider it.''

Nora's gaze swept the room. She was startled to see
Charly was crying. "Charly, what is it?''

Charly shook her head. "Nothing, I'm happy for
Paige.''

"You're not usually this emotional,'' Taylor told her.
These two spent the most time together, as they both
lived in Elmwood. "You have good news too, right,
about Serenity House?''

"Not anymore. Jeez, I thought we'd be celebrating an
expansion, and now Serenity House is being investigated.''

"Investigated?'' Paige asked. "By whom?''

"The state." She shook her head. "One of the residents was caught with pot a few weeks ago. We had to ask her to leave. Ten days later, someone else ran away."

Nora reached over the table and covered Charly's hand. "Those are typical group-home setbacks, sweetie, I told you that. They happened when I was in charge, too. No one will fault you for it or stop the expansion."

"Not by themselves, no. But…something else happened. Something that *was* my fault." Charly's face reddened. "The night after the fund-raiser, I asked another counselor, Linda, to cover for me. I was supposed to do twenty-four-hour supervision, but I had somewhere else to go. Linda agreed to fill in, but then had an emergency at home. She called with a message that she had to go to the hospital, and assuming I'd get it, she left the house."

"She left the girls alone?" Nora asked.

"Yes, for a few hours. She said I was always checking up on them, and her son had been rushed to the hospital for a broken arm. She wasn't thinking clearly because she was upset." Charly sighed. "I didn't check in that night."

Jade eyed her carefully. "Where'd you go?"

Charly twisted the wedding ring she still wore two years after her husband's death. "I was with Trace McCall."

"*The* Trace McCall?" Darcy asked. "Oh, be still my heart."

Taylor swooned along with Paige.

Jade said, "So, 'fess up, what'd you do?"

"Jade, that's none of your business," Paige told her sister.

"Is he good in the sack?"

Taylor blushed. "*Jade.*"

"We weren't in the sack, smarty." Charly's eyes got dreamy. "We did go to the Boxwood Inn where he was staying, but nothing happened." She paused. "Much."

"Oh, God." Jade was giggling. "A night at the Box-wood with America's number-one sex symbol, and you did nothing *much?* I'll never believe that, girlfriend."

Charly sobered. "Never mind what I did or didn't do. I've paid dearly for the evening. The girls were left alone for a few hours and Emma Perry, the resident who just came to us from Elmwood, snuck out. Anabelle's little friend, Ariel, tried to stop her. But Emma went anyway, and was picked up by the cops for drinking behind a bar on Main Street. The newspaper got wind of it. Now the state's investigating us."

Nora said, "This will work out, dear. We'll get Seren-ity House's lawyer, Jillian Sullivan, on it."

"We were thinking of asking Nathan to help if that's not enough." Charly looked to Anabelle. "Your being upset tonight has to do with him, doesn't it?"

"Yes."

With surprising gentleness, Jade said, "What's going on, honey? Tell us why you're so upset. You look like Julia Roberts in *Sleeping With the Enemy.* Battered."

Anabelle stared at her friends. "I *feel* like I've been battered. By past ghosts." She stood. "Let's go in the living room where the fire is."

Once they were resettled, Anabelle leaned against the back of the couch in front of the fire and sipped her wine. She stretched out her jean-clad legs and folded her arms across the Seattle P.D. sweatshirt she wore. "Years ago, I had an affair with Nathan, when I was Kaeley's nanny. He promised to leave Olivia, and he didn't."

All the women frowned. Several pithy remarks were made.

"Why on earth would you choose to work for him now?" Paige asked.

"Because there were extenuating circumstances then." She looked at Nora. "Things even you don't know about, Nora."

"Nora knew about the affair?" Darcy asked.

"Yes, she and Dan got me out of Hyde Point and found me a job in Seattle."

Silence.

"In any case, I didn't return to Hyde Point because of him." She glanced around. "And because my brothers are still in town. But when I got shot, I couldn't resist coming home to recuperate with Nora and Dan."

"That's understandable." Jade looked puzzled. "But I still don't understand why you'd go work for Nathan. You weren't really rethinking your future, were you, like you told me and Charly at Rascal's?"

Anabelle looked at Nora. "I'm so sick of the secrecy, Nora."

"Then tell them what's going on. They can be trusted."

Her shoulders sagging, Anabelle shook her head. "Nathan's being stalked. Because of my experience in undercover work, I volunteered to be his bodyguard."

"That's why I felt your gun," Taylor commented, "when you were so upset at the hospital, and I put my arm around you."

Anabelle smiled sadly. "Yes. It's been excruciating. I took the job because I never stopped caring about him. I should have known we couldn't stay away from each other. One thing led to another…we got stranded Thursday night…God, history repeated itself. He's engaged, I slept with him." She shook her head. "I never learn."

"Oh, sweetie." Nora hadn't known this and it made her angry all over again at Nathan.

"I love him. I never stopped loving him."

"He's a shit to have slept with you when he's engaged to Barbara." Jade's tone was vehement.

"Yeah, well, he said he loved me, too." She shook her head. "Just like the last time."

"Don't you believe him?" Taylor, who put great stock in true love, asked.

"Now that I've had time to calm down, I really don't know what I think. The situation has so many parallels to the last time, it threw me."

All the girls and Nora listened as Anabelle told the group about Barbara and R.J.

Jade said, "You're star-crossed, like Romeo and Juliet."

"Or maybe I'm just Shakespeare's fool. If you knew how vulnerable I felt a few hours ago...when the same thing happened, when I had no control over it, just like the last time. God, I vowed, *vowed* this would never happen to me again."

"You can stay here, honey." This from Taylor.

Nora added, "Or come home with me."

"All right. But I have to go back to Washington tomorrow."

"Screw him," Jade said. "He'll have to get another bodyguard."

"Yes, he will. But it'll take a while. Meanwhile, I'm going to protect him."

"Dan can go with him," Nora suggested.

"Dan has a life here, Nora." Anabelle shook her head. "No, I'll see this through until Nathan can get somebody else."

"Is it over between you?" Darcy asked.

She swallowed hard. "I don't know, Darce. All I know is that what fragile trust I was building in him didn't hold up very well in the face of what happened with Barbara." She turned to Nora. "What's wrong with me, Nora? Won't I ever really trust anybody again after what happened to me when I was young?" She glanced around the room. "Do you guys?"

"I do," Paige said. "I trust Ian now."

Darcy chimed in the same about Hunter.

Taylor said, "I trust Nick. But there's something between us, something I can't put my finger on. I don't trust *myself* with that."

"I trusted Cal," Charly added. "But now, other men…"

"Like superstar Trace McCall?"

"Oh, yeah. Sure. Trust *him?* No matter what he says—" Charly broke off abruptly and she flushed a deep red.

"He *says?*" Jade dropped her empty wineglass to the rug on the floor. "You talk to him?"

"He…calls sometimes."

"Sometimes?"

"Guys, Anabelle's in crisis." Charly scowled. "Let's stick with her question." She focused on Jade. "How about you, Miss Nosy? Do you trust men? Anybody?"

Drawing in a breath, Jade locked gazes with Paige. "I trust Paige, of course, though I didn't always and I'm sorry for that. And now I trust you all." She shook her head. "But can I trust men? Doesn't look that way. I ended it once and for all with Beck and I think he's going to go for custody of Jewel."

"Oh, no." Taylor was horrified. "And just when you were getting things together?"

"We'll get a good lawyer, sweetie," Nora said to Jade. "I told you that."

Jade's eyes teared. It was so unexpected to see tough-guy Jade turn emotional, everybody hushed. "I couldn't live without my daughter. I'd die if he took her. Maybe I'll chuck getting my teaching degree and leave Hyde Point. Disappear."

"No, stay and fight him." Paige grabbed her hand. "We'll all help you."

Jade sighed. "I don't want to talk about it anymore." She turned to Anabelle. "Do you feel any better?"

Nora saw Anabelle look around the room. "Yeah, I do. We've all survived horrible things. I'll survive this. So will you, Jade, and you, Charly." She nodded to Taylor. "If things aren't perfect between you and Nick, they're near to it."

Headlights broke the darkness outside. "Hmm. Looks like the guys are back." Taylor stood and crossed to the window. She peered out.

"Is it them?" Paige asked when Taylor stilled.

Taylor turned. "No, it's Dan's car."

Nora swore softly, shocking them all. "Nathan will be with him, Anabelle."

GIVEN THE EVENTS of the last forty-eight hours, Nathan was at the end of his rope. When they pulled into Taylor's driveway, and Dan turned off the engine and faced him with old and familiar disapproval and distrust on his face, Nathan knew he was ready to snap.

"I'll say it again. I'm totally against this. I don't want you to see Anabelle tonight."

"I've got to see her."

"Haven't you hurt her enough, man?"

"I had no choice."

"That's what you kept saying the last time, Nathan. I'm pissed as hell that you're involved with her again. It's unforgivable, after what you did to her ten years ago."

"I told you there were reasons why we couldn't be together years ago that she understands."

"Yeah, so you said." Dan's tone indicated he clearly didn't believe Nathan.

And suddenly, Nathan couldn't take it anymore. He'd lost Anabelle once. He'd lost Dan once. He wasn't going to lose either of them again. So he took one of the biggest risks of his life.

"I gave Anabelle up last time because Olivia blackmailed me." The words stuck in his throat. They'd choked him before, and they were choking him now. "Kaeley isn't my biological daughter, Dan."

Total, tense silence.

Finally Dan said, "Oh, dear Lord."

Nathan needed to get it out fast. "When I told Olivia I was in love with Annie, she produced a birth certificate and paternity tests to prove some other guy was the father. So I had DNA tests done. They confirmed what she said." He swallowed hard. "She said she'd make sure I never saw Kaeley again if I left. It would have been bad enough never to see my daughter again. But I would have sacrificed my *life* before I'd have left Kaeley alone with that monster of a mother."

"Instead," Dan whispered harshly, "you sacrificed your happiness."

"No, I sacrificed *Anabelle's* happiness. Just like I'm doing now." He looked over at the one person who, next to Kaeley and Annie, meant more than anything in the world to him. "Tell me, at least, that you understand why I hurt Anabelle the last time. Rage about now—I've been irresponsible—but at least tell me you understand about then, Dan.'' He swallowed back the emotion in his throat. "I need to hear that now. I need…you now.''

From the dim confines of the car, Dan sighed heavily. Nathan didn't know what he'd do if Dan berated him again. Then he felt a strong hand grip his arm. "Of course I understand. You made the right choice back then, Nathan. The only choice.''

"Thank you for that.''

"And I can't imagine how bad this is now for you, being thrust into such a similar position.''

"It's Anabelle I'm worried about. It must be…'' He pounded his hand on the dashboard. "I can't bear to think what she's feeling now.''

"She doesn't trust easily.''

"I know, and I *promised* her she could trust me on this.''

"Well, she can, can't she? After the treatment is under way with R.J.? You'll tell Barbara you're in love with Anabelle, won't you?''

"Yes, I'll tell Barbara. But what's going to happen to Annie in the meantime? She's a lot more fragile than she lets on.''

"I know.'' He nodded to the house. "Let's go see.''

Taylor swung open the door before they rang the bell. Behind her were the Serenity House posse—Jade, Paige, Darcy and Charly. Anabelle was nowhere in sight.

"Where's Nora?'' Dan asked when Nathan just stood there.

"She's in the den with Anabelle.''

"I…'' Nathan looked to Dan, who laid a hand on his shoulder, then back to the women, gathered to protect their friend. "I need to see her.''

"I'm not sure that's such a good idea, Congressman."
Jade's tone was full of frost.

"Look, I appreciate your protectiveness. God knows,
she needs it from me. But I won't leave here without
seeing her."

Finally they let him into the house. Taylor showed him
to the den. He knocked, then opened the door. Anabelle
was standing with her back to him, and Nora faced him
down. She stood tall, a mama defending her cub. "She
says she'll see you, though I don't think it's a good
idea."

"It's...I...I don't know what to say, Nora, except I
have to talk to her."

With a last glance at Nathan, Nora left; the click of
the door closing echoed loudly in the room. Nathan
waited a moment, then said, "Annie?"

Her shoulders stiffened slightly at the nickname. Nathan approached her. As he got closer, he saw her wrap
her arms around her waist—poor armor against his actions. Still he came up and grasped her shoulders.

He said, "I'm so, so sorry, love."

"It's not your fault, Nathan." Her voice was raspy and
raw. He wondered if she'd cried today.

"It wasn't last time either, but that's where your mind
went, didn't it?"

Still facing away from him, she nodded.

"I'm sorry there are so many similarities to the last
time."

"She even..." Her voice cracked and Nathan thought
he might lose it. "She even said some of the same things
Olivia said."

"Oh, Annie."

Anabelle shook her head. "I know, I shouldn't do

this…'' She pivoted around then and what he saw sucker punched him in the gut so much he gasped for breath.

She looked exactly as she'd looked the last time.

''But it was too similar, it was…*is*…too much like the last time.''

He wouldn't go down without a fight. He grasped her shoulders. ''Listen to me. There *are* similarities to Olivia and Kaeley. I'm engaged, the welfare of a child is at stake. But I'm not married, and I'm not going to marry Barbara. When this is over for her, I still plan to break it off. I won't sacrifice you for her, Annie. Not like I did for Kaeley.''

Amber eyes stared blankly at him.

''Tell me you believe me.''

Nothing.

''Annie, tell me.''

She clasped her arms tighter around her waist. She didn't say anything.

''Annie.''

''Did you make love to her?'' Anabelle blurted out.

''What?''

''Did you make love to Barbara?''

He must have heard her wrong…but he could tell by the expression on her face he hadn't. ''You've got to be kidding me.''

''No, I'm not.'' She swallowed hard. ''Ten years ago, before I left Hyde Point, Olivia told me you hadn't stopped having sex with her, even after you fell in love with me and told me you had.''

''I assured you I had.''

''Last night, you came down in just a robe… Barbara said you always fell asleep after sex… She wondered if she would ever enjoy it…''

He shook his head sadly. ''I didn't sleep with Olivia

or Barbara. Olivia lied for obvious reasons. I can't fathom why Barbara would tell you that, except for—''

''She didn't tell me, I surmised it.'' She explained the events of last night.

''Well, Anabelle,'' he said defeatedly, ''you were wrong. I had boxer shorts under my robe. We'd been talking about never enjoying life again... I fell asleep because I was worn out. But if you could possibly think that of me now...''

''Nathan, I can't tell you I trust you if I don't.''

The words were razor sharp and cut deep. He ran a shaky hand through his hair. ''I can't believe this. I thought after Belhurst... We should be *past* the doubts.''

''We should be. I'm sorry, but I guess I'm not.''

He didn't know what to do with this information. He was so caught up in making sure she was all right, in worrying about her being hurt, he didn't plan for what to do if he couldn't make this right. How, *how* could she have thought this of him?

He stepped back. ''What will you do?'' he asked woodenly.

''You have to get another bodyguard. I'm sorry, I can't protect you adequately.''

''Dan's already told me that. He's going to look into it. And Monday, I'll see what I can do.''

''I'll stay with you until someone else comes.''

''Fine. We'll fly back to D.C. tomorrow as scheduled.''

She nodded.

Then he remembered something and it made his stomach roil. ''Are you still going to break it off with Rob tomorrow? When he comes to Washington?''

''I—I hadn't thought that far.''

Oh, God, she really meant this. She didn't trust him.

Perhaps he was foolish to have believed she ever would, after what had happened to her at such a young age. He'd been the first man to make love to her. Could his betrayal ten years ago have affected her irrevocably? Beleaguered, exhausted, he stepped even farther back.

"Dan's staying with you tonight?" she asked.

"Yes." Panicked by the thought of losing her, he whispered, "Come with us."

"No, I'd rather stay with Taylor."

He nodded. There was no more to say. Slowly he raised his hand and brushed her cheek.

Then he turned and walked out of the den.

THE ENVELOPE was a pure, crystalline white. Very appropriate. Carefully, he set down his Manhattan, a crutch that he needed more and more lately, and donned his gloves. Soon the deed would be done. It was already sealed up tight. Ready to go.

Remembering 9/11 and its aftermath had sparked the idea. Nate had been distraught by the attacks—one of his close friends had been in the Pentagon on that day—and equally upset by what had happened in Washington in the aftermath. The congressman's grief was real.

His wife's voice intruded. He hid the envelope, quickly, and whipped off the gloves.

There was a knock on the door, to which he replied, "Almost done, dear."

And he was…almost done. Almost all done.

CHAPTER THIRTEEN

At 6:00 A.M Monday morning, Anabelle watched Nathan, accompanied by Dan, come toward her inside the Elmwood airport terminal. Nathan was so handsome in a navy suit and light-blue shirt. She closed her eyes briefly to shut out the sight of him—along with all the feelings that rushed to the surface when she looked at him—and tried to concentrate on the day ahead. They would go directly from Reagan Airport to the House Chamber, where the Standards Committee would be meeting in three hours. As he got closer, she noted the lines of strain around his mouth, and his eyes were muddy with fatigue. He hadn't slept any better than she had.

He drew up to her, nodded curtly, then turned away. His distance and—was it anger?—rubbed already sore wounds raw. Not that she blamed him. She'd said she didn't trust in him, and he was hurt by it.

Dan hugged her. She held on. "You okay?" he asked.

"I'm fine." She glanced at Nathan who had crossed to the window. "How is he?"

"A mess."

Shaking her head, she sighed heavily.

"Maybe you should talk to him, honey."

"Nothing to say, Dan." She kissed him on the cheek. "Thanks for everything."

"I'll call you tonight."

Dan said goodbye to Nathan—they hugged, causing Anabelle to look away again—then left. Silently, Nathan picked up his briefcase and headed to the inner terminal; she had to jog to catch up to him.

The building was almost deserted. They went through security and made the long trek through the airport. All the while they said nothing to each other. At the gate, Anabelle took a chair in the corner, Nathan checked their tickets, then joined her.

"The plane's on time."

She straightened the severe black pants and cashmere sweater she wore. "Oh, good."

His face was full of thunderclouds, which he seemed no longer able to hold back. "I can't believe this, Annie."

"Don't, Nathan, please."

"I'm angry."

"Yeah, I can tell. I'm not so happy myself."

"It's not the same as with Olivia."

"How…how do I know that, Nathan? How do I know Barbara won't be able to keep you, like Olivia did?"

"You've got to trust me on this."

She didn't say anything.

"Like you said you would at the Belhurst Castle."

She shook her head.

"You should be able to get past this."

"Because you say so?" Temper simmered beneath all the hurt. "Life doesn't work that way."

"Not because I say so, because we love each other." He shook his head. "Goddamn it, Annie. At least tell me you've decided to break it off with Rob today. After you've had time to think about—"

"I don't know what I'm going to do about Rob now."

"How can you say that to me?" When she didn't respond, he stood, said, "I'll wait over there for the flight to be called," and strode away.

The atmosphere was tense on the flight to Washington, on the cab ride to Capitol Hill, and as Nathan left Anabelle to go to the Standards Committee room. All the while he didn't speak to her again, hardly even looked at her.

He was really hurt.

"What the hell happened to you?" Zeke asked when he came to take over for the day as Nathan's bodyguard so she could spend some time with Rob.

"I got run over by the past," she said.

He tipped up her chin. "This—" he nodded to the chamber where Nathan met with the committee "—was a mistake."

"You have no idea how true that statement is."

His dark eyes were warm with compassion, making her throat clog. "We're working on finding a new bodyguard," he said gently.

"Good." She smiled. "I've got to go pick up Rob." She started away.

Zeke called out, "Belle?"

She pivoted.

"Don't do anything rash. Some things a guy can't forgive."

She smiled sadly. "Thanks for caring."

Anabelle remembered Zeke's advice as she watched Rob coming toward her in the Reagan International terminal. He was tall and lanky. Today he wore jeans and a sweater she'd gotten him for his birthday. He looked young and uncomplicated.

Just what she needed.

When he spotted her, his face lit up. He rushed over, swung her up and around, then buried his face in her neck for a moment. She shivered. He misinterpreted it.

"Me, too, baby." And then his mouth covered hers. It was a carnal kiss, reminding her of the good sex they'd had. She tried to remember that and return the kiss. As they broke apart, he hooked an arm around her neck and they headed out of the airport. "Where can we go, babe? I've missed you so much." He scowled. "You should have let me come to Hyde Point."

Oh, God. Still, she tried. She leaned into him. But it felt wrong. She hadn't thought this out, hadn't let herself consider what was going to happen when he came to town if she didn't break it off. The hurt Nathan had caused her had overshadowed everything. Again.

Anabelle took him to Nathan's town house. She didn't know why she'd chosen Nathan's place, except that it seemed safer somehow. They went directly upstairs; he tore off his coat, and hers, then grabbed her.

She avoided the kiss this time, so he reached for her sweater. "It's been so long..." The pretty, black cashmere came over her head and dropped to the floor.

The time at Belhurst Castle came back to her...

I missed your body so much, Annie.

She gasped as Rob's hands closed over her bare ribs. "You feel so good..."

You feel so good, Annie. Nothing ever felt this good...

Rob's mouth was in her hair as his hands sought the zipper on her slacks. "Anabelle, baby, I'm dying..."

I'll die, love, if I ever lose you again...

Oh, God, what was she doing? She stilled his hands. "Rob, wait."

"No way."

"Yes, please, I have something to tell you."

AT NINE THAT NIGHT, another cab drew up to the town house. From inside, Zeke and Nathan exited. The cold air slapped Nathan in the face, a fitting backdrop for what he saw when he looked up at the Colonial structure. He stopped in his tracks.

"What?" Zeke asked gently. The guy had been solic-itous all day; Nathan sensed Zeke knew the gravity of what was occurring.

"The lights are on. Upstairs." He swallowed hard. "In her bedroom."

Campoli shifted from one foot to the other.

"How could she bring him back here?"

"Maybe she's alone."

"His plane doesn't leave till eleven."

"She's a complicated woman," Campoli said. "Have a little faith."

Did you have sex with Olivia…did you make love to Barbara?

"That, my man, is the one thing we can't seem to man-age between us." He shook his head. "Let's go in. I'm not going to freeze my ass off out here like some lovesick teenager staring up at the prom queen's window."

Nathan stalked to the door, unlocked it and stepped inside. Zeke shed his jacket, hooked it on the coat tree and headed for the living room. Nathan hung up his coat and was closing the closet door when a rumble came down the staircase. Pivoting, he saw a man pause on the bottom step.

Shit, she was a magnet for good-looking guys. He was about her age, tall and muscular. His curly brown hair was a mess—from Anabelle's hands?—and his clothes were wrinkled. Like a jerk, Nathan just stared at him.

Rob stared, too, then said, "You're Hyde, aren't you?"

Nathan nodded.

Then Rob drew his arm back and plowed a fist right into Nathan's face.

Pain splintered from his jaw to every nerve cell. "What the—"

Nathan was slammed against the foyer wall. His head clouded and the room darkened for a moment.

He heard yelling—Anabelle, then Zeke.

Slowly he became aware of being sprawled on the floor and Anabelle hovering over him. Her face was full of worry. "Oh, God, are you all right?"

He tried to nod, but pain rocketed through him with the gesture. Looking up, he saw Campoli behind Rob, his arms locked around the guy's chest. "Hold on, cowboy," Zeke said. "It's over."

"It's far from over." Rob strained at the bonds of Zeke's meaty fingers. "You bastard," he said to Nathan. "You slept with the woman I planned to marry."

Forget it. Nathan wasn't going to lie there and take this. He sat up, supported by the wall. "No, I slept with the woman *I* planned to marry."

The guy tried to shake off Zeke's grip. "Let me go. I won't hit him again."

"All right, man," Zeke said, "but if you touch the congressman, I'm taking you down."

Rob towered over Nathan instead. "I thought she was over you. I didn't even know who she was guarding until tonight." Again he spat out the words. "Well, this isn't finished. She's just mixed up—you confused her like you did before. When she gets back to Seattle, we're going to work this out.''

''Rob, please, I told you—'' Anabelle's voice was a hoarse plea.

''No, no more.'' He yanked her up and away from Nathan. ''Come on, you're coming to the airport with me.''

She looked torn.

When Nathan started to protest, Rob moved forward.

Zeke said, ''Stay back.''

''Fine. I'm done with him,'' Rob spat out disgustedly. ''And so is she.''

He grabbed Anabelle's coat, then took her hand and dragged her out of the house.

Nathan felt as if he'd just landed in Oz. He turned to Zeke. ''Holy mother of God.''

''I gotta say, Congressman, there's never a dull moment with you around.''

ANABELLE RETURNED to the town house at midnight, beleaguered and more confused than she'd ever been in her life. Inside the foyer, Zeke approached her. ''You okay, babe?''

''Hell, Zeke, this is a goddamn circus.''

''I know.'' He chucked her under the chin. ''Should I stay?''

''No, we'll be all right.''

He watched her for a minute. ''I'll work harder on getting the new bodyguard. We should have somebody in place in a day or two.''

''Good.'' She glanced toward the house. ''How is he?''

Zeke shook his head. ''You've both about hit bottom.''

He shrugged into his leather jacket. "I'd try to pull each other out, if I were you." He kissed her cheek. "Lock up."

She secured the house, then leaned against the door. Closing her eyes briefly, she thought about the man she'd just hurt.

I'm sorry, Rob, I can't do this.

I love you. Leave him now. I'll make you forget him.

It's not that simple. In any case, I can't let you think we're going anywhere.

I won't listen to this. He'd headed for the gate. *We'll talk when you get back to Seattle.*

She heard rustling in the living room and walked out of the foyer. Nathan was at the sideboard. He turned when he heard her come in. He was fishing ice out of a bucket, putting it into a small towel. She entered the room and crossed to him. Up close, she could see his lip was swollen. His green gaze on her was intense. She reached up and touched his jaw. He flinched.

"I'm sorry."

"That's okay. My whole jaw is sensitive."

"Put ice on it."

He held up the towel. "Yeah." He went to the chair and dropped down. Laying back, he closed his eyes and lifted the ice to his mouth.

Anabelle leaned against the sideboard and folded her arms across her chest. "I meant I was sorry for what Rob did. He was upset."

"Why did you tell him about us?"

Pushing away from the furniture, she wandered to the window and looked out into cold January night. "He wanted to make love." She bit her lip. "I couldn't."

"Thank God."

She circled around. "It doesn't mean anything about us."

"The hell it doesn't." He grimaced, the vehemence of his statement obviously hurting his jaw.

"Doesn't this make it all the more obvious how wrong we are together, Nathan? We keep hurting everybody. The scene with Barbara in the hospital...Rob...even Dan. It's so seedy."

"Don't say that. Please. Don't do this."

"I'm sorry. I can't say I trust you if I don't. It may not even be a rational thing. With our past, with all that's happened...maybe it's just an insurmountable hill I'll never scale."

He stared at her, long and hard. "Then that's a crying shame. Because I love you more than I ever loved a woman in my life. But you're right, if you don't trust me, nothing else matters. The odds are against us anyway, so without that, we're sunk." He stood and gave her a last look. "I'm going to bed." He headed for the door and disappeared into the hallway.

She wanted desperately to go after him. To call him back. To say she'd try to work things out with him. But suddenly ghosts were there, crowding her...

Her brother Aaron, big and bulky, slapping her across the face. *You're a slut, just like your mother.*

Her brother Al, *Let me in, you little whore...*

The look on her father's face, when she was five, and he simply walked out on her, leaving her with her brothers...

Olivia laughing at her. *What were you thinking...*

Barbara, *You can't have him...*

And suddenly, Anabelle got mad. For ten years, she'd worked at forgetting all those things, at building a new life. And then, at Belhurst Castle, she'd shaken loose of her past and was able to make baby steps toward trusting Nathan. So what if she'd been thrust into a situation similar to before? She should have been able to handle it.

But she couldn't. It was a flaw, it was an inadequacy; she'd caved under the ghosts of the past. Hyde Point's legacy still clung to her.

Damn it, she was tired of the ghosts, tired of the past haunting her. She wanted to be free of all that permanently. So, in the silence of Nathan's town house, she vowed to conquer those ghosts, even if she couldn't work things out with Nathan. She vowed to win this battle with the insecurity of the girl she used to be once and for all. Somehow she was going to overcome it.

THE NEXT MORNING, Nathan felt as if he'd been run over by a train, and Anabelle looked as if she'd been in the same wreck. They were going to have a hell of a time explaining the condition of his face to his staff, hell, to all his colleagues.

Right now he didn't much care. How could a man lose what was most important to him and still keep caring? Disgusted at his wallowing in self-pity, he entered his office in Longworth. Anabelle, behind him, was quiet, had said almost nothing since they'd bumped into each other this morning at the coffeepot.

Perhaps too much had already been said.

A harried Hank Fallon met him in the outer office. Barely glancing at him, Hank had his nose buried in a document. "Nathan, good, you're here. I've got—" He looked up. "Holy shit, what happened to you?"

"I ran into a door in the dark."

Hank's gaze flared. "I've seen fat lips from punches before. What's going on?"

"Leave it, Hank." He started to his office.

Hank blocked Anabelle's path when she went for the desk. "It has something to do with you, doesn't it?"

"Get out of my way, Hank." Anabelle's voice was cold, but Nathan detected the underlying weariness in it.

"Something hasn't been right since you came to work for us. And now Nate looks like he's been wrestling with street punks. You're involved."

Anabelle looked to Nathan.

He sighed. "Join me in my office. It's going to come out anyway." *Since I'm getting a new and public bodyguard.*

"Nathan, I don't think…" Anabelle began.

He didn't wait for the rest of her comment. He drew Hank inside and closed the door. "You're right. I've been keeping secrets." He walked to the sideboard and poured them both coffee. Handing a mug to Hank, he nodded to the chair in front of his desk. "Sit. I'll tell you everything."

They sat.

"I'm being stalked and Anabelle's my bodyguard."

Hank sputtered coffee on his pristine white shirt. "Excuse me?"

Sighing, Nathan explained the situation. Hank was stone-faced but Nathan could see the temper rise in his eyes. When Nathan finished, Hank said, "I was kept in the dark because I was—I am—a suspect."

"Everybody's a suspect. Even my brother."

Hank let a few choice expletives fly.

Nathan's cell phone rang. Immediately he thought of Barbara, and R.J. He snatched it up. "Hyde."

"Nathan, it's Zeke. I got you a new bodyguard. He can start tomorrow. But he's big and brawny and won't cut it as a staff member."

"It doesn't matter anymore."

"Fine, then. See you later. Oh…wait…something else just came in. Did you know that ten years ago Hank Fallon ran for a seat in the House of Representatives in Idaho and lost?"

Nathan eyed the man before him. "Ah…no, did that ever come out in the checks?"

"No, it didn't."

"Interesting."

Zeke paused. "Is someone with you?"

"Yes."

"I'm coming over. We'll talk when I get there."

Even more on edge, Nathan asked Hank to let him tell the other members of his staff about Anabelle. Hank agreed, had a few more questions, then left in a sulk. All the while, Nathan wondered if Hank was after him out of some twisted sense of not having achieved his own goals, while Nathan had gotten his. He sighed and sat back in his chair. Things were falling apart around him and he couldn't seem to hold them together.

In a moment, Anabelle opened his door. She had an odd expression on her face. "Nathan? You have a—"

His brother Drew barreled through the door, almost knocking Anabelle down. "I want to talk to you."

"Drew, what are you doing here?"

"I flew down this morning to see you."

Nathan glanced at the stack of things Drew held in his gloved hand. "What's that?"

Drew looked down and seemed surprised to see he

carried Nathan's mail. "Oh, I picked up the mail on the way in."

Nathan smiled. His brother simply couldn't stop taking care of him. As his campaign manager, he'd routinely attended to details that were technically Mark's domain.

Reaching out, Nathan took the letters from Drew. "Usually Mark goes through the mail and gives me what I should look at, but he's out sick today."

"I can go through it." Drew's tone was odd. "After we talk."

"I'll do it." Anabelle, who'd been watching the exchange, crossed to them. She reached out to take the mail and Nathan gave her a look full of feeling. Apparently it distracted her, because some of the correspondence dropped on to the floor.

She leaned over to pick it up and froze. Her hand hovered over the pile. Cool and calm, she said, "Nathan, I want you to get up and go to the other side of the office. You, too, Drew."

"What the hell?" Nathan stood. Staring down, he saw a mass of letters spread over the floor. One had opened. There was white powder spilling from it.

The events following 9/11 quickly registered in his mind.

"Oh my God," Nathan said. He looked up at Annie. "Do you think it's anthrax?"

Drew said, "Anabelle, let me—"

"Move! Both of you," Anabelle yelled. "Get on the other side of the room. But don't leave this office."

Her tone was brisk, professional and urgent. He stepped away from the desk, about ten feet back. Drew accompanied him, saying, "Something's obviously wrong, Nate. Why would *she* deal with it? I should be the one to take care of you.''

Nathan looked at him askance. ''Why should you?''

''I...''

They were both distracted when Anabelle flicked open her phone and dialed security. She said simply, ''I need help in Congressman Hyde's office. Send a HazMat team.''

IT WAS LIKE A SCENE from a science fiction movie. Having procedures in place from the anthrax scares in the House and Senate, a team arrived quickly at Nathan's office. The images were surreal. Yellow-suited men trained in hazardous material cleanup swarmed the office. They circled the offending letter, discussed it, then brought in a sealable, leakproof container, where they dumped all Nathan's mail.

Meanwhile, Anabelle, Drew and Nathan stood by, openmouthed, in shock. Drew seemed the most upset. ''I brought the freakin' mail in,'' he said, cursing vividly.

''It's not your fault.''

''I could have prevented...''

Nathan lay a hand on his brother's arm. ''Drew. It's all right. There's nothing you could have done.''

After a while, the HazMat guys approached them. Nathan, Drew and Anabelle were instructed to remain where they were until the white powder was tested for anthrax. No one was to enter or leave the offices. A sweep of the mail room and other potentially affected places would be made.

So the three of them waited in the sitting area. Nathan made some calls, and answered more—apparently news spread and the whole Longworth Building was in a lock-down, much as it had been a year and a half ago.

Nathan and Anabelle didn't talk until all calls were answered and Anabelle had alerted Zeke. When they were done and seated on the couches, Drew said, "What's going on? This doesn't seem like a surprise, Nate."

Nathan shot Anabelle a quick look. She nodded. He said, "Drew, there are some things I've kept from you. I'm being stalked."

Drew stared at him stonily, then shook his head. "I thought we were past this." He glanced at Anabelle. It was a stern father's disapproving look. "After we bridged the gap ten years ago."

"We are. I'm sorry. But I was instructed to keep this quiet."

"By whom?"

"The FBI."

"To keep it quiet from your family?"

"I'm sorry."

"I insisted on the secrecy, Drew." Anabelle didn't know why she felt the need to defend Nathan.

"You knew."

"I'm his bodyguard. Or I was. We were just about to replace me with someone new."

"You're his bodyguard because you're a cop?"

"Partly. And also because I could fit in undercover easily. We've been thinking the stalker is someone Nathan knows."

Like you.

"Then why are you being replaced?"

Nathan jumped in. "It's personal."

Drew paused, his gaze darting from Anabelle to Nathan. "You two?" He shook his head. "Not again."

Anabelle stood and crossed to the other side of the room. She heard Nathan say, "It isn't the time for this, Drew."

"Is it ever, Nate? Do you ever have time to take me into your confidence?"

"I'm sorry. I—"

Just then, the HazMat director strode into the office.

Without his G suit.

They all looked up in surprise.

The guy shrugged gray-suited shoulders. "It was a false alarm. The white powder was flour not anthrax."

"Somebody wanted him to think it was anthrax, though, right?" Anabelle asked.

"Yes. Somebody wanted to scare you, Congressman. Any idea who?"

CHAPTER FOURTEEN

AT THE END OF THE WEEK, Nathan was back in Hyde Point. He stood across from Anabelle in the room where, ten years ago, he told her Kaeley was not his child and he couldn't leave Olivia. The atmosphere was equally as tense today, perhaps more so since they had choices now. "So, you're really leaving?"

Without turning to face him, she stuffed clothes in a suitcase. Little Rosy scampered at her feet, then jumped on the bed and woofed softly. She petted him. "Yes, I'm leaving."

Leaning against the jamb, Nathan stuck his hands in his pockets so he wouldn't reach for her. "Is there anything I can do to make you stay?"

She stilled. Her shoulders hunched then they began to shake.

Crossing to her, he grasped her upper arms. "Annie…"

"No, don't, please, this is hard enough as it is."

"Sweetheart, if it's so hard, you shouldn't be leaving."

Her sigh was heavy and burdened. When she pivoted around her eyes were hollows of darkness and her cheeks were wet. "Nathan, we blew it again." When he started to speak, she pressed her fingers to his mouth. "No, don't argue. It's my fault, mostly. I can't get beyond my hang-ups about trust. Maybe I'll always distrust people—

men—because of how I grew up. We've just got too many strikes against us.''

"We'll work on it. Together.''

"We can't. You've got to take care of Barbara now. I'm obviously not capable of weathering that.''

"You're the strongest woman I know.''

"Do you really know me, Nathan? Who I am now?''

"I know your core, the woman you always were.''

Breaking away from him, she sat on the sofa bed and picked up the dog, nuzzling him. ''No, you knew a young and impressionable girl. I'm not her. I'm jaded and cynical now.''

Because he couldn't think of anything else to say, he whispered, ''I love you.''

"I love you, too.''

"Not enough. If you did, you'd stay. Work on this.''
She shook her head.

The phone rang. He turned away and whipped the phone out of his pocket, checked the caller ID. ''It's Barbara, I have to answer it.''

Anabelle stood, put the dog down and snapped the suitcase shut. ''Go ahead.'' She grasped it in her hand. ''I'll bring this to my car.''

"Promise me you won't leave yet. Until we talk more.''

"Answer your call.''

She was gone before he could say anything more. He clicked on the phone. ''Hello, Barb.''

"Where are you?'' She sounded frantic.

"I'm home.''

"You're supposed to be here to visit with R.J.'' Ever since the anthrax scare, Barbara had worried about his safety. As he talked to her, Nathan crossed to the window and stared out. Anabelle was at her car. In the light from the outside lamps, he could see her place her suitcase in the trunk.

Please, come back. Let's try again.

"Nathan, do you hear me?"

"Yes, Barb. I'll be at your house shortly."

"All right."

He clicked off.

Anabelle slammed the trunk and turned to stare at the house. She cocked her head, stood still for a moment. Then she circled the car to the driver's side and opened the door. As she slid in and started the engine, Nathan's heart felt as if somebody were choking the life out of it.

As she drove away, he thought maybe it had stopped beating, his chest hurt so much. The taillights disappeared, and Nathan sank onto the sofa and buried his face in his hands.

ANABELLE HAD ONE last stop to make. She'd already said goodbye to almost everybody. Nora and Dan were the hardest. Except for Nathan.

Don't think about that.

She'd had lunch with Charly and Taylor at Taylor's house yesterday. She'd managed some time with Darcy and Paige, too. Now she was headed for Rascal's to bid farewell to Jade, who was working tonight. They weren't able to get any time together before now, so Anabelle had promised she'd stop by on her way to the airport. Still reeling from her problems with Nathan, from the anthrax scare, and from all the sad goodbyes, Anabelle was distracted as she parked and headed into the bar. It was early, so only four or five cars inhabited the lot.

The place was empty except for a few isolated patrons.

Jade stood behind the bar talking with Hunter. They were in serious conversation. Anabelle knew they'd gotten close; the Serenity House sisters and their guys had formed a tightly knit group since Nora's wedding. Once, Anabelle had hoped Nathan could have been part of it.

Jade saw her first. "Well, look who the cat dragged in."

"Hey, darlin'."

"Hi, guys."

"Come to say goodbye?" Jade asked with none of her usual sass. Much of it had fled in light of Beck's impending custody battle for Jade's daughter.

"Yep." Anabelle sank onto a chair. "I'll have a soda."

Hunter went to get it. Jade leaned over and braced her arms on the counter. "You look like hell."

"I feel like hell."

"Sometimes that happens when you're not doing the right thing."

"Sometimes that happens when you *are* doing the right thing." The women shared a knowing look.

"I'm gonna miss you," Jade said.

Anabelle's eyes narrowed. "You sticking around here?"

"Yeah, she is." This from Hunter. "Running away never solved anything." He took a bead on Anabelle. "Darcy says *you're* running."

"I am, I admit it."

"Serenity House girls seem to have that tendency in common," Jade remarked.

"Yeah, I guess."

"Bartender?" someone called from the other side of the room.

Anabelle turned just as Hunter said, "He wants another Manhattan. I don't think he should have any more."

"Cut him off, then," Jade agreed.

They were talking about Drew Hyde, who sat in a corner booth, giving new meaning to the phrase "drowning in your beer." He was holding up an empty rock glass.

"How long has he been here?" Anabelle asked.

"Today?"

"What do you mean?"

"He's been here every night this week. Not driving, though. He's taken cabs or calls his wife to come get him."

"What does he do?"

"Gets quietly drunk." Jade watched him. "There's something about that guy that gives me the creeps."

Anabelle's antennae perked up. "I'll be right back." Standing, she crossed the room and approached Drew's booth. "Hello, Drew."

Up close, he looked bad. His normally meticulous suit was wrinkled and his tie was undone and hanging around his neck. His short hair was disheveled. "Well, if it isn't the femme fatale."

"Excuse me?"

"The only lady who makes my brother dance."

Privacy, and maybe shame, urged her to run away. Something else made her stay. "Can I sit down?"

"Why not?"

"You're hurting, aren't you, Drew?"

"Yep. I'm hurting. But not for long. Just garnering my courage."

"For what?"

"Nothing. I'm a sloppy drunk." He studied her. "Heard from Kaeley recently?"

"Yeah, she called me tonight."

"She used to call her uncle, too. Not anymore. Everybody ditches good old Drew eventually. Even his own…" His eyes moistened. "Never mind."

"Nathan needs you, depends on you, Drew."

Reaching out, he grabbed a pack of cigarettes Anabelle hadn't seen and lit one. "When it's convenient."

"What do you mean?"

"Nothing. So, what's going to happen between you guys?"

"I'm leaving town."

"Nate never said anything to me about that. He never says anything at all." Drew sat back in the booth and closed his eyes. The action made his suit coat gap.

And Anabelle saw, in the inside pocket of the jacket, the butt of a small gun.

Oh my God.

He started rambling then. "I can never be enough for him, you know? From the day his father married my mother, I tried. Even my mother liked him better." He opened his eyes. "I need another drink."

"I'll get it for you." She slid out of the booth. Glancing at Hunter and Jade, she thought about keeping them safe, felt for her own gun, then realized she'd left it in the glove compartment of the car since she was no longer playing bodyguard. "I'm going to the ladies' room first, then I'll get your drink." She'd use her cell phone from the rest room.

He nodded wearily. She walked casually to the rest room where she dug into her purse for her phone. Shit, it wasn't there. Now she remembered leaving it on the seat of the car.

Think. She'd go out the side door to the car. Call Dan, or the police. Call Nathan's bodyguard to warn him. Slowly she crept out of the bar. She reached her car in no time, glad for the cover of darkness. Unlocking the door on the passenger side, she grabbed her phone and punched in Dan's number.

Thank God he answered. "Dan, I think I know who the stalker—"

The phone flew from her hand. She was yanked from behind, caught in a headlock. She could smell booze and cigarettes—then felt a gun at her temple. "Get in the car, Anabelle. We're going for a ride."

Anabelle didn't move.

He jammed the gun into her flesh. "Give me your keys and get inside."

She remembered her advice to the Serenity House girls. *Don't go willingly. The place he's going to take you…*

Anabelle stiffened but said, "Okay." Having a gun at her head put a different spin on things.

Slowly she dug in her purse and took out the keys. He reached for them before she could activate the small pepper-spray container she used as a key chain.

Throw the keys…

She jerked her arm and managed to avoid his hand. She threw the keys away but was afraid, given his restriction on her, they didn't go far. Drew swore. Steel hit the back of her head. Pain sliced through her skull and her eyes blurred. Half-dazed, she crumpled to the ground. Her arms were yanked behind her back; something soft and satiny went around her wrists.

She heard the jangle of keys, then was yanked up by the neck. She struggled...but was forced into the car. Tires squealed and the parking lot whizzed by.

Anabelle shook her head to clear it. Her hands were tied, and Drew was talking.

"He doesn't appreciate me, Anabelle. That's the problem. I've admired him so much, loved him like a real brother, and he ignores me. First he favored Jack. Then Dan. I can't seem to gain his confidence. It almost happened when he lost you, but then Dan came out of his funk..." Drew trailed off, genuine hurt in his voice. "I thought if he was in danger, he'd turn to me, I could help, then..."

Oh, God. "Where are we going?"

"What?"

"Where are we going?"

"I don't know. I don't know what to do with you. I didn't plan this."

Where's he going to take you and what he'll do is worse than what will happen if you cause an accident...

"I'd do anything for Nathan, you know. *Anything.* I even let him keep Kaeley."

"What do you mean, keep her?"

Drew laughed, a crazed sound, like a man possessed by something or someone else. "Kaeley's my daughter. I'll bet you didn't know that. You were so close, he *loved you so much* and you didn't even know that."

"Drew, Kaeley isn't your daughter."

"She's not Nathan's."

"I know. Her father's Joseph McLean. He was a man Olivia almost married. She had a farewell fling with him just before she and Nathan got married."

"That's not true. Olivia told me Kaeley was mine."

"You had an affair with your brother's wife?"

"No, she seduced me. Once. I was freakin' eighteen years old. She seduced me the night before the wedding, after the rehearsal dinner."

"Oh, God."

"A few months later she said Kaeley was mine." He waved the gun. "She is. If you know she isn't Nathan's, why do you say she isn't mine?"

"Olivia had paternity tests to prove Nathan wasn't the father, in case she ever needed the evidence. McLean's name was documented on them and the birth certificate. Afterward, Nathan had his own DNA tests done, too."

"I don't believe it." He pointed the gun at her. "You don't know. *I* know. I know Nathan had my child. I wouldn't have cared, but he didn't take me in…he didn't…" Tears started to stream down his cheeks. The gun wavered. He pressed on the gas pedal.

What was he going to do? Crash them? Shoot her.

Cause an accident.

Before he could go any faster, and because they were alone on the road leading to Spencer Hill, she lifted her legs and jarred the steering wheel. The car veered off to the right…

They speeded up…

The wheel twisted and they headed into an embankment.

It was just like the night they drove back from Kaeley's play in Syracuse. Only this time Anabelle's hands were tied, so she couldn't protect herself.

She saw Drew hit the windshield.

She slammed against the door.

The door sprang open.

She hit the ground, banged her head, hard.

Then, there was an explosion that rocked the earth.

NATHAN STOOD by Anabelle's bed and watched her sleep. Numbness had settled over him like an icy blanket. And he was glad for it. She hadn't regained consciousness after she'd been abducted by the stalker and thrown from her rented car. Just before the gas tank exploded.

Ironically, they still didn't know the identity of the culprit; they'd recovered only a charred body. From Anabelle's call, Dan figured out that she was with the stalker. The police had swarmed Rascal's.

Anabelle's car was not in the parking lot. Neither Jade nor Hunter had seen her leave, which was odd. Figuring the stalker had gotten her, the police had put out bulletins, and Dan had called Nathan to warn him of what had gone down. After an interminable forty-five minutes, the call had come in. They found Anabelle's car on the side of Spencer Hill. They'd discovered the driver's remains, and a critically injured Anabelle on the shoulder of the road. He and Dan met the ambulance at the hospital three hours ago. Nathan stayed by her bed as soon as they'd let him come into her room.

He picked up her hand. It was frigid. Bringing it to his mouth, he kissed it. "You were right, sweetheart. We don't belong together. All our being together does is hurt you." Physically and emotionally, he'd caused her more pain than any person could ever forgive.

"Please, love, please get better. Then I'll let you go. I won't try to stop you. I—" The numbness receded, replaced by a sharp pang of remorse so great it almost leveled him.

The door to the small ICU room opened and Dan came in. "How are you holding up, buddy?"

Nathan ignored the solicitation. "Did you talk to the doctors?"

"Yeah, with Paige and Ian. Anabelle has a head injury, but no internal bleeding. They say we just have to wait for her to wake up."

"I did this to her." Nathan looked at Dan. "I should have stopped this crazy bodyguard scheme after she got hurt in the first incident coming back from Syracuse."

"Nathan, you're—"

"No!" He sliced the air with his hand. "I'm responsible for this. She was eighteen when she came to me from Serenity House, and I've done nothing but hurt her. Now, if she doesn't—" His voice broke.

"She's going to make it." Dan's tone was ragged and a little bit desperate. His eyes were stricken.

"She's like your daughter. If you lose her…"

"I won't lose her. And I won't lose *you*. You're important to me, too, and the three of us are going to pull through this."

Nathan remembered when his older brother, Jack, died. Right here in this very hospital. It had also been a car accident. Nathan had been fourteen, Dan almost twenty-six. Nathan was crying in the hallway and Dan had come to find him. Dan had held him, cried with him, and told him that he'd be his big brother the rest of his life.

They had tried to bring Drew into the circle, but at eleven, Drew had stood on the outside looking in, and wouldn't let anybody comfort him.

Once again, Nathan and Dan sat together in the hospital, watching the woman they both loved. Praying. And, after a few more hours, their prayers were answered. She stirred. Nathan, half-asleep in the chair, still holding her hand, felt her move. He bolted upright. Dan was already on the other side of the bed.

In a gravelly voice, she mumbled, "Nathan?"

"Right here, sweetheart."

"My head hurts."

"I'll bet it does."

Her eyes were glazed. "What...what..." She asked for water. Sipped. Took a few moments to collect herself. Then her brain seemed to clear. "Oh my God, Drew."

Dan asked, "Drew?"

"Drew's dead, isn't he?"

"Why would Drew be..." Nathan's voice trailed off.

Drew? You've got to be kidding. He's my brother, for God's sake.

Anabelle was wide awake now, and looked to Dan. For a cue?

"Tell us, honey," Dan said gently.

She gripped Nathan's hand. "I'm sorry, Nathan, Drew was the stalker."

He couldn't take it in. For a moment, he just stared at her. Then he said, "No, you must be mistaken."

"I'm not. I found him at Rascal's. He was drunk. He started babbling. I saw he had a gun in his suit coat. When I went to my car to call Dan, he followed me."

Nathan felt chilled. "No, Jade said he was at Rascal's and left before you did. Annie, please, don't tell me he tried to harm you. He didn't...oh, God."

Dan circled the bed and placed his hand on Nathan's shoulder.

Nathan asked, "Why? *Why?*"

"He said you never paid enough attention to him. You never gave him a chance. First you preferred Jack, then Dan, over him as your confidant. He said he just wanted your approval, your attention." She sat up more and winced. "He was half out of his mind, Nathan. Something was wrong with him mentally."

"This was all my fault, too."

"No. It was fate, circumstance. With a little help."

"What do you mean?"

She looked torn. "Olivia seduced him when he was eighteen. All this time, he thought Kaeley was his. She told him that."

"Why would she tell him that? We verified the father."

"She was a terrible woman, Nathan," Dan said.

Anabelle added, "So it wasn't your fault."

He looked at Anabelle trying to take everything in. "Oh, yes, yes, it was." With that, he turned and walked out of the room.

"ARE YOU SURE you want to do this, sweetie?" Nora smiled at Anabelle from where she stood across the room snapping her suitcase shut and hefting it down to the floor.

"Yep. I'm all packed and set to go."

Nora sat on the edge of the bed. "It's only been two weeks. You sure you're ready to return to Seattle?"

"Uh-huh." She glanced around the room where she'd stayed when she first came to Hyde Point in November. "It's been an interesting few months."

"It has."

"Is Dan here yet?"

"Yes, I heard him come in." Nora smiled. "I'm going to miss you."

Anabelle went to Nora and hugged her. "I'm going to

miss you, too." She was going to miss a lot of things in Hyde Point. Who would have thought?

"Will you see Nathan before you leave?"

Glancing in the mirror, Anabelle tugged down the light-gray sweater that she wore with matching slacks. "No, he made it clear at the funeral he didn't want to talk to me. See me. I think it hurts too much." And he'd been with Barbara, who was doing a fine job of comforting him. It had killed Anabelle to watch that.

"Give him time, honey, he lost his brother."

"It's over, Nora," she said sadly. "There was too much baggage between us already. He's right, this thing with Drew was the last straw."

"When you love somebody, you should be able to handle the baggage."

"Like you and Dan." She shook her head. "Nathan and I just weren't as strong as you two."

Nora helped her cart her luggage downstairs and into the kitchen, where Anabelle stopped dead in her tracks. Nathan was there with Dan, leaning against the counter, sipping from a mug of coffee. He looked up when she entered.

The ravages of death and guilt had taken their toll on his handsome face. It was deeply creased. His eyes were bloodshot, and his forest-green sweater and khakis hung on him.

She was hit by a blast of love and the need to comfort so hard, she almost couldn't control it.

"Hi." His eyes locked on her face. "I came to say goodbye."

She smiled sadly. "I'm glad you did."

Nora took Dan's arm. "We'll give you two a minute alone." They left quietly.

"How are you feeling?" Nathan asked achingly.

"All better. It takes more than a knock on the head to keep me down."

"That's good." He glanced around the room, sighed. "This is hard."

"I know."

"So you're going back to Seattle?"

"Yeah."

"Will you go undercover right away?" There was strain in his voice, worry in his eyes.

"I don't know. I've had about all the intrigue and suspense I can handle for a while."

"I can see why."

"How about you?"

"I'm heading to Washington tonight. Two weeks away put me behind."

"I hear R.J.'s doing well."

"Yeah, responding to the treatment."

"Barbara was really there for you during all this, despite what she's going through."

"Yes, she was." He sighed. "I'm still going to break it off. I'm just waiting until the last of R.J.'s chemo."

"Ah."

"How about you? Have you spoken to Rob?"

"Yeah, I'm done with that, too."

"Ironic, isn't it? We'll be free of attachments yet we'll never be free of the past."

She sighed. Crossing to him, she slid her arms around his waist and lay her head on his chest. His arms were strong and warm as they encircled her. Resting his chin on her head, he whispered, "I'm sorry, Annie."

"Me, too."

She drew back. "Will you be all right?"

He swallowed hard. Nodded. "You?"

"Yeah."

He kissed her forehead, and she stepped out of his arms. "Goodbye, Nathan."

"Goodbye, love."

The endearment weakened her. But before she could give in to the incredible feeling of loss, she pivoted and walked out of the room.

After one last goodbye to Nora, Anabelle and Dan made their way to the car. She slipped into the front seat. Before she could buckle her belt, she heard a yipping noise. Turning, she saw Rosy, the gorgeous Irish setter pup, in a small travel crate in the back seat. "Dan? Did Nathan give the dog to you and Nora?"

He reached out and grasped her hand. "No, honey. Rosy's for you. Nathan wants you to have him."

That did it! She burst into tears and fell sobbing into Dan's arms.

CHAPTER FIFTEEN

As soon as Anabelle picked Kaeley up at the airport she knew something was wrong. The girl's usual perky personality was subdued and the smudges under her eyes indicated she hadn't been sleeping. Since Kaeley had been excited about spending the first four days of her April break in Seattle, Anabelle was worried about her mood. They made small talk until they reached Anabelle's apartment. Once inside, where they were greeted by an exuberant Rosy, Anabelle asked, "Okay, kiddo, what's going on? You look like you lost your best friend."

Kaeley promptly burst into tears and threw herself into Anabelle's arms.

"Oh, honey, what is it?"

"Jon and I broke up."

"Aw, sweetie, I'm sorry." She was. She knew Kaeley and Jon were close and it had seemed they had a fairy-tale relationship. Anabelle should have known those didn't exist.

"Come on, sit down." She drew Kaeley to the tapestry couch, where the dog promptly jumped up and began to lick their faces. "What happened?"

Blue eyes sparkled with tiny, starlike tears. Holding on to Rosy, Kaeley sighed. "He said we should see other people. That I was young, and he was my first serious relationship. Before it went any further, I should date different guys. To see if Jon's what I want."

"Well, is that so bad?"

"No, it isn't. I didn't like it, but I agreed." Tears began to course down her cheeks. She swiped at them with the sleeve of her Syracuse University sweatshirt. "Then he slept with his ex-girlfriend."

"Oh, Kaeley."

"She'd been hanging around him for weeks, calling him, asking him to meet her. I was so stupid, I believed it when he said he was trying to get rid of her. I even believed it when he said breaking up for a while was in *my* best interest." She started to sob now. "When all he really wanted to do was screw her."

"Are they back together?"

Kaeley laughed a very adult, womanly laugh. "No, he came to me right away and *confessed* what he'd done. Said he'd made a huge mistake, he didn't even know why he did it. He was sorry and he wanted to ditch the dating-other-people thing, get back together and make plans for our future."

"What did you say?"

Her blue eyes cleared and she slapped her hands on her jeans. "Are you kidding? I told him to go to hell."

A small smile escaped Anabelle's lips. Kaeley Hyde was something else.

"So you're upset because it just happened?"

"No, I'm upset because I love him. I wanted to marry him. I *trusted* him."

Anabelle picked at the lap blanket on her couch. It was one she'd gotten at the Women's Rights National Park visitors' center. "And you think now you can't trust him?"

"At first I didn't, but after I talked to Daddy about it, I'm not so sure anymore."

Daddy, whom Anabelle hadn't heard a word about in the six weeks since she'd left Hyde Point. Dan didn't mention Nathan on the phone, and Anabelle had refrained from asking Kaeley. But Anabelle had suffered in the six weeks they'd been apart, and had second-guessed herself a thousand times about leaving. She missed everything about him—how his eyes twinkled with humor or darkened with desire. How he touched her casually and what it felt like when he was inside her. Sometimes she missed him so much, she cried—*she* who never cried.

"What did your dad say?"

"That life was short. That people make mistakes. That losing a person you love is worse than anything in the world." The girl scowled, an expression so much like one of her father's that it hurt Anabelle to look at it. "He didn't mean Mom, I know that for sure. They were never happy together. It sounded like he lost somebody he loved, though."

He did.

"Annie?" Kaeley stared at her, studied her face. Then her eyes widened. "Oh my God, it's you, isn't it? You're the woman Daddy lost."

"Honey, I don't think—"

"Now it all falls into place. Since you left he's been morose. I go home a lot because Uncle Drew died. I thought Daddy's mood was because he lost his brother. But it's because of you, too." Then Kaeley clapped a hand over her mouth. "Oh, God, I just realized. He was sad forever after you left ten years ago. Even though I was little, I sensed how unhappy he was. It happened then, between you, didn't it?"

Anabelle didn't want to lie to the girl but she and Nathan had had an illicit affair and she didn't want to taint Nathan in his daughter's eyes. "We fell in love when I was your nanny, honey. It's why I left when you were little." Sitting back into the pillows, she drew up her knees and hugged her legs tightly. "It's the real reason I offered to be his bodyguard."

"Then why did you leave again?"

"Sometimes the past won't go away. Old hurts can't be made up—" Anabelle stopped suddenly, realizing what she was doing. Her advice could be crucial to this girl's happiness.

"What?"

"Well, I was going to say that the past can't be made up for. But honey, I'm not sure that's true for you and Jon. People *do* make mistakes. And you seemed so happy with him. Like your dad said, you could be giving up the love of your life."

Thoughtfully, Kaeley petted Rosy's pretty red coat. "Daddy was the love of your life, wasn't he? It's the reason you never married anyone else."

"Yes."

"Then why did you give him up this time?"

Anabelle looked at Nathan's daughter. "Sometimes I don't know."

SPRING HAD COME to Hyde Point, and Nathan was glad. Often early April was a winter wonderland in the Southern Tier, but it appeared the weather gods had given the little town a break. As he jogged down the street leading back to his house, the warm air and signs of spring made him smile.

Those smiles had been rare these days. He was finally recovering from the stalking and Drew's subsequent death enough to function. One of the reasons for the upswing in his mood had been Nora Whitman, who'd hovered over him since the funeral. She'd talked him into getting some help from a private counselor in dealing with his guilt. The therapy was working, though he had a long way to go. As he approached his home, he was thinking about his plans for the future.

The first thing he'd done was talk to Barbara. As soon as R.J. had been out of the woods, Nathan had gone to her house to confess his feelings for Anabelle. He'd found her with her ex-husband, Rick. They'd been having lunch when Nathan stopped by...

"Nathan? What are you doing here?"

"I'd like to talk to you, Barb."

She looked nervous.

"Aren't you feeling well? Did something happen with R.J.?"

"She's feeling just fine," a male voice said from behind her. "And so is my son."

Nathan glanced over Barbara's shoulder to the dinette to see Rick Benton rise from the table.

"Nathan, come on in." Barb brought him to the dining room.

Benton moved closer to his ex-wife and gently grasped her shoulders, clearly staking his claim.

Barbara looked up at him. "Rick, I'd like some time alone with Nathan."

"I want to stay while you tell him."

"No, please go into the den and wait."

Stepping back, Rick stuffed his hands in his pockets. "All right." He faced Nathan. "You can't have her, Hyde."

When Benton was gone, Nathan sat down at the table. "Those were the exact words you said to me about Anabelle."

"I know. I'm sorry." She glanced over her shoulder. "I didn't plan for this to happen."

Well, I know that feeling.

"But Rick and I have been together so much because of R.J., and then we got the good news about his remission." She shrugged helplessly. "Finally, we admitted we still loved each other."

Nathan reached out to grasp her hand. "It's okay, Barb. Things haven't been right between us for a long time."

"I know." She sighed. "I was going to bring this up sooner, but your brother died, and I didn't want to abandon you in the middle of all that."

"I understand. More than you could possibly know."

He'd confessed his feelings for Anabelle then...

Life had a funny way of working out, he thought as his house came into view. Then, he stopped short. Somebody was sitting on his front steps. A man. As he got closer, he saw it was Jon Jamison, Kaeley's erstwhile boyfriend. Stifling violent fatherly urges, Nathan approached the guy who had hurt his little girl. "Well, this is a surprise."

Jamison looked up at him. His face was gaunt, his eyes stricken. The guy had obviously suffered. Nathan had seen the same signs in his own mirror.

"Congressman Hyde," Jamison said by way of greeting.

"What do you want?"

"To see Kaeley." He stood, a little shaky. "I've been calling her cell phone, but she doesn't answer."

"She didn't come home for spring break."

Kaeley had gone to Seattle, which just about broke Nathan's heart. Mostly he tried not to think about Anabelle and what they'd lost. No, what they'd both willingly given up, his therapist had reminded him. But when Kaeley decided to visit Annie and talked incessantly about what they had planned, the feelings of loss swamped him. It was especially hard at night, when he couldn't get to sleep. He wanted Anabelle with him so badly he ached with it.

"Where did Kaeley go?" Jon asked.

Folding his arms over the front of his fleece jacket, Nathan stared down the younger man. "I'm not very inclined to share that with you, Jamison. After what you did to her."

"She told you?"

"Yep. And right now, I feel a lot like punching your face in."

The man deflated. "Go ahead, I couldn't feel any worse than I do now."

Don't bet on it, kid.

"I think I'll restrain myself. For now." Taking pity on the guy, he said, "Want to come in?"

Jamison nodded. They entered through the side door and were greeted with loud yips. Elly scampered across the floor. Nathan wondered how Rosy was doing, if Anabelle liked having the dog or if it reminded her too much of him. She'd sent her thanks by way of Dan.

Nathan grabbed beers from the fridge then joined Jamison at the table. "Do you want to talk about it?" Nathan asked.

The guy messed up his curly hair. "I don't know what to say. I made a mistake. I hurt her, I know that. But I want to make it up to her." He met Nathan's eyes directly. "I want to spend the rest of my life making it up to her."

"What you did is tough to make up."

"I know. I was weak, and stupid, and it never should

have happened.'' He peeled at the label on the bottle. ''Do you think some things are just unforgivable, Congressman? That you can hurt somebody so much, she'll never forgive you?''

''I'd like that not to be the case, Jon,'' he said, thinking of Anabelle. ''Truthfully, I'm not sure.''

''She'll never trust me again.''

''Maybe. Maybe not.'' He saw Annie, at Belhurst Castle, promising to trust him. She couldn't follow through on it, though. Maybe betrayed trust could never be restored.

Jon slapped the bottle down on the table. ''Well, I'm not giving up. Not without a fight. I've let my guilt color everything for weeks. But I'm a long way from letting her go.''

Nathan stared at the man before him.

The man who obviously had a lot more grit and determination than he himself had. The thought took hold in his head and wouldn't shake loose.

''Well, buddy, Kaeley's coming home tomorrow morning to spend a few days with me.''

Pure hope—and love—shone in the guy's eyes. ''Think I could drive back down here? See her?''

''I think you could stay here tonight, if you want to.''

''Yeah, I would.'' He watched Nathan. ''Can I ask you something?''

''Sure.''

''Why are you being helpful in this? Most fathers…I mean, if they knew what I did…they'd deck me and kick me out.''

''I've made mistakes, Jon. I've let people down I care about.'' He stood. ''And I lost the only woman I ever really loved because of those mistakes. If you and Kaeley were meant to be together, I'm not going to be the one to keep you apart.'' He stared at the young man. ''But if you hurt her again, I'll probably have to break your arms. Just remember that.''

''I won't hurt her again, I promise.''

Nathan knew Jon couldn't promise that, but he felt better knowing he'd given the boy the best advice he could. For Kaeley. Even though Nathan had made a lot of mistakes, he was still a good father. The thought warmed him.

KAELEY LOOKED OVER at Anabelle from the window seat of the plane. ''Are you sure you want to come back with me? You know, after what you told me about Daddy?'' They were halfway to Hyde Point, so it was a little late for the question, but Anabelle answered it anyway.

''I'm positive. I'd been thinking about coming home anyway. Ariel, my friend from Serenity House, is getting some kind of poetry award this week at school and it would be fun to see her get it. And it's Paige's daughter's birthday. She and Ian are having a celebration for Mara. Paige invited all the Serenity House original residents.''

Kaeley played with her hair, which was longer now, and flowing way past her shoulder. ''Will you see Daddy?''

''I don't know, honey.'' The thought scared her to death. She took Kaeley's hand. ''Feel any better than when you came to Seattle?''

''Yeah.'' Kaeley stared out the window. ''Our talks helped.''

They'd discussed life and the nature of men for hours over ice-cream sundaes, during shopping expeditions, and sitting on top of the bed in the guest room with Rosy cradled between them. Anabelle loved this girl so much.

"Life isn't black and white, is it?" Kaeley commented. "It's gray."

"Yeah, it's gray all right. A lot of different shades."

The plane landed and Kaeley went ahead to wait for their luggage, while Anabelle visited the ladies' room.

Coming out, she ran smack into a big, hard male body. One she recognized. Immediately, her insides contracted and her heart sped up. Those shoulders and that chest, encased in an airport-maintenance uniform, were just as big and menacing as Anabelle remembered them.

"Hey, lady, watch it…" The voice trailed off. "Well, well, well, lookee here. If it isn't little Cinderella, all grown up."

Anabelle stared up into the face of her stepbrother Al Crane. She stood immobilized, watching him. For a brief moment, she was thrown back fifteen years, when she'd run into the bathroom to escape him. She had the urge to flee into the airport rest room now.

"You've changed." Al eyed her lasciviously. "Filled out right nice."

The sleazy nuance of his tone shook her out of her reverie. She gave him a glaring once-over. "So have you." He was bloated and jowly. Years of hard drinking had worn on him. "Not for the better, I might add."

"Hmm. Has the little kitten gotten claws?"

"You might say that."

His face contorted. "Think you're hot shit now, don't you?"

"What do you mean?"

"I knew you were back in town a few months ago. That you were some big-shot cop in Seattle and had gotten hurt. Then all that mess happened with Drew Hyde. Still, you needed good old Nathan to protect you."

"Protect me? What are you talking about?"

"As if you didn't know. He came to see me when you got back in November. He threatened me, said that if I didn't stay away from you, he'd find a way to put me in a cage where I belonged."

Anabelle thought about not seeing Nathan all those months she was home, and the fact that he was still looking out for her.

Al continued to spout off. "He don't scare me, though. I go after what I want, when I want." He glanced around at the airport. It was fairly deserted this early in the morning. He stepped forward.

Anabelle held her ground.

"I always wanted you, little girl." He raised a beefy hand to her jaw. "And maybe, just maybe—"

He never got to finish his sordid suggestion. Anabelle shoved him back against the wall. He outweighed her by at least fifty pounds and was a head taller, but in no time she had her hand against his windpipe and her knee hovering at his groin. "You ever, *ever* get within touching distance of me again, tough guy, and I'll make sure your cruel hands—" she lifted her knee higher "—and this equipment here never hurt another woman again."

His eyes bulged as she cut off more of his air.

"Got it?"

He didn't answer.

She rammed his head against the wall. "Got it?"

"Yeah," he squeaked.

"Good." She let go and stepped back. "I *have* changed, big brother. I'm not the girl I was when you used me as a punching bag. Don't forget it."

And, as she walked away to find Kaeley, her own words stayed in her brain. She wasn't that girl anymore.

It was time to start acting like the woman she'd become.

ANABELLE STOOD in front of the Winslow Place, watching the sun sparkle off the black shutters and kiss the new gray siding. The house was bigger than she remembered it. Its peaks and rooflines stood proudly in the air. Her gaze traveled to the turret, barely visible from the driveway where she'd parked her car behind Nathan's.

I'm not the girl I used to be…

Why did you give him up this time…

She made her way around back, under big maples just beginning to bud, and over grass that had already turned green. Passing by daffodils peeking out from the stalks, she smiled. Rebirth and new life were good omens.

She was amazed at the changes she saw in the back of the house. There was a stone patio right off the kitchen. A wooden swing that reminded her of the one on Serenity House's porch stood at one end, and Anabelle wondered if its fancy woodwork was Hunter's.

Pounding came from the turret. Nathan must be inside.

Everything I did in the Winslow Place I did for you.

Drawing in a deep breath, she stilled a moment, remembering other words he'd said when she was just coming out of unconsciousness…

I did this to her. I'm responsible for this. She was eighteen when she came to me from Serenity House, and I've done nothing but hurt her.

Would Anabelle be able to convince him to give them another try? She pushed open the turret door and found him inside. He was on his hands and knees pounding some boards into place on the beautiful new hardwood floor. The turret receded and she only had eyes for him—his strong back, his arms bulging in the white T-shirt he wore with jeans. Suddenly she couldn't wait to talk to him.

"It looks beautiful," she said when the pounding ceased.

His head snapped around and he dropped the hammer. His face registered shock, and then a look so poignant it almost brought her to her knees. "Annie." He breathed her name reverently. Then he stood and faced her. The jeans rode low on his hips. His chest muscles were outlined in the shirt. Her eyes riveted on him. "What…what are you doing here?" he asked.

"I wanted to see what you'd done to the place." Dumb, but her hands had started to shake and she couldn't think clearly.

"How did you know I was here?"

"A certain young man waiting at your house told me. Of course, he could barely get the words out, he was so nervous at seeing Kaeley."

"I know the feeling."

"I flew back with your daughter."

"I gather that." He watched her. "Why?"

"I wanted to see Ariel. And Paige's daughter's birthday is today…. Oh, hell, I came back to see you, Nathan."

He closed his eyes and swallowed hard. For a minute Anabelle panicked. Would he send her away?

"I won't let you send me away. Not without a fight."

"I—"

"I know the last time we saw each other you said it was over, all we did was hurt each other. But I decided I'm not going to accept that."

"Annie, I—"

"Look, we hurt each other, okay. We've got a lot of baggage. All right. We can help each other deal with it." She folded her arms over her chest. "Isn't it worth another shot to see if we can make it work?"

"Will you just—"

"I love you, Nathan. More than anything in the world. I want to live here in this house, sleep in this turret, have your babies and—"

He strode across the room and grabbed her. His mouth came down on hers in a deep, sensual, avaricious kiss that made her head spin and her body go soft. She returned it with equal fervor.

After a long time they separated, both gasping for air. She smiled, tears forming in her eyes.

"Don't cry," he said, brushing his hand down her face. "I didn't know how else to shut you up. I have some things to say, too."

"I won't let you—"

He kissed her quickly again. "Hush and listen. I love you, too. And I've missed you more than I can say. More than the first time you left me."

"Oh, Nathan, me too."

"We made a mess of things, Annie, but we can fix them. I know we can. We'll beat the odds this time. We'll make it work."

She glided back into his arms. Buried her face in the soft cotton of his T-shirt and breathed him in. His hand came to her hair and tangled in it.

"I can't believe this is happening." His voice was still raw.

"Hmm." She nosed his chest. "Think there's something I can do to...um, make it more real?"

He clasped her bottom, his touch hot, even through the jeans she wore. Clamping her to him, she felt him swell against her. "Oh, I think there is."

She drew back. "Here?"

"Ah, here, anywhere you choose, love."

She glanced to the side. Saw the winding staircase that

had been lovingly refinished. "How about up there, in the bedroom?"

"Oh, yeah."

"Take me upstairs, Nathan, I can't wait."

"Well, then." He kissed her nose, stepped back, and still clasping her hand, led her to the steps. He started up first, tugging her behind him.

As they climbed the staircase, she watched Nathan's broad back and confident steps, then took a good look at the turret. Smiling, she realized she did indeed feel like a princess here. And she'd be damned if, this time, she didn't hold on to her prince.

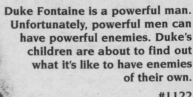
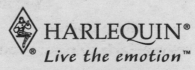

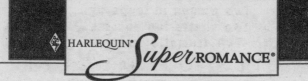

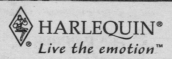

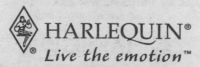

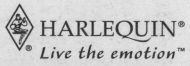

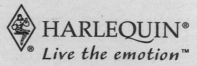